Rescuing Samantha

Heidi M. Thomas

Heidi M. Thomas (signature)

SunCatcher Publications

To Kerrington –
Enjoy Samantha's
rescue story –

Praise for *Rescuing Samantha*

"Heidi Thomas brings us a story about a young woman facing life's trials in rugged Montana. But "Sam" has the gumption of her grandmother and great-grandmother, to persevere and overcome. She is also compelled to rescue horses and young people.

There is drama and true-to-life dialogue in Thomas' smooth writing and the reader will become immersed. It is a joy to watch along with the characters how God brings "mysterious" blessings to their predicaments.

This is also a story of rural America that many of us long for—neighborhood rodeo, BBQ, homemade ice cream, reverence for the Star-Spangled Banner, fiddles and dancing, and (mostly) friendly neighbors. Readers will love this story." ~ Denise F. McAllister, MAPW, Atlanta, GA. Freelance editor, Member of Western Writers of America and Women Writing the West.

"Samantha's dream of raising thoroughbred horses goes askew, but a new venture of rescuing horses and saving damaged teenagers brings fresh life to her new Montana ranch. Add in a dash of romance, a friend in a wheelchair, a mystery, and Heidi Thomas has penned another winner!" ~ Rose Miller, author of *Girls Can Be Cowboys Too!* vol i and ii

"Samantha Moser leaves city life to return to her roots in Montana's ranch country. Obstacles threaten to shatter her dream. Will her longing to restore her roots win out against outside forces? A highly suspenseful and heartfelt novel of depth." ~ Mary Trimble, *Maureen*

"Another delightful Montana story, coming full circle from Cowgirl Dreams. Heidi M. Thomas has another hit on her hands." ~ Brenda Whiteside, author of the "Love and Murder" series

Other books by Heidi M. Thomas

Cowgirl Dreams series
Cowgirl Dreams
Follow the Dream
Dare to Dream

American Dream series
Seeking the American Dream
Finding True Home

Nonfiction
Cowgirl Up! A History of Rodeo Women

Praise for the Cowgirl Dreams series

Cowgirl Dreams: "...Brings heart, verve and knowledge to her depiction of the intrepid Nettie. A lively look at the ranch women of an almost forgotten West." —Deirdre McNamer, MFA English Professor, University of Montana, *Red Rover, My Russian,* and *One Sweet Quarrel*

Follow the Dream: "I enjoyed this bittersweet novel with its accurate depiction of the lives of cowgirls in 1930s Montana and its tender portrait of a marriage." Mary Clearman Blew, award-winning author of *Jackalope Dreams, All but the Waltz: A Memoir of Five Generations in the Life of a Montana Family,* and *Balsamroot: A Memoir*

"In her poignant tale of Nettie Moser's diligent pursuit of a dream, Heidi Thomas gives a stunning example of what it means to "Cowgirl Up." *Follow the Dream* is a dynamic story of a woman's strength and determination that is sure to inspire as well as entertain."—Sandi

Ault, award-winning author of *Wild Sorrow*, in the *WILD* Mystery Series

Dare to Dream: "Finding our place and following our hearts is the moving theme of *Dare to Dream*, a finely-tuned finish to Heidi Thomas's trilogy inspired by the life of her grandmother, an early rodeo-rider. With crisp dialogue and singular scenes we're not only invited into the middle of a western experience of rough stock, riders and generations of ranch tradition, but we're deftly taken into a family drama. This family story takes place beginning in 1941 but it could be happening to families anywhere - and is. Nettie, Jake and Neil struggle to find their place and discover what we all must: life is filled with sorrow and joy: faith, family and friends see us through and give meaning to it all. Nettie, or as Jake calls her, 'Little Gal' will stay in your heart and make you want to re-read the first books just to keep her close. A very satisfying read."—Jane Kirkpatrick, *a New York Times* Bestselling author and WILLA Literary Award winner of *A Flickering Light*

Cowgirl Up: A History of Rodeo Women: "The best kind of history lesson; Informative and entertaining. Thomas does a great job of showing the lifestyles of these women in a very male dominated world, and how through hard work and determination they gained the respect of many people not only in the U.S., but throughout the world. You can't help but be impressed with the toughness of these women, who competed even with broken bones and other injuries. An eye-opening look at the world of rodeo, and the accomplishments of these women. –John J. Rust, author of *Arizona's All-Time Baseball Team* and the "Fallen Eagle" series

Praise for *Finding True Home*

"This sequel to *Seeking the American Dream* continues Heidi Thomas' heart-tugging saga of the life of a World War II war bride as she struggles to adjust to life on a Montana ranch, where family is everything and neighbor helps neighbor through the toughest situations. Struggling through isolation, prejudice, and self-doubt, Anna Moser finally finds peace, acceptance, and her true home through a lifetime of love and sacrifice." – Donis Casey, author of the Alafair Tucker series

"*Finding True Home* is the author's fictional story of her mother, a woman who emigrated from Germany after World War II. Transplanted to a difficult life on a Montana ranch, she finds everything foreign, and believes the neighbors there do not trust her. While she is different, she holds on to feeling that way long after people have ceased to notice. She raises three children who all differ in personality and tries to hold them close, long after they have flown the nest. Thomas makes the events of life seem very personal. Watching the older generation dying off and the new one taking their place, moved this reviewer to tears many times. This coming of age story of an adult woman makes you realize it is never too late for love to triumph." –Linda Jacobs, author of the "Yellowstone" series novels

"This addition to Heidi M Thomas's body of work is sure to captivate readers as much as previous books in the series. She gives readers rich and accurate accounts of obstacles young women faced eighty - ninety years ago. Young women who desperately wanted to step out of society's restrictive molds. Thomas shows us how Montana women aspiring to participate in male dominated roles faced their fears and naysayers with determination and courage." – Karen Casey-Fitzjerrell, author of *Forgiving Effie Beck* and *The Dividing Season*

Praise for *Seeking the American Dream*

"Heidi Thomas's latest novel grips the reader from the first opening sentence, as her nurse-protagonist struggles to face the wretched suffering in war-torn Hamburg during the final days of WWII. From there, her sweeping saga takes her away from Europe's lurching efforts to rebuild, and into the building of her own new life in America. From the perspective of a hard-working, and still bright-eyed young woman, we participate in America's own next chapter." – Mara Purl, best-selling author of the Milford-Haven Novels

"Once again, I open the pages of a Heidi Thomas novel and I'm transported to another time and place. From post WWII Germany to the sometimes-brutal Montana ranch life, Seeking the American Dream explores one woman's journey as she faces impossible odds to live her dream. Ms. Thomas is excellent at period literature. You won't be disappointed."—Brenda Whiteside, Author of The Love and Murder Series

A SunCatcher Publications book

Cover Design by Jason McIntyre
www.TheFarthestReaches.com

Library of Congress Cataloguing-in-Publication data is available on file.

ISBN: 978-0-9990663-3-1

Printed in the United States of America

10 9 8 7 6 5 4 3 2 1

DEDICATION

I dedicate this book to the "something special" between women and their horses, the healing, comforting bond they forge. So many western women have found a unique friendship with their horses, and my grandmother in the 1920s was no exception. Many broken hearts have been healed when hoofbeats and spirits unite.

ACKNOWLEDGMENTS

I thank God for gifting me the writing gene, my family for their continued support and encouragement, the teachers and editors who believed in me, my fellow Women Writing the West members, and my critique group who has given me such valuable feedback: Sally Bates, Leta McCurry, and John J. Rust. Thank you also to my beta readers, Mary Trimble and Brenda Whiteside for helping make my work better.

"My grace is sufficient for you, for my power is made perfect in weakness." 2 Corinthians 12:9

CHAPTER ONE

FOR SALE OR LEASE:
360 acres prime pastureland. Ingomar, MT.
Great starter ranch. Call Teresa Knudson 555-2589.

Samantha Moser's heartbeat echoed every bump in the dusty country road. She was coming home.

Even though she'd never seen this ranch, its history was as much a part of her as the blood pulsing through her veins. Her great-grandparents had once owned this piece of Montana. Made a new beginning here. Realized a dream here. Sam could hardly breathe, and it wasn't just the dust swirling through the open windows of the car. This might be her chance for her own new beginning.

"Yikes." Teresa Knudson let out a yelp as her car hit a large pothole. She swerved to avoid another.

Sam glanced at the real estate agent, dressed in boots, jeans and western shirt. She guessed Teresa's age about twenty-five or six, about three or four years older than she.

Scrapbook pictures from the 1940s and '50s, when Great-Grandma Nettie and Grandpa Jake lived here, conjured images. A white two-story house with a wrap-around porch. A leafy cottonwood tree in front where a hammock swung. And a tall, classic red barn with white trim, horses in the corral. Sam rubbed her sweaty palms on her jeans. *I can't wait to see it.* Teresa said it was a "fixer-upper," but surely a few repairs and a coat of paint would spruce the place up.

"How much farther?" Sam was ready to get out and walk if it would get them there faster.

"Just over this little hill." Teresa steered around another rut.

The spring-fresh prairie spread around them like an endless sea, broken only by undulating hills until it reached the low horizon, seemingly the end of the earth. This is how Sam remembered her childhood in Montana, before her family moved to Arizona. This is what had been calling to her since she was ten: *Come home, come home.*

Teresa finally turned off onto a narrow track, and they jounced through a gully and up a low rise. Sam's stomach swooped with the motion. She leaned forward as the place came into view.

And gasped.

Silhouetted against the white-hot blue of the eastern Montana sky, the old house's doors and windows gaped like a toothless old woman who has lived too long without proper care. The barn listed and sagged, gray weathered boards showed missing panels, and weeds grew over fallen corral fences.

"Oh my." Sam's dream image faded like the remaining patches of red paint. A cloud covered the sun.

"Well, it's got great bones." Teresa's cheerful voice sounded forced. "And look at that rich pastureland."

They got out of the car, and Sam gazed beyond the buildings. A slight breeze waved through the tall grass. A sage hen chuckled from the gray-green brush. No other houses marred the landscape. No dull traffic roar interrupted the rustlings of the prairie. The sun shone again. All the tension she'd been holding inside began to melt.

She pictured her great-grandparents on their horses, bringing in a bunch of cattle for branding. Frisky white-face calves. Mamas lowing plaintively. An electric thrill ran through her. The images changed. Instead of peeling paint and fallen fences, she could again picture a bright red-painted barn and a newly-fenced pasture filled with sleek Thoroughbred mares and their spindly-legged colts.

"Oh, it's beautiful," Sam whispered.

Teresa coughed, but quickly regained her composure. "Yes, it is. Can you picture yourself living here?"

Sam smiled at her. "Absolutely. This is family history. What better place for my horse ranch? I have to have this place."

"You do?" The woman's tone was incredulous for just a second, then she swiftly changed back into Realtor mode. "Of course you do. I knew you were the right person."

Sam laughed, almost giddy. Then she sobered. "But the buildings. Wow. They're in worse shape than I anticipated. I wouldn't be able to live here."

"Oh, don't worry about that. If you want to rent a place in town, I can help you out there."

Sam scuffed the toe of her boot in the dirt. "But I'd really want to live here. If I sign a lease with Jack Murdock, do you think he'd work with me to fix up the buildings?"

"You know, I think he'll be willing to make some kind of deal." Teresa leaned closer to Sam and lowered her voice, as if sharing a secret. "He's been trying to sell this property for years. He just decided to lease it out, so I think he'll talk. And I know some excellent contractors in Miles City. I'm sure they can make it habitable in no time." She fished her cell phone out of her purse and turned in a circle, looking for reception. "Darn. No cell service out here. We'll have to go back to Ingomar to call."

Sam nodded. "I'd like to lease with an option to buy. And my fiancé Kenny is a building contractor. We could do the work, if Mr. Murdock would give us a price break."

After a quick walk-through of the dilapidated barn and peering through the dust-covered windows of the house, nothing she saw changed her mind. Sam followed Teresa back to the car. Every nerve ending in her body tingled. This could be it. A place to start over, to forget the failures, the accident. She shut her eyes against memories, then opened them again, and began shoring up the slumping barn in her mind.

Driving back over the eight miles to the tiny town, Teresa kept up a lively chatter. "You know, I think my grandparents knew your great-grandparents. I remember them talking about Jake and Nettie's love of horses and rodeo."

Sam glanced at the other woman. "So, you're a native."

Teresa laughed. "More or less. I grew up here. When I graduated high school, I couldn't get away quick enough. Moved to Missoula for college but dropped out my sophomore year to go into real estate. But," she downshifted to drive through a rutted washout, "something out here kept calling to me. I just moved back a few months ago."

Sam's heart warmed. *This woman understands.* "Me too."

"Yeah. Must be something in the wind." Teresa laughed again. "What kind of ranching do you plan to do?"

"I have a rescued Thoroughbred mare, and I want to start a breeding ranch." Sam amazed herself with the confident tone. She would do this. She *could* do this.

"A rescued horse? That's awesome." Teresa glanced into the rearview mirror. "What a cool dream. You know, I've just known you a couple of hours, but I feel like we have some things in common." She paused a moment. "And, I guess I wouldn't feel right if I didn't warn you it's going to be a tough road. Montana, and especially this part of Montana, isn't the best place to make a good living."

Sam waved off her comment. "Oh, I know what I'm getting into. I grew up on a ranch about fifty miles northwest of here, near Horse Creek. I was helping out as soon as I could walk, almost. My parents and grandparents sold the

4

spread about twelve years ago and moved to Arizona." She smiled at the other woman. "I'm not worried." Her words belied the flutter just under her heart.

Teresa glanced at Sam with raised eyebrows. "Okay."

Leaving the rutted road, the car bumped down an equally rough "main street" with only a few ramshackle, boarded-up buildings. Teresa parked in front of the Jersey Lilly Bar and Café. She pulled out her phone again. "Good. I can make that call now. Why don't you go on inside and order us a Coke, my treat."

Sam walked into the dim, cool bar that smelled of stale cigarettes and beer. She ordered soft drinks from the bartender, the only person in the room, and sat at a table near the window. This move wouldn't be easy. In fact, if not for Kenny, she would have no financial backing. She smiled, anticipating their new life together. And the peace that came over her when she gazed at the prairie landscape was priceless.

"Yes, ma'am." Teresa's shout directed Sam's attention to the door where the agent scurried into the bar toward her. "He'll go for it. Lease with option to buy, one month down with four months' gratis on the lease for fixing up the buildings."

Sam flashed her a thumbs up. "Let's do the paperwork."

Teresa had a big grin. "Oh, that's great. I had to do a bit of fast-talking and old-fashioned horse-trading, but Jack is ecstatic." She laid out the papers on the table and took a sip of her drink. "So, I'll add the new terms here, and then we'll meet tomorrow, and you can sign the new contract."

After going over the wording and nodding her approval, Sam fished her cell phone from her jeans pocket. "I've got to call Kenny now and tell him. He'll be so excited. He's always wanted to be a cowboy." She punched buttons and listened to the phone ring somewhere on a jobsite in Phoenix. "Oh, and Aunt Monica, too. She's the one who told me about this."

Teresa held her glass up to clink with Sam's. "This is so great. To the rescuer of horses. And houses too."

The next day after she'd scribbled her name on the last line, butterflies kicked up dust inside her stomach. Sam swallowed hard. *Oh my gosh, what have I gotten myself into? This will be a huge undertaking. What if I fail? Again.*

No. She squared her shoulders. *I gotta do this. My dream will work out. I know it will.*

CHAPTER TWO

Sam bounced on the pickup seat beside her fiancé. "Just wait till you see it." She felt like a ten-year-old about to meet her first horse.

Kenny turned his Arizona-bronzed face toward her and flashed a white-toothed smile, the one that always made her knees turn to chocolate pudding. "Well, if you're this excited about something, it's got to be good. But man, this is desolate country. We haven't seen a single car since we left Ingomar."

Sam giggled. "That's part of its charm, hon. We won't be living in our neighbor's hip pocket." She sobered. "The buildings are in pretty bad shape, though. But making this place come to life will be fun. We'll fix it up together."

Kenny downshifted and drove up the low rise to the abandoned ranch. He pulled up in front of the sagging house, turned the ignition key, and sat, his mouth agape.

Sam gulped. *What if he just wants to turn around and go home?* She put on a bright smile. "Well?"

Kenny shook his head. "Holy cow."

"C'mon, let's go look at it, see what we need." She got out, walked to the weathered porch that ran the length of the house, and tested each board with a tentative shoe tip before placing her full weight on the steps. The wood creaked but held.

"Wait. It looks pretty bad," Kenny called. He slammed the pickup door shut. "Be careful."

Ignoring the warning, she left him inspecting the foundation, stepped cautiously once again across the warped porch and unlocked the door into the kitchen, greeted by the musty-dusty smell of old buildings. A gray coating of dust covered the cabinets, and cupboard doors hung askew. Paint and wallpaper curled from the walls. Sawdust insulation spilled out of the cracks like stuffing from a tattered rag doll. Faint scuffling noises inside the walls told Sam that the only residents of this house for many years were mice.

Crunching across fifty-some years of detritus from intermittent renters and neglect, Sam moved into the living room.

Her gaze took in the warped floor and broken windowpanes. Thinking of pictures from long ago, she almost expected to see the floors strewn with bright Navajo rugs and the couch covered with horse blankets and pillows. She glanced into the first-floor bedroom and the tiny adjoining bathroom. Moving to the stairs at her right, Sam wiggled the banister.

Then she tried the steps, one at a time. They felt fairly sturdy.

At the top, a horseshoe-shaped landing opened to two bedrooms tucked under sloping rafters where she could walk upright only in the center. The only things left were porcelain shards from a broken washbasin and the iron head of a bedstead, rusted and spotted with bird droppings.

Can we really do this? But Sam remembered the pictures her aunt showed her of this house—warm-looking, homey— and of her petite great-grandmother clad in jeans and boots. Instead of dirt and debris, Sam saw the promise of once-again gleaming wood floors, of soft quilts covering antique bedsteads.

Gramma Nettie—so courageous, living through the hard times and trying to be a rodeo rider. She never gave up. *Not like I did. I couldn't even make it through one year of junior college.* Sam chewed her bottom lip. *Well, I have a dream too.* She peered out the broken window at the outbuildings below. Someday her champion horses would fill the barn and run in the pasture.

Excitement coiled inside her. *I want to live here. I have to do this. I can't go back to live in the city. Nothing left for me, no friends, no family. I'll just dry up and blow away there.*

Sam descended the stairs two at a time and stopped in the middle of the living room. Golden dust motes danced in the sun that slanted through the large windows.

Kenny stood in the entryway, taking in the mess. "Well, it's got great windows. And that porch is awesome—you just don't see those old-time wrap-around porches anymore. The foundation'll need shoring up, though."

"How much do you think it'll cost?"

Kenny shrugged, and a grimace creased his face. "A few thousand, I suppose." He gestured toward the shedding walls. "We'll have to replace all the wallboard. And a lot of the flooring. We'll have to get a camp trailer or something to live in while we work on it."

Sam danced in a circle. *He's getting into it too.* "I know. And plaster. And paint. And sanding and cleaning. Oh, but it'll be so pretty when we're done." She stopped and gave him a quick kiss. "And it'll be our home."

He twirled her around and caught her. "Yeah. That's the important part. I love that you have a dream, and we're going to make it happen together." He smiled and pulled her closer, into a long, smoldering kiss.

Hope exploded in Sam's chest.

CHAPTER THREE

Sam wrestled the steering wheel as the old pickup churned slowly through the snowdrifts in the pasture. Kenny stood in the back, feeding out flakes of hay bales to the band of hungry cows that swarmed the vehicle.

The wind kicked up suddenly and sent a fresh swirl of snow across the windshield. Although still early afternoon, the sky darkened to twilight, the leaden clouds reaching down to envelope the gray horizon. Sam shivered and turned up the heater fan, then put the wipers on. What a winter so far. Only the end of December and they'd been fighting snow for two months already.

Kenny thumped on the cab roof, and she stopped to let him get in. "Criminy, it's cold." He pounded his arms to restore warmth. "Doesn't this heater work any better than that?"

Sam grinned. "Poor Kenny. Miss your Arizona winter?"

He snorted. "I didn't know they made temperatures this low. Well, we've done our duty for the day—how long do we have to feed Jack Murdock's mangy cows?"

"People help each other out here—it's what we would do, even if he wasn't giving us a nice break on the lease for feeding them."

"Yeah, I guess." Kenny shook his shaggy brown hair. "At least it's his hay."

"We don't need the land yet, anyway... until we get our horse herd built up." Sam pushed her boot against the accelerator. "I'd guess we're in for another big blizzard. Let's get you home and feed you something hot."

Another gust of wind rocked the truck and snow came down heavier. Sam peered through the diminishing visibility and plowed through drifts, the vehicle swerving and bucking. Kenny sat hunched against the door, arms crossed, his face dark and glowering. She sneaked a glance. He looked like a cowboy—wide shoulders and slim hips—but he was a city boy.

"You'll get used to it." Sam swallowed. *I hope.*

"I doubt it."

Sam peered out the windshield, barely able to see where they were going.

"Do you know which direction is home?"

"Of course." *I think I do.* The wipers ineffectively moved clumps of ice across the windshield. She held her shoulders rigid. They should be getting to the gravel road back to the ranch by now.

Finally, Sam felt the terrain smooth out somewhat. *Ah, thank goodness.* Now she knew where they were—just a mile to the house. She accelerated toward home.

"Aren't you going a little fast?" Kenny looked at her with a frown.

"Since when are you a backseat driver? Don't you want to get home where it's warm?"

The pickup suddenly fishtailed on the icy road. Before Sam could react, they swung around in a half circle, bumping over ruts. She bounced. Her head hit the roof. White sheets of snow sprayed over the hood and covered the windshield. The pickup came to an abrupt stop in the ditch, buried in snow up to the windows.

She sat, stunned. Then she turned her head to Kenny, his legs splayed against the floor, hands braced on the dashboard. He stared back, mouth open wide.

"Kenny? Are you all right?"

"What… the heck… were you trying to do, kill us both?" The words spat from between clenched teeth.

She frowned. What kind of reaction was that? "Course not. The road's icy. Rutted. I couldn't—"

11

He hmphed and looked out the window. "I suppose you expect me to get out and shovel now."

Sam slumped in the seat. *Why is he acting this way?* Was this the man she loved, who loved her, who wanted to spend the rest of his life with her? He was acting like a jerk, not the kind, loving guy she'd known for the past three years. Her heartbeat thudded. She bit back the temptation to say, "Cowboy up! Act like a man!"

"I'll take a look. You stay inside where it's warm for now." She pushed the door against the drift. It wouldn't budge. Rolling down the window, she peered outside. Wind-driven snow stung her face like needles. "We're buried pretty deep. We're not going to be able to dig out."

"What d'you mean?" Kenny's scowl deepened.

"We're not far from home. We can follow the fence line and not get lost in the blizzard." Sam's stomach knotted like a noose. *I hope.*

"You're crazy. We'll freeze to death." His tone slid into a whine.

"Well, the gas tank is almost empty. Nobody's going to be coming down this road for days. We could freeze in here— less than a mile from home." She forced control into her voice, while all she wanted to do was collapse into his arms and feel comforted.

"You and your big ideas to move out to the middle of nowhere." Kenny heaved out a breath. "All right. You're so smart, lead the way."

Sam crawled out the window, Kenny following. She pawed through the snow in the bed of the pickup to find several lengths of discarded twine from the bales, tied them together, then knotted one end around her waist. "Tie the other end to yourself, so we don't get separated."

Kenny complied without a word. Sam squeezed his shoulder. *He's cold and he's scared. So am I.* She tried to smile. "Ready, Freddy?"

He gave a short nod. "Let's go."

She waded through the waist-deep snow toward the fence, barely able to make out the dark ghostlike shapes of the fenceposts through the swirling storm. Each step was a giant effort. Beads of sweat popped out on her forehead and promptly froze. Her nose was a lump of ice. With stiff fingers, she pulled her knitted hat lower and adjusted her neck scarf higher.

One step at a time. She pushed forward. *I can do this. If Great-Grandma Nettie could do it, I can.* She glanced back at Kenny. *Can he?*

The wind intensified. Sam lost sight of the elusive gray posts and stopped to peer through the driving snow.

"Where are we?" Kenny's muffled shout blew past her on the wind.

"Hang on. We're almost there." But her own words held no comfort for her. Were they lost? Had she turned in a circle? She trudged forward again. *Trust your instincts. It's gotta be here.* Her heart pounded. She'd heard plenty of stories about people freezing to death mere feet from their door.

Sam stuck her arms out in front of her, feeling her way like a blind person. Then her mittened hand hit a post the same moment she finally saw its dark shape. *Whew. I was right.* She turned to Kenny. "Okay, we're practically home free now."

Hand over hand, she pulled herself along the wire. Having something to hold onto gave her strength. *Almost home. Almost home.* She kept up the chant with each slogging footstep.

They trudged for what seemed like hours, pushing and stumbling through the drifts. Sam's overboots filled with snow, her hands so numb she could hardly feel the fence. *Did I turn the right direction?* Surely they weren't headed away from the house. How long had they been out here? An hour? Two?

"How much farther?" Kenny's shout urged her on.

"Not far now." *I hope.* She pushed harder. Her breath came in gasps. Then her boot hit a sagebrush root or something buried in the drifts. Her momentum carried her forward, and she fell face first into the snow. *I'm so tired. I can't go on.* She could just lie there and go to sleep. It would be warm in the deep snow, in a cocoon, soft and peaceful.

Kenny's mittened hands fumbled at her arms. "C'mon, Sam, you gotta get up. Don't quit on me."

She tried to swat him away. "No. Leave me alone. Tired."

"Sam. We're almost there. Come on, don't give up now." He pawed at her shoulders, his voice frantic. "Let me lead and break trail awhile."

Sam squeezed her eyes shut. The snowdrift was so soft, so warm, so comforting. But Kenny's voice kept intruding, waking her, prodding her. She blinked. *Oh. Freezing. Snow. Gotta get home.* She shook her head clear and allowed him to help her to her feet. They switched places. "Thanks, Ken." With tears of gratitude freezing beneath her lashes, she followed him mutely through the dark gray tunnel of the storm.

Then Kenny stopped abruptly, and Sam bumped into his back. "What?" She looked up. They'd run right into the side of the barn. A chuckle burbled up in her throat. "Oh, thank God. We made it."

She felt her way to the door and gratefully stumbled inside. Flipping on the light switch, she stood for a moment, savoring the light and the warmth of just being out of the wind. Memories of stories about her great-grandparents, Grandpa Neil and Grandma Anna flashed in her mind. They'd had close calls like this in blizzards too.

Kenny stomped in. The snow caked on his legs fell in clumps to the floor. Sam did the same. Little balls of ice stuck to their knitted scarves and hats. She grabbed an old broom and brushed him off. "Hey, you okay?"

He shrugged. "I guess."

Behind them, a horse blew and whinnied.

"I'm coming, Sugar. Hold on." Sam turned on a heat lamp and sat beneath it on a hay bale, rubbing her hands together. She patted the bale. "Come sit, get warmed up a little before we make the trek up to the house."

Kenny lowered himself like an old man and sat beside her, hunched and shivering.

Sam reached inside his coat and snuggled close, trying to combine their body heat. He stiffened and turned his head away. She withdrew and held her hands under the infrared bulb. Worry skittered through her mind. Why was he acting so strange?

Warmth from the lamp prickled needlelike sensations back into her fingers. She massaged her hands and Kenny's. He groaned as the feeling returned. "Oh, man, that stings!"

The horse nickered again. "Okay, Sugar Lump. I'll feed you." She picked up a bucket, dipped it in the oat bag, and walked to the mare's stall. "You're a lucky old nag—get to be in here, out of the storm." She held out a handful of the oats, smiling as her rescued Thoroughbred moved gentle lips over her palm.

Sam dumped the rest of the oats into the trough and ran a hand down the mare's neck, withers, and over the lumpy, malformed front leg—the result of a racetrack accident a couple of years ago.

"Yeah, you don't know how lucky you are—you were on your way to the glue factory for sure." Sam picked up an elastic bandage and wrapped the horse's knee.

"Lucky your grandparents bought her for you," Kenny muttered.

"Yup. Pretty cool eighteenth birthday present." She smiled, a hitch in her heart. Her beloved Grandma Anna and Grandpa Neil had passed away shortly after that, within six months of each other. Their hearts were so intertwined, one couldn't live without the other. *I want that too.* Sam sneaked a look at Kenny.

She patted the horse's withers. "Okay, Sugar, rest easy and stay warm."

Kenny stood by the barn door, shoulders hunched, kicking at the straw on the dirt floor. "I swear if we were the last three beings alive on earth, you'd eat me before you'd lay a hand on that horse."

Sam could tell he was trying to make a joke, but he wasn't able to disguise his impatient stance. "That's right, big boy. So you'd better watch your step." She laughed. "C'mon, let's follow the clothesline up to the house. That stew I made yesterday is going to taste awfully good warmed up."

Inside, changed into dry clothing, they sat, still shivering, in the living room near the fire in the propane stove, and spooned from bowls full of hot stew. Kenny had quit shaking, but the silence between them hadn't thawed.

CHAPTER FOUR

Sometime during the night, the wind stopped its howling, but the morning sky remained full of gray, threatening clouds. When Kenny came downstairs from his room, Sam dished up big bowls of oatmeal. "We'd better get that pickup dug out before the next storm hits."

He grunted. "I suppose."

Heavily bundled against the cold, they trudged through the white undulating terrain, using their shovels as walking sticks. The air was still and frosty and the hairs inside Sam's nose felt like miniature icicles. Kenny broke trail through the deep snow-covered road. Sam followed in his tracks. The mile to where the pickup sat stretched interminably. She could barely recognize the terrain. Then a huge white mound off to the side appeared. "There's the truck. You can't even tell it's blue under all that."

Kenny sighed and scooped a hard-packed shovelful of snow. "This could take all day." His face darkened with a scowl.

"Yup. It might." Was he giving up already? Sam brushed snow from the top of the cab with a broom she'd brought and dug a hole alongside until she could open the driver's side door. Then she joined Kenny at the rear, digging a pathway back to the road. Sweat beaded on her forehead and froze. She pulled her knitted cap down farther. Plant the shovel, bend and scoop, throw the snow to the side. Over and over.

Kenny stopped and stretched his back with a groan. "We've been at this for an hour and it doesn't look like we're making any progress."

Sam straightened and looked back at the road. "Oh, but we have—we've come a good six feet. Only about six more to go." She grinned. "C'mon. I'll race you—last one dug out to the road has to push."

Kenny glowered. Then he laughed. "All right, Miss Smarty, you're on." He went back to digging with a fury. Snow flew around them as each tried to outpace the other. Grunting and panting, Kenny dug. Puffing and groaning, Sam kept up with him until the last couple of feet. *I think he's actually enjoying this.* Then she feigned exhaustion, working slower and slower.

Kenny hit the hard surface of the road and flung his shovel with a triumphant shout. "I beat you!"

Sam picked up a handful of snow, packed it quickly, and threw it at him. "You cheated. Your path is narrower than mine."

"Oh, bull it is." He grabbed the shovel and threw a blade full of snow at her. Sam launched herself at him, and they fell into the fluffy drifts, scuffling and laughing.

Sam sat up, still giggling. "Okay. You won, fair and square. You get to drive, and I have to push."

"Oh no, you don't. I'm not going to have anybody come along and see me sitting in the pickup with you out there pushing. No way." He stood and gave her a hand up. "Let's go do this."

While Kenny dug a path around to the front of the truck, Sam got into the cab and ground the ignition. After several tries, the engine finally caught. Shifting into reverse, she slowly depressed the gas pedal. The pickup moved a few inches, then the wheels spun.

She let up on the gas and opened the window. "Okay, I'm going to try to get this thing rocking. So, watch yourself."

Kenny nodded. He pushed while she gunned the engine, then let the truck settle back, then gunned it again until the truck moved—just a little. For every few inches gained, the wheels dug deeper into the snow, and Sam stopped while Kenny put hay from the back under the tires for traction. Four or five more inches, dig some more, try again.

Then with one mighty push, Kenny doubled over with a shout. Sam cut the engine and leaped out. "What happened?"

"My back." Kenny groaned. "I can't straighten up."

"Oh no." Sam took his arm. "C'mon, can you get inside? We have to get this pickup out to get you home. If you can drive, I'll try pushing."

Kenny's face was white. His teeth chattered. Hunched over, he made his way painfully to the door and tried to step up into the cab. "Aarrggh." He sank into the snow. "You're going to have to go home and call for help."

"No. Kenny, you have to get in this pickup." Sam plucked at his sleeve. "You'll freeze to death out here. At least get inside so you can run the heater while I go home and call somebody." For the first time, she missed having cell phone service. *Darn this remote country. What did Great-Grandma and Grandpa do?*

She looked frantically around the white nothingness. No trees. No branches to rig up a travois. What was left in the pickup bed—a rope, a chain, an old board perhaps? Rummaging through the snow and scraps of hay, she pulled out a dirty, torn tarp. Now what? She surely couldn't pull Kenny all the way back to the house on that.

He groaned. Sam pulled the knitted cap from her head and threw it on the ground. *What am I going to do?* "Hang in there, Ken, we'll figure something out." Maybe she could at least wrap him with the tarp, and he'd stay warm enough until she came back. She pulled it around to where he lay, took off her overcoat, and covered him.

"What're you doing? You can't walk a mile without a coat. I can get..." Kenny tried to push himself up with one arm but fell back with a grimace.

"Well, I'll be running, so I'll be warm. But you need this." She rolled him to one side, tucked the tarp under him and wrapped him inside. "I'll be back soon."

Shivering now, Sam put her hat back on, stood, and waded through the snow to the road. Once she found their tracks from earlier, she started to run—slow and clumsy. Thoughts whirled through her head. The nearest neighbor lived five miles away. Would they be stuck too? Ingomar was eight. Too darn far away.

Sam stumbled and fell, getting a face full of snow. *Crumb!* No cell service. Only one vehicle, only one horse that she couldn't ride. What had she been thinking, moving out here? She hoisted herself up, bent over to catch her breath, then took off jogging again.

In the distance, she heard the low roar of an engine. Sam stopped to listen. The noise faded. Probably an airplane. *Gotta get going.* She shoved back her mitten cuff—no watch. Must have dropped it in the snow. Sam moved forward, slower now, her energy flagging, her arms numb with cold. *Can't stop, can't give up. Kenny is going to die out there.* Fear spurred her on.

Finally, she saw the house and with renewed strength, she ran up the slope and through the door, not stopping to shake off the snow. She grabbed the phone with one hand and the short list of neighbors' numbers in the other. Horace Jones. The old widower lived the closest. With shaky fingers, she punched in the number. It rang. And rang. No answer. *Dam.* Her finger ran down the list. Buck Gilbert. Ten miles away. Well, better than nobody. Again, no answer. How was Kenny faring out there in the cold? *Oh, Lord, watch over him.*

Sam punched in the number for the Jersey Lilly—*maybe that's where everybody is.*

Then she heard the engine again. She peered out the window through the murky grayness and caught a glimpse of a vehicle. *Somebody's coming.* Sam slammed down the receiver, grabbed a coat, and ran outside, down the lane to the country road. Old Man Jones with his snowplow came up the road. *Oh, thank you, Lord.*

Sam waved her arms, jumped up and down, and yelled. Her pant legs shed clumps of snow.

Her seventy-year-old neighbor finally saw her and pulled the vehicle to a stop. "Howdy there, Samantha. What're you doin' out here?"

"It's Kenny. The pickup's stuck and we tried to get it out and he hurt his back and couldn't get in the truck and I left him in the snow and I tried to call you and you weren't home and ..." Sam ran out of breath. "Oh, please, can you help?"

"Sure thing. Hop in. We'll go get 'im." Horace gunned the engine and pushed snow out of their path, clearing the road to where the stuck pickup rested.

Sam sat on the edge of the seat, her hands fisted on her thighs. *Oh please, be all right, Kenny. Please be alive.*

Horace braked, and Sam leaped from his truck. "Kenny! Kenny! Are you all right?"

Kenny pushed himself up with one arm. "Yeah. A little cold. Glad you're back."

Horace ambled around the side of the pickup. "So, threw your back out, huh?"

Kenny grunted. He didn't look up at their neighbor.

"Okay. Let's get you up and in the truck. Get you warm." The old man grabbed Kenny under the arms and Sam took his feet.

He sputtered and squirmed. "I oughtta be able to do it myself..." But then he grimaced in pain.

Together they carried him to Horace's warm vehicle and propped him as comfortably as possible on the seat.

"Might as well be in Siberia," he mumbled.

Horace grabbed a chain from the back of his truck and hooked it to Sam's. "Jump in there, and let's see if we can get 'er outta here."

The chain tightened. Sam pressed the gas pedal, and Horace pulled the pickup smoothly out of the ditch. Once back on the road, he unhooked the chain. "There ya go, little gal. I'll bring Kenny on up to the house and help him get inside."

At the house, Kenny opened the pickup door, stretched one leg out, and moaned. Pulling his other leg around, he slid down from the seat and stood, hunched over, a hand on the frame. Sam slammed her door shut and ran over to him. She and Horace each got on one side and helped him inside to the rocking chair by the stove. Kenny continued to look down and mumbled about the cold, the snow, "...this God-forsaken country."

Sam steeled herself against his complaints. She turned to her neighbor. "Oh, Mr. Jones, thank you so much for your help. I didn't know what I was going to do."

"Aw, call me Horace. It was nothin'. Figured I'd better get out and get that road plowed out 'fore it snows again."

"Well, you came along at just the right time." Sam's hands shook. "Let me put the coffee on and I'll broil some burgers."

"Coffee sounds mighty fine, but you don't need to be fixin' me no supper."

Sam touched the old man's arm. "Please. It's the least I can do."

CHAPTER FIVE

Kenny spent the next couple of snowbound days in bed. Lying in the snow had provided a great icepack for his pulled muscles. Sam massaged his back, and he gradually began to loosen up—physically anyway. An emotional chill still emanated from his core.

One evening, he limped downstairs to join her by the stove. He eased into the rocking chair with a sigh. "Sam …?

"What's wrong? Are you still hurting?" She leaned forward, concern fluttering her heart.

"Well yeah, but… Sam… you know I love you?"

"Of course. And I love you too." She frowned. Something in his tone sent a flicker of worry through her.

"We need to rethink this plan to live out here… in the middle of nowhere." Kenny shook his head. "I had no idea this land was so harsh. We could've died in that blizzard."

Sam bit her lip. "Yeah. But we didn't."

"And then, what if Horace hadn't come along? I coulda froze to death laying out there in the snow."

"B-but Horace *was* there. Neighbors take care of each other out here."

He leaned his head against the pillows. "This is not living. What about this *existence* makes the struggle worthwhile?"

"My… our dream—to raise Thoroughbreds…"

Kenny blew out a long sigh. "How is that ever going to happen? You and I both know it's an impossible dream. We're miles from any shipping point, miles from vets, miles from… everything! It's forty miles to Forsyth and the nearest hospital, for cripes sake." His voice rose. He pounded a fist on the chair arm. "And how are you going to get the money to buy a stud, or even afford a stud fee to start this wonderful herd of yours?"

Sam stared at him in shock. "Mine? I thought this was your dream too." He'd been so supportive, so enthusiastic when she found out the old family ranch was for lease.

"No." Kenny spat the word. "This 'dream' has turned into one big nightmare, that's what. It'll never happen. We could kill ourselves trying."

"No, honey." Sam knelt on the floor beside him. "Listen. Please. I know this winter has been rough so far. But you'll feel different in the spring. Sugar will be ready to breed... and... we'll figure out the finances... together. There's building going on in Forsyth—you can find lots of work with your skills." She peered into his face, her eyes stinging with tears. *I don't seem to be getting through to him.*

He looked at her from beneath lowered brows. "We didn't plan this very well. Please, let's rethink this. Let's go back to Phoenix this winter and regroup—talk to the banks there, maybe get a loan, figure out how we're going to do this."

"Kenny..." Sam heard the exasperated tone of her voice and stopped. "Okay. I admit we didn't think ahead very far, but when I found out this place was for lease... well, I couldn't let it go. This is my history. This is where I want... need to be. We can build this ranch together." She smiled. "Just remember the original homesteaders. They didn't have much more than we do."

He snorted. "And look at the abandoned sites all over the country. I can't live like this. I want a secure future—for us, for our children. I want to live in civilization and not have to eke out an existence from an unforgiving, hostile land."

Sam took his hands in hers. "Oh, Kenny. I'm so sorry this is so tough. I guess I didn't realize how different Montana would be for you. I grew up here, so I knew what to expect. But, really, once you get through this winter, you'll see... things will look up, it'll be better. And next winter probably won't be so hard."

She stood and kissed his forehead. "Why don't you sleep on it? You'll feel better tomorrow. I've got to go check on Sugar before I turn in."

The next morning, the sun came out and the snow glistened and shimmered as far as Sam could see. As she set up the coffeepot and turned on the gas under the frying pan, she glanced out the window and saw Horace drive by, plowing the road again. She smiled. *Nice to have a neighbor like that.*

Hearing Kenny clomp down the stairs, she dished up a big plate of eggs and bacon. "Ready to tackle the feeding again?"

A thump brought her around sharply. Kenny stood in the doorway, a suitcase on the floor beside him. "No."

A stone-like weight sank through her chest. "Wha... what are you doing?"

"I'm going back to Arizona. I can't do this."

Sam lowered the plate to the table as if it weighed a ton. "What do you mean?"

He shrugged and lifted his hands in mock defeat. "I'm not cut out for this life—this struggle for each day's existence. And I'm not going to help you down the road to failure. That's what this is—a dead end. If you come to your senses, I'll be in Phoenix."

Little white lights exploded behind Sam's eyes. "Kenny..."

He picked up his suitcase. "Will you please take me to Ingomar? Maybe I can catch a ride with the mailman to the airport in Miles City."

***

The plane soared into the crystal blue sky, as Sam clenched her hands until her fingernails bit into her palms. Anything to keep the tears from coming. Kenny was gone. She turned from the window, walked through the small, empty lobby, and out to her pickup.

Her mind blank, she drove through the blinding snowscape and found herself parked in front of the house before she realized where she was. The house they'd spent months fixing up together.

Sam sighed. Last summer had been so much fun while they sawed and hammered, stripped walls and floors, cleaned and painted to get the old house into livable shape. Their dreams were alive, vibrant. But Kenny had changed. The energetic, hopeful jokester disappeared after the novelty of his first snowstorm wore off. She'd thought surely when spring came, he'd regain his old spirit. Tears prickled, and she bit her lip. She knew how long and hard Montana winters could be from when she was just a kid. But when the snow and ice thawed, people were renewed along with the greening of the prairie.

Inside, she brewed a cup of tea and took it into the living room to sit in the rocker by the stove. She should go out and feed those cows before dark, but she couldn't bring herself to move.

It was like having her horse suddenly spook, falling from that firm, safe place in the saddle, and being dragged with her boot still stuck in the stirrup.

How could she not have known him? She pounded her thighs with tight fists. Kenny had loved riding with her in Arizona, going to horse races, talking about the fillies and colts they'd one day have, to watch grow and mature, to sell. And later read about their wins.

What a stupid fool she'd been to think he could adapt to life so foreign—from Phoenix to Podunk, Montana. To think that love would overcome their differences.

The closest thing she'd ever experienced to this pain was when her old gelding, Apache, suddenly died. She hadn't been able to save him.

The vet had come to do an autopsy. He'd peeled back the layers of hide, fat, and muscle, reached into the stomach and pulled out yards of moist yellow intestines, then a black, bloated piece. The horse had a twisted gut.

She curled forward in the rocking chair and hugged her arms over her own churning insides. Kenny was right—at least about being miles from everything. But her dream wasn't impossible. It couldn't be. *I can make this happen. I know I can.*

She bit back tears and rocked into the darkness.

***

Sam trudged through the loneliness of the morning to the barn, her head down, watching one foot move in front of the other. Inside, she filled the oat bucket and walked to Sugar's stall. The slender brown mare rested her head over the gate and fluttered her nostrils.

She stroked the horse's soft neck. Then she buried her face in Sugar's silky mane. "Oh, baby. It's just you and me now."

Sugar nuzzled Sam's shoulder as if she understood.

After feeding and brushing the horse, she let her out into the corral for exercise. Sunshine spotlighted from a clear blue sky. The hills shone in the white distance. With a deep breath of the clean, crisp air, she drank in the beauty, relief flooding her body. This is what she wanted, needed—to be back in touch with the land, the animals—not the heat and bustle of Arizona cities. This is where her dream would come true. She didn't need anyone else. After all, she had Great-Grandma Nettie's blood. And Grandma Anna's strong German instinct for survival. She had survived WWII and cancer. Sam could do this—she would show Kenny.

With a smile on her face, Sam strode to the pickup. She could load this truck and feed those cows by herself. She gave one quick, resolute nod, jammed the lever into gear and drove to the haystack.

CHAPTER SIX

Spring arrived overnight, water gushing from the hills as snow melted in the warmth of a Chinook wind. Everywhere she went, Sam waded through a sea of mud. Finding a dry spot to feed the cattle grew harder and harder. But with sunshine came hope and the promise of green grass, new calves, and her dream.

Since Kenny left, Horace stopped by every day and they helped each other with their feeding chores. He was like Grandpa—down to earth, seasoned, and wise. Grandpa Neil had lived his life in Montana much like this, until he and Grandma Anna sold their ranch and moved to Arizona.

"I'm going to work on getting my Thoroughbred herd started this year." Sam gazed out the pickup window at the hills she pictured some day dotted with gangly-legged colts. "Sugar looks like she's strong enough to breed now."

Horace gripped the steering wheel as they bounced through the ruts. "What's your plan?"

"Well, I need to come up with some money to buy a stallion or at least to pay for stud fees. And since I'm not making any money out here—yet—I guess I'll have to go see if I can float a loan at the bank in Forsyth or Miles City."

Horace nodded. "Sounds like a good idea. You might even go back to Foster, where your grandparents banked. Small town—they'll probably remember your family."

Sam shook her head. "I'd rather not go back there. My memories as a kid aren't so fond. I was happy when Mom and Dad decided to move to Arizona when I was ten." She chuckled. "But here I am, back in a rural Montana community. I guess things weren't so bad as all that."

***

The banker in Forsyth wanted to know what Sam could use as collateral. "A broken-down racehorse? No, I'm sorry, we can't lend money on that alone."

Miles City and Billings bankers sang a similar refrain. "Racehorses in this part of the country?" A lift of an eyebrow and a smirk signaled that they thought Sam must be crazy.

The First National Bank of Foster hadn't changed much since she'd been here as a child, collecting her lollipop when Mom stopped to make a deposit. It was the only bank—in the only town, for that matter—thirty-some miles from Dad's and Grandpa's ranch at Horse Creek.

Sam entered the small brick building. The same cracked green plastic chairs adorned the lobby, and she swore the same fake Philodendron plant stood in the corner—probably with ten years worth of dust. She smoothed her skirt—was it too tight? Too short? She'd much rather be wearing jeans.

The face of the young man who strode toward her now looked familiar. Jerry Osborn, son of Gerald Osborn II. Even the bankers were the same—at least the same family.

"Samantha Moser." He took her outstretched hand in both of his. "How good to see you again."

She smiled. "Likewise." Yeah, wasn't this the ornery kid who beat up all the ranch kids when they were about six or eight? Or was that his brother Nate?

He led her into his office and motioned to a chair. "What can I do for you today?"

Sam crossed her black-stockinged legs, another concession to this project, and leaned forward. "I'd like to take out a loan to buy a racehorse."

Jerry's eyebrows arched, and his eyes widened for just a moment before his face settled into his normal banker's repose. "Racehorses? Out here in the middle of nowhere?" Then his façade cracked. A smile tugged at the corner of his mouth, grew, and he laughed. Soft chuckles at first, then guffaws.

The same answer as in Forsyth, Miles City, and Billings. Sam stood. "Thank you for your support, Mr. Osborn. You'll not be hearing from me again." She turned abruptly and marched out of the office, through the dusty lobby and into the muddy street of the nearly deserted town.

"He'll be begging for my accounts one day," she muttered through clenched teeth. He was even a bigger bully now than when they were kids.

She jumped into her pickup, snagging her nylons on an exposed seat spring, slammed the door, and gunned the engine. The tires spit gravel as she backed out of the diagonal parking spot on Main Street and sped toward the highway. She couldn't get out of this half-horse town quick enough.

The forty miles over rough, unpaved roads did nothing for her temperament. Sam seethed all the way home. Bankers! What did they know anyway? Just because no one successfully raised Thoroughbreds in this part of the country didn't mean it couldn't be done. Not all horses in Montana had to be ranch or rodeo stock. She pounded the steering wheel. She'd come up with the money another way.

But what could she do? A sigh escaped her throat. Ever since she was about twelve, she'd focused on nothing but pursuing her dream. Before she grew into her five-foot seven-inch frame, she'd thought of becoming a jockey. Oh well, dreams can change. But not this one. *I have to do this.* She couldn't let Kenny think she was a failure.

The late afternoon sun sank toward the low horizon. The clear blue sky filled her periphery like an inverted bowl, with streaks of orange and gold painting the edges. Montana truly was "Big Sky Country."

How was she going to get the money to stay here? Her savings wouldn't last long and without Kenny helping pay the lease... A breath fluttered from her lips. She'd dropped out of college, preferring to work in a stable—around horses—to earn money. No stables around this country. Waitressing? Sam wrinkled her nose. Where? The Jersey

Lilly, with its clientele of about five regulars? Drive all the way into Forsyth every day? *Crumb.* Well, she had to earn money somehow.

Mom and Dad didn't have the money, struggling up there on their off-grid homestead in Alaska now. Besides, they thought she was crazy to move back to Montana like this. Grandma and Grandpa—they'd shelled out a thousand bucks for Sugar's adoption fee—but they were gone now. Nor Aunt Monica—even though she was a best-selling author with her books about Grandma Nettie, that didn't mean she had a lot of money.

Sam pulled up in front of the old house and sat. Hire herself out as a ranch hand? She knew how to do that. But the few ranchers left in this country were self-sufficient—didn't seem to need any help or helped each other. Besides, they were all older men who would probably bridle at the thought of hiring a woman.

She got out and slammed the door. A man would have been given a loan by now.

***

Booting up her laptop, Sam did an internet search for "stud fees." Why hadn't she started this sooner? If she didn't get some money put together soon, it would be too late to get Sugar bred this year. Her dream had been to buy a stallion and start with a breeding pair. But she'd done research on buying a stallion months ago and nearly fell off her chair—she'd need $100,000 or more. Well, that was out of the question, especially with bankers' attitudes the way they were.

Her search brought up several breeding farms in Kentucky. She clicked on one. First on the list was a descendent of the famous Seattle Slew, winner of the 1978 Triple Crown. She peered at the screen. "Holy cow." Three hundred thousand dollars for a live foal. "I don't think so."

Sam scrolled down to the end of the list. Here was one for $5,000. Hmmm. That might be a little closer to her price range.

The phone rang.

"Hey, babe." Kenny's voice kicked up the butterflies in her stomach.

"What are you doing?" She tried to sound nonchalant.

"Just working. Lots of construction down here. Phoenix is growing fast."

"So… that's good, I guess…" She bit her lip. "Any thoughts on coming back here now that it's spring?"

"Aw geez, Sam. I'm so busy—got more work than I can handle, practically. I don't see how I can leave this opportunity to—"

"Live in poverty with me?" Sam finished for him. "Yeah, I figured."

"Now, Hon, it's not like that. I want to be with you—I miss you. Why don't you come back down here and help me with my construction business, and we can build up a nest egg so you can start your horse ranch? Let's face it, babe, we weren't ready."

Sam sighed. He just didn't get it. This state, this way of life, this feeling of home—this was her lifeblood.

Long after the conversation ended, Sam sat, her shoulders slumped. Kenny was probably right—she'd gone into this adventure without a concrete plan. *Darn it, why did he have to leave?* Five thousand might as well be five hundred thousand—she didn't have either amount. Her meager savings wasn't going to last long. She *had* to find a job.

CHAPTER SEVEN

Once again, Sam donned a dress and stockings and drove to Forsyth. She wandered down Main and Front streets, stopping at every café and restaurant—all eight of them, including the Dairy Queen—to ask about work.

"Gosh, honey. Wish I could, but there aren't that many jobs in this town—I have more applicants than I can ever use." The reply from the owner of Buff's Bar and Cafe became a repeated litany as Sam trudged down the street, ruing her choice of heels.

After buying a soda at the Dairy Queen, she wandered down a side street. *I knew this was going to be a wild goose chase.* But what else was she going to do? Go back to the Jersey Lilly and see what they might suggest? Maybe this fall, during hunting season, they'd be needing some help. What about this summer? She needed a job now. Sam sipped wearily on her soda.

Spying a bench in front of City Hall, she gratefully sank onto it with a sigh, enjoying the warmth of the spring sun. She gazed around at the town—planters optimistically filled with flower starts, strips of greening lawn between the boulevards, trees blossoming with new leaves. Yes, this town was a long way from what Kenny thought of as "civilization," with a population of less than two thousand. Yet the residents were trying. And that's what Sam had to do. She couldn't give up, like Kenny did. No way could she go back to the city. She loved life here. This country was in her blood.

She swiveled around to look at various flyers in the window—an all-town garage sale coming up next weekend, a dance at the Legion Hall, a meeting of the Rosebud County Cattle Women. Then she saw one titled "Riding Instructor Wanted." Sam stood to read the small print. The Parks and Rec department was instituting a summer horseback riding class. "Inquire Within," it said.

Sam set her empty cup on the bench and strode to the door. This might be something she would be qualified to do. She grasped the doorknob and pushed. The door was locked. She glanced at her watch. Noon. Closed for lunch. Okay. She'd go back to the Dairy Queen, grab a burger, and come back.

At 1:15, Sam stood at the still-locked door, peering inside. Boy, they took long lunch hours around here.

"The mayor's out of town and the secretary is sick today." A voice came from behind her. Sam turned to see a jeans-clad woman smiling at her. "I don't know where the rest of the crew is—I think maybe a conference or something."

Sam's shoulders slumped. "Oh. I see." *Figures. Just my luck.* "Thanks." She jotted down the phone number and walked back to her pickup.

The next morning, with buoyant anticipation, she dialed the number and called back several times before someone finally answered.

"I'm calling about the riding instructor position you posted," she said.

"Oh yeah. Guess we need to take down that flier. Sorry, but we didn't get the funds we needed for the program."

Sam hung up the phone with a sigh. *Well, might as well drive to the Jersey Lilly. It'll be tourist season soon. And it is closer to home.*

Billy Cole, the proprietor, welcomed her as she stepped into the darkened beer-scented saloon. "Hey there, Sam. Can I pour ya a cold one?"

"No thanks, Billy. It's a little early for me yet. Maybe some coffee, though." She admired the massive dark cherry back bar with mirrored shelves lined with colorful bottles. "Where did you say that bar came from?"

34

Rescuing Samantha

The bartender poured her a cup of coffee. "All the way from St. Louis by boat, early 1900s." He wiped a bit of dust from a corner knick-knack shelf.

"It's beautiful. You don't see these much anymore." Sam took a sip. "And what about the name 'Jersey Lilly?' Seems an odd name for this part of the country. Is there some significance to that?"

Billy picked up a bottle and replaced it in its proper spot. "Yup, there's a story all right. You ever heard of Judge Roy Bean down in Texas?"

She shook her head.

"Well, your education is sorely lacking." He chuckled. "He was a colorful old west character, lived just this side of the law, established a saloon, and ended up being appointed Justice of the Peace along the Pecos River. They called him 'the hanging judge'."

Sam raised her eyebrows. "Sounds like a character, all right."

Billy refreshed her coffee. "Well, to make a long story short, he fell in love with Lilly Langtree, a British actress he never even met. So, he named the saloon for her, hoping she'd come there some day."

"Did she?"

"Not as far as anybody knows. Anyhow, the original owner of this place liked the story and named it after Judge Roy Bean's saloon." He ran a wet cloth over the counter in front of her. "Lunch?"

"No." Sam took a deep breath. "I'm looking for work. Just wondered if you could use an extra hand."

"Gosh, it's a might slow right now." He paused, picked up a glass, and studied it against the light. "But... maybe come mid-June, when school's out and people start travelin', I might need somebody Friday and Saturday nights."

She nodded. That was a good two months away, but it was the first remotely positive response she'd had yet. "I'd be interested."

"Okay. I'll give ya a call." Billy ran water into his wash sink. "Say, you're a good horsewoman, aren't ya?"

"Yeah, I know my way around the back of a horse."

"Well, ya might check with Clyde Bruckner. He runs a dude ranch, gives horseback rides to city slickers in the summer. He might could use a hand."

Sam brightened. "Hey, that sounds right up my alley. Thanks, Billy, I'll do that."

***

Clyde took off his hat and ran a hand over his short, gray-speckled hair. He appeared to be in his late forties, actually a bit younger than most of the ranchers around here, who pretty much ran close to Horace's age. He looked her over from head to toe. Sam shuffled her booted feet, waiting for a reply. *Sure, the ol' fart has to ogle me first. I ought to...* She bit her tongue.

"So, you've got experience with horses, huh?"

Sam nodded. "I've been around horses all my life, on the ranch till I was ten, worked in stables ever since."

"W-e-l-l, I dunno. You're a..."

"I know. I'm a girl. But I can handle horses." She straightened to her five-foot, seven-inch height. *I can do this.* "Tell you what, why don't I work with you for a couple of days, show you what I can do."

Clyde lifted his black eyebrows. "Hmm." He whacked his hat against his leg to dust it off and put it back on. "I suppose. I could use some help right now gettin' ready."

"Okay." She smiled. "You got a deal."

The rancher led her at a brisk clip past the big rambling ranch house and the bunkhouse cabins with new cedar shake siding to the corral where several horses milled, nipping at each other, kicking up dirt. He pointed at a black gelding. "Coal Dust. He's new with me this year, and I haven't had a lot of time to get him ridden down so he don't buck off the first dude who tries to mount him." He indicated the barn with a tilt of his head. "Gear's inside. Go ahead, saddle 'im up."

A test. He wants to see what I can do. Sam stepped into the musty dimness, paused to let her eyes adjust, and then grabbed a bridle hanging from the wall. Spying a sack of oats nearby, she scooped a handful into her jacket pocket, and went back outside. She approached Coal Dust who turned and walked into a corner away from the other horses. With the bridle hidden behind her back, she grabbed some of the oats from her pocket and held them out, palm up. The gelding eyed her but stretched his neck out to sniff. He took a step closer, then lipped the treat gently from her hand.

"Good boy." She rubbed his nose and up his face to his ears, while reaching around his neck with the bridle in her other hand. "There now." She eased the bit between his teeth, fastened the buckles and led him to the barn where she saddled him. Then she led him out and walked him around the corral several times. Conscious of Clyde watching, Sam took the horse through the gate and mounted.

As she swung into the saddle, Coal Dust shifted sideways and crowhopped. Sam clenched her knees to the saddle and pulled up on the reins. "Whoa, boy. Whoa now." The black settled into a walk. "All right. That's better." She kept her voice low and calm. "Feeling your oats a little, huh?"

She nudged him into a trot, frowning at a rougher-than-normal gait. A greenhorn sure wouldn't like that. A canter followed, then a stumbling lope. *Something's wrong.* Sam checked which side his gait was leading. That seemed okay, so she pulled him to a stop and dismounted. She ran a hand down his legs, looking for cuts and bruises. "You look okay. What's got you lame?"

Talking all the while, she leaned against him and lifted first one foot, then another. "Ahh, here's the culprit." A stone had become lodged alongside the soft frog of the hoof. She reached into her pocket for her ever-present hoof pick. Prying the metal prong under the rock, she gently worked it out, then cleaned dirt and grass from the foot.

"There, that's better." Sam let his hoof fall back to the ground and patted the gelding's neck.

"Hey, good catch." Clyde's voice startled her.

"Oh." She turned her head toward him. "Thanks. He seemed a little off."

"Yeah, I could see that when you started ridin'. I just haven't had time to work with him." The rancher touched a finger to his hat brim. "Appreciate it."

Pride bubbled up in Sam. "Any time. How about I take him back to the barn and treat his foot—make sure it doesn't get infected—and maybe trim his hooves a little?" Coal Dust nuzzled her shoulder.

"Sounds good." Clyde grinned. "Well, Miss Sam, I think you've got yourself a job. I'll put you on the payroll today."

"Thanks." Sam willed herself not to yell out loud and jump up and down like a schoolgirl. But she couldn't keep a big grin off her face. She had a job! "How much?"

Clyde gave her a bemused look. "How about we start you out at half-pay till the dudes get here, then bump you up." He named a figure that made her wince.

She knew how much work she was in for and that hardly seemed worth her while. "How about starting out at full-pay, with a raise after the first guests—after you see how I handle things."

"Hmm. I dunno." He scuffed his boot in the dirt.

Sam pulled herself up to full height. "You saw what I did with this horse. I can handle anything you give me."

Chuckling, the rancher shook his head. "Okay. You drive a hard bargain, Missy. But it sounds fair enough." He stuck out a calloused hand, and they shook on the deal.

CHAPTER EIGHT

Through the next several weeks, Sam divided her time between her home chores and helping Clyde get tack oiled and repaired and riding the horses to make sure they wouldn't buck the city folks off.

In June, the first group of dudes arrived for their vacation experience on a "real" ranch—businessmen from Boston—one with two hyperactive kids and one with an overweight, shy boy; cautious, over-dressed wives, and nonstop discussion of business deals. Samantha grinned, listening to their almost-comic "Bahston" accents, "R" pronounced as "ah," and "AH" as "er."

"Y'all ready to play cowboy?" Clyde asked them in a mock Texas drawl, with a wink at Sam.

"Yeah, yeah!" The younger kids screeched and raced toward the corral where the horses eyed them with a look that Sam thought was disdain.

"Slow down," she called. "You don't want to spook the horses."

The heavyset boy, who looked about ten, hung back beside his mother and whispered something.

The perfectly coiffed woman sniffed at the manure odor wafting on the breeze and brushed an imaginary speck of dust off her stiff-creased new blue jeans. "Do we really have to ride those... mangy horses?"

"Oh, come now, Martha." Her husband flashed a fake-looking smile.

"But Bobby can't—"

"You agreed this would be a nice change for us." Her husband handed them both straw cowboy hats. "Be adventurous, Martha. Bobby... be a man. Develop some *cojones*, for heavens sake."

Sam sighed. She and Clyde had their work cut out for them.

"C'mon folks. Time's a'wastin'. Let's get you all saddled up." While Clyde went to help the group saddle their horses, Sam walked over to Bobby who hung back, his face white, head down.

"It's okay if you don't want to ride. You don't have to."

He looked up, tears in his eyes. "I don't? B-but my dad..."

"Don't worry about it. We'll keep your dad busy. Have you been around horses before?"

Bobby stared down at his feet again. "Mom took me for English riding lessons, but I fell off the first day." He sniffed and wiped the back of his hand across his nose. "I sprained my ankle. It hurt."

Sam nodded. "I'll bet it did. You know what—I got bucked off the first time I tried, too. So, you're a little scared of those big animals, huh?"

He kicked at his instep with a shiny new cowboy boot.

"Well, it helps when you have a gentle horse. How about I introduce you to Ginger? She's a really small horse, and she loves kids."

The boy drew inward.

"It's okay. You don't have to ride her. Just come here. Let me show you something." She led him to the smaller corral and took a couple of cake pellets from her pocket. "Here, Ginger." She held the pellets in the flat of her hand, and the little mare barely kissed her palm as she ate them. Then she handed more to Bobby. "Just hold them out in your hand, flat, like I did."

Still snuffling, he reached out, but snatched his hand back as the horse came close.

"Hold still now. She won't bite you." Sam put a hand on his shoulder. "Try again."

This time, he let Ginger move her lips over his palm, then giggled. "It tickles." He looked up at Sam. "Can I do it again?"

41

"Of course. You can pet her nose too." Sam demonstrated, and he followed. "There, good."

"It's so soft." The child's eyes were wide.

Sam picked up a brush and swiped it gently over Ginger's back. "She's pretty dusty. How would you like to stay here and brush her down, get her coat all nice and shiny?"

Bobby took the brush, reached out slowly, and ran it along the horse's neck.

"It's okay. She likes brushing. She won't hurt you." Sam glanced over at the corral where Clyde was getting the group ready. "Listen, while I go out on the ride, why don't you get her all spruced up. There are some kittens in the barn too. I see Mrs. Bruckner is coming down now, and she'll probably have some lemonade for you."

The boy grinned shyly. "Okay."

Out of the corner of her eye, she saw the dad shake his head, but he turned away and headed toward his horse. *Good. At least he didn't put up a fuss.*

***

The ride went smoothly, despite Sam's fears that the two rambunctious kids would scare the horses or fall off or get bored. She gave them pointers on standing up slightly in the stirrups when the horses trotted so the ride wouldn't be so rough.

"Have you been riding for a long time?" the girl asked.

"I'll bet not as long as Mr. Bruckner," her brother put in.

Sam laughed. "No, not as long, but most of my life, since I was younger than you guys." She leaned forward. "You know what, my great-grandmother used to ride steers in rodeos."

The kids' eyes got saucer-wide. "She did? Have you done that?"

"No, not me. That's a pretty tough thing to do—to stay on the back of a big ol' bucking animal like that. I prefer well-trained saddle horses."

As they trotted back toward the corral, she saw Bobby inside the fence, currying Ginger. Mrs. Bruckner stood in the open barn door with a kitten in her arms, watching.

Sam smiled and rode up to him. "Hey, Bobby, good job."

His round face split into a wide grin. "This is fun. She's really nice. I like her."

Martha led her horse up next to Sam. "Thank you," she whispered. "I didn't know how he would deal with this so-called vacation."

Sam nodded. "I think he'll be all right."

"Look, Mom. I'm brushing the horse."

"That's good, Bobby. I'm glad."

"And, c'mere, let me show you the kittens." The boy dropped the currycomb and ran toward the barn, motioning for his mother to follow.

"Bobby—" Martha pointed, but he'd already stopped and turned to pick up the tool.

"I'll put it away, Miss Sam."

"Okay, Bobby."

"And, Miss Sam?"

"Yes?"

"Maybe, tomorrow, maybe I can try to ride her?"

Sam grinned. "Tomorrow it is then. You show your mom those kittens. See you later."

***

One evening at the end of the week, the phone rang. She considered not answering, afraid it might be Kenny again. *Unfinished business.* She grimaced, preparing herself, and answered. It was Horace.

"Hey there, little gal. How's the dude herdin' goin'?" He had a chuckle in his voice.

"Oh, it's going." Sam laughed with relief. "I'm glad to get rid of them. But… I gotta tell you, there was this little kid who was scared to death of horses, and I…" She hesitated. Was she bragging? But she was proud of Bobby and wanted to tell somebody. "I, well, I helped him get acquainted with a gentle mare, and he was actually riding before they left."

"Well, I'll be jiggered." She heard Horace slap his thigh. "I ain't surprised. Yer good with animals, I'd just bet my bottom dollar you'd be good with kids, too."

"Yeah. I don't know. I never did anything like that before. I guess it feels kinda good."

"Course it does. I'm prouda ya."

***

After the Boston dudes left, Sam had a couple of days to herself. She spent much of her time at the barn, brushing Sugar, trimming her hooves, and even took her out for a few short rides.

"Your leg seems a little stronger, girl." Sam melted into the smooth gait of the lithe racer, although she still detected a slight limp. "I don't know if I'll ever get enough money saved up to get you bred, but at least we can ride together sometimes, huh?"

As if in answer, Sugar stretched her neck against the reins and lengthened her stride. Sam let the mare run a bit, reveling in the freedom, with the wind blowing through her hair. She could forget all her problems as long as she was riding. But she didn't want Sugar to overdo. She reined her in again. "Good girl. That was fun. We don't want to risk your leg too much."

Topping a rise, Sam took in the wide expanse of green-gold prairie, rolling hills, and blue, blue sky. She inhaled the fresh, fragrant air. Then a sharp glint marred the peaceful horizon. Sam drew up on the reins. Across the pasture, near the neighbor's fence, sat a white pickup with dark tinted windows, black lettering on the door. A man leaned out of the window holding something up to his face.

Her heart thudded. What in the world was he doing?

Before she could ride down the hill to investigate, he ducked back inside, put the vehicle in gear, and roared away.

Sam sat still, her buoyant mood deflated. A gun? No, more likely a camera. A tourist? Boy, he'd have to be really lost to end up way out here. But the lettering on the door... A cloud passed over the sun. Sam clucked to Sugar and turned toward home.

***

In the dusty-lavender evening, Sam brought a glass of lemonade and her great grandmother's scrapbook out to the porch. She ran her hand over the brand "N hanging J" burned into the leather cover. Nettie and Jake. How they must have enjoyed sitting out here together, planning rodeo schedules, what to do next with their cattle, content with each other's company. Sam turned the pages of the old geography book that Great Grandma Nettie had used to paste photos, newspaper clippings, poems, and sketches. Nettie did everything with her husband. She was a cowgirl through and through, felt more at home on the back of a horse than behind a dust mop, at least that was the picture Aunt Monica had painted in the books she wrote about her grandma.

Sam sighed. She would love to be able to talk to Grandma Nettie, ask her all kinds of questions. How did she stay so strong in her convictions, even when her mother was so against women rodeo riders? How did she find a man in the 1920s unconventional enough to accept her as a fellow cowhand? Sam had a feeling she and Gramma Nettie would've gotten along just fine.

The phone rang, and Sam went inside to answer.

"Hey, babe, how you doing?" Funny how Kenny's voice always sent skitters through her nerves. It used to make her weak in the knees, but now she simply wondered what he wanted.

"Oh fine. How about you?"

"Great. Just great. My construction business is going gangbusters—I've had to hire three more guys this week just to keep up. Can you believe it?"

"Yeah. I can. You're a good businessman and a good contractor. Never had any doubt you'd be successful... with whatever you did." Sam pressed her lips together. If only he had put his mind to building a ranch with her.

"Say, I had a thought. Why couldn't we compromise— spend winters here in Phoenix and summers there?" Kenny's voice took on a wheedling tone.

Sam rolled her eyes. "I can't, Kenny. I have livestock to take care of year 'round." No. She didn't want to go back there... maybe ever. She shut her eyes against memories.

A melancholy ache formed a hollow inside her. Kenny should be here with her, planning their future. The internal bleeding of a broken heart didn't heal up as quickly as the scrapes and bruises of falling off a horse. *He's so stubborn.* He claimed to still love her, but he wasn't willing to be with her—not here, anyway. *And I guess I don't love him enough to be with him there.*

Sam reached inside a high cupboard, brought out a bottle of vodka, and poured a generous dollop into her lemonade. Something had to fill this void—at least numb the pain. She walked back out to the porch and sat in the worn rocker, watching the purple twilight pull part of her dream into black shadows.

CHAPTER NINE

Clyde greeted Sam with a cheerful wave. "Ready for the next batcha dudes?"

She grinned. "Sure. Bring 'em on."

"Well, another family's coming in a coupla days. Up for helping me patch the corral fence?"

"You bet. So, are you going to use that wild horse for rodeo stock?"

"That's the plan. Oughta earn me some bucks... so t'speak." The middle-aged man chuckled at his pun. He opened his pickup door, climbed in, and turned the key. "Can you locate my toolbox? Should be in the barn." He drove toward the corral.

When Sam joined Clyde with hammers, staples, and wire, he'd already unloaded several posts and poles, grabbed a shovel, and started digging a hole. She helped him seat the post and tamp the earth firmly around it.

He shoved his hat back and wiped the sweat from his forehead. "That oughtta hold for a couple dozen years. The old one'd completely rotted off."

"No wonder the fence didn't stop that horse."

Each grabbed one end of a long pole, and Sam held it in place while Clyde fastened it to the post. "Funny thing. Ran across some city guy takin' pictures out on the buttes the other day."

Sam did a double take. "Really? Young guy with a movie camera?"

"Naw, regular camera. Young? Well, younger 'n me—early to mid-thirties, I'd guess."

"Hmm. I had someone nosing around on my place yesterday. But he took off before I could talk to him."

Clyde pounded a nail into the pole. "This guy mumbled somethin' I ain't quite sure what about. Figured he was some city dude takin' pitchers of his vacation." He chuckled. "I told him to watch out for rattlesnakes. Didn't take him long to hightail it outta here."

***

At home in the evening, she went straight to the barnyard to brush Sugar and take her for a short ride. The mare always came to the fence with a warm, rumbling nicker. Feeding her a handful of carrots, she ran a palm over Sugar's velvety nose, up her blaze face to scratch the base of her ears. The mare leaned her head into Sam's arm like a cat. She could almost hear the horse try to purr.

"Well, girl, I've got about five hundred dollars socked away so far to get you a baby next spring. Would you like that?"

Sugar bobbed her head up and down along Sam's shoulder. She laughed and stepped wider to regain her balance. "I think you *would* like that."

When she finally made her way inside to fix a quick bite of supper, the light on the answering machine blinked rhythmically in the darkened kitchen. In deference to the nostalgic origins of this house, she'd kept the old-fashioned wall phone.

The first message was from Kenny with the same old question: "When are you coming back to Phoenix?" Sam blinked back the sting in her eyes. "I'm not, Kenny. When are you going to get that through your thick skull?" She punched the erase button.

The second message was from a Teresa Knudson in Forsyth—the name sounded familiar, but she couldn't quite place it. Puzzled, Sam tapped out the number.

"Thanks so much for calling me back." The woman's voice bubbled over the line. "Remember me? The Realtor for your place?"

"Oh, yeah. Nice to talk to you again."

"You said you have a rescued horse, didn't you?"

"Yes, that's right." Sam frowned, waiting.

"Well… I don't know how to go about this but thought you might have some ideas. I was in the Miles City area today. I drove by this place—apparently nobody lives there anymore—I thought I might be able to get a listing. But there's a horse in a tiny fenced area…" The woman paused.

"Uh-huh…?" Sam prompted. *What's she trying to tell me?*

"It's terrible. There's no grass left. The water tank was nearly dry, and the windmill shut off. And the horse…" Her voice caught. "It doesn't look very healthy."

Sam's heart flip-flopped. *Oh, the poor thing.* "Did you report it to the sheriff?"

"Ah, no… I… I didn't know what to do. My first thought was of you. I did turn on the windmill, though, so it could get some water."

"Good. That's good." Her thoughts whirled. "Listen, since you witnessed this, and it's in another county, you need to call the sheriff there. They can probably find out who the owners are and contact them."

"Oh, sure. It was just… the only thing I could think of was taking the poor thing away. But I have no place to keep a horse. I'm sorry to have bothered you, but I remembered your horse, so…"

"No, no. That's fine. I'm glad you called me. I really hate to hear about things like that. Let me know what you find out, okay?" Sam hung up and slumped into a chair. Her heart ached for that abandoned horse. She couldn't stand to see an animal suffer. *I'm such a softy.* As a child, she was always rescuing something—a bird with a broken wing, a bunny whose mother had been eaten by a coyote, or even the runt of the litter of kittens in her grandpa's barn.

Sleep eluded Sam that night as she tossed and turned. *How could anyone leave their horse like that without feed and water? Gosh, I hope he didn't drink too much after Teresa turned on the water.* When she dozed, images of emaciated

49

horses galloped through her half-dreams. *Did I tell her the right thing to do? Maybe I should do something.* Finally, about 4 a.m., she gave up, dressed, and called the real estate agent. "I'm sorry to wake you so early," she apologized to the sleepy-voiced woman, "but can you give me directions to where that horse is. I'm going to go take a look at it."

"Oh, I'm so happy to hear that. The sheriff's office said they'd send an animal control officer out in the morning, but somehow I don't know if that'll be enough."

After feeding Sugar and eating a hasty breakfast, Sam loaded several hay bales in the bed of her pickup and started the ninety-mile trip to Miles City. When she had cell service, she called the Custer County Sheriff's Office.

"Oh yes," the dispatcher said. "We had a call on that last night. We'll send animal control out when he comes on duty at nine."

"Well, I'm on my way now. Have the officer meet me as soon as possible." Sam hung up before the woman could ask what business she had there.

Following Teresa Knudson's directions, she drove the twisting, dusty roads beyond the town for another fifteen miles. The sun rose steadily in the sky, spreading its warm glow over the green-gold prairie. Ranch houses were few and far between out here, and Sam was beginning to think she was lost, when she finally saw the windmill silhouetted against the clear azure sky.

Near a dented, rusting water tank stood a dust-caked horse, its head down in a look of abject despair. Sam moaned softly and swallowed a lump in her throat. She parked her pickup by the fence and walked toward the horse. Flies blackened its rump, but the gelding made no move to flick them away with his matted tail. His hipbones protruded from a concave flank, and the outline of his ribs stood out.

"Oh my gosh. This is horrible." A chill shook her. "You poor thing. What am I going to do?" She walked to the water tank—empty. The windmill spun in the breeze, and water trickled from the pipe, but the old tank was leaking too much to hold water.

Sam glanced at her watch—7:30. The animal officer wouldn't be there until nine. But she couldn't just stand there and do nothing. She went back to her pickup, retrieved the bucket of pellets, and dumped them on the ground near the horse. Then she filled the bucket with water and climbed through the fence, approaching the animal slowly. As she set the water in front of him, he finally raised his head and sniffed, then dipped his nose into the cool wetness.

After he'd drunk, the glaze in his eyes seemed to lift somewhat. Through the dirt and flies, his ragged coat showed streaks of reddish brown with a black mane and tail—a bay. Sam retrieved a handful of cake pellets and offered one on her palm. The horse nuzzled the treat weakly and dropped it. Sam tried again. This time he took the pellet and chewed, seeming to savor the food. She fed him the rest of her handful, then went back to the pickup for a bale of hay.

By the time the animal warden truck arrived about 9:45, the horse was munching, his tail now occasionally flicking at the flies.

The heavyset officer eased out of his truck, a travel cup in one hand, a clipboard in the other. His name badge read Madison. "Mornin', ma'am. What's the problem here?"

Sam stood, arms akimbo. "Well, I think it's pretty obvious. Look at this horse—skin and bones. He's been abandoned. No food or water for who knows how long."

The warden creased his forehead. "Well, looks like he's eatin' now."

Sam bit back the urge to punch the guy. "That's because I just gave him some hay."

Madison took a sip of coffee. "And what's your relationship here? Are you a neighbor?"

"No. I live at Ingomar. But I have a rescued racehorse, and the real estate agent who found this situation called me."

"Oh. I see." The officer nodded. "And you thought you'd ride in and rescue the poor thing."

"Well, no... not exactly. I advised her to call you. It's your jurisdiction. I thought maybe you could find out who the owners are."

"Yeah, probably can." Madison set the cup on the hood of his truck and pulled out a pen. "What'd you say your name was?"

Sam narrowed her eyes. "I didn't say... But it's Samantha Moser." She gave him her phone number. "I'd appreciate a call when you find out what's going on here."

"Uh-huh." He ambled to the fence, peered at the horse for a minute then wrote something on his clipboard. Back at his truck, he picked up the coffee cup, opened the door and climbed in. "Thanks for your concern, ma'am, but a word of advice—don't be gettin' in the middle of something here. I'll look into it." He drove away in a cloud of dust.

Sam closed her open mouth. "Well, I'll be..." *That son-of-a-gun probably won't do a darn thing. Criminy. My hands are tied. Gotta go through the legal channels first.* She stomped to her pickup, unloaded the rest of the bales into the small pasture, and headed back into Miles City to find a small tank or something that would hold water. *The least I can do to alleviate the poor guy's suffering.* Tears stung her eyes, and she swiped at them with the back of her hand.

***

Sam's dreams filled with grotesque images—the mysterious photographer leered at her, his face morphed into Kenny's, laughing as he dragged the carcass of her childhood horse, Apache, its intestines spilling out, onto a pile of starved equine bodies. She screamed to stop, but he ignored her.

She sat upright in bed. Her sweat-dampened nightshirt clung to her breasts. "Oh. Just a dream. A horrible dream." She scrubbed her hands through her tousled hair and tried to shake the images away, but they persisted. Like a pesky mosquito whining through a summer's night, the nightmarish pictures came back every time she lay down.

Finally, she got up, went to the kitchen and poured a finger of vodka. Tossing it back in one gulp, she poured another, then another, as if to wash away her sins—Apache, the horse she couldn't save; Kenny, the relationship she couldn't save; the starving horse she might not be able to save....

CHAPTER TEN

The next morning Sam dragged herself out of bed to go to work at Clyde's. Her head ached, and she moved as though swimming through Jell-o. *I shouldn't have had that vodka.*

"Mornin', Miss Sunshine. You're lookin' a might peaked today." Clyde greeted her at the corral. "You up to buildin' more fence?"

Sam tried to put on a bright smile, but her face felt like cracking plaster. "Sure. Let's finish this."

They went through the motions—digging holes, setting posts, hammering staples—without conversation. Sam stopped frequently to take long draughts from her water jug. The sun beat on her head like a fiery drum.

Finally, Mrs. Bruckner called them to come to the house for lunch. Clyde put down his tools, rested a booted foot on the bottom rail and peered at Sam from beneath his battered hat brim. "Yer awful quiet today. Somethin' happen?"

She shook her head, regretting the quick movement. "Naw, I'm fine."

They walked in silence to the house, where Clyde's wife served up a hearty beef and vegetable soup, thick slabs of homemade wheat bread, and butter. "You're pretty quiet today, Sam. Are you feeling all right?" the motherly Mrs. Bruckner asked.

"Oh yes, I'm fine, thanks. Just a little tired. Didn't sleep too well last night." Sam smiled. "But your wonderful food is making me feel human again."

Back at the corral, she scooped up a handful of staples. As she turned to help Clyde, she stumbled on a dirt clod and dropped the nails. "Sorry." She bent to pick them up.

Clyde gave her a sidelong glance, then went back to work on the fence.

Sam stood and stared off toward the rippled horizon. Had she given Apache enough hay and water to last a few days? Would the animal officer go back out to check on him?

Already she had given the bay the name of her beloved dead horse.

Clyde spoke up. "Would you get me that wire-stretcher out of the back of the pickup?"

Sam started and dropped the staples again. "Oh crumb! Sorry. What'd you say?"

"So, somethin' *is* eatin' at you, huh?"

She gave a deep sigh. "Yeah, I guess."

Clyde nodded. "Thought so."

"It's a horse."

"Uh-huh?"

Fighting back tears, she told him about the abandoned animal. "I don't know what to do. I can't drive almost two hundred miles every day to feed the poor thing, and the animal warden pretty much warned me to mind my own business."

Clyde slapped his thigh with a loud whap. "Danged city law enforcement types." He shook his head, his mouth set in a grim line. "Them owners oughtta be strung up. But you try to help an' you're likely to end up in jail."

"I know." Sam pulled her hair back and fastened it into a ponytail. "But I kept dreaming about it all night."

"W-e-l-l, as much as I'd like t'drive over there and knock some heads m'self, guess I'd say wait a coupla days, see what the sheriff's office says."

She nodded. "I dunno. What if they won't do anything? He could die while I'm sitting around here, waiting."

Clyde put a calloused hand on her shoulder. "You do what you gotta do, Missy. I'll help if you need it."

That evening, she rushed into the house to check her answering machine even before going to see Sugar. No blinking light. Sighing, she went out to do her chores. Her mare greeted her with a happy rumbling nicker, and she threw her arms around the horse's neck, burying her face in the thick mane. "Oh, Sugar. What am I going to do about that poor horse?" Sugar nuzzled her pockets, looking for a treat. Sam fed her the carrots she'd brought and gazed into the animal's liquid brown eyes. "There, but for the grace of God, go you." She gave a little laugh. She'd rescued one horse. Could she save another?

When the phone rang later, she jumped to answer. It had to be the animal warden.

"Hey, babe."

Kenny. Sam sat heavily in her chair.

"So, when you coming back to Phoenix?"

She closed her eyes. *Always the same question. Every time he called.*

"I... I'm not coming back, Kenny. I can't."

His voice softened. "I miss you."

"I've missed you too. But we've talked about this. You don't want to come back here. This is my home now. It's my dream. And you don't seem to share it."

"What about finding a ranch up north at Sedona or Prescott or even Flagstaff—you'd get your snow there."

"Kenny..." She squeezed her eyes shut. *It's not about snow!* "We both know land is horrendously expensive there. This place was available—for practically nothing, since we fixed up the house and barn. My great grandparents once lived here... you know all this. You know how important Montana is to me."

"I don't get it. Whatever happened to 'stand by your man'?" Exasperation edged his voice now.

"What about 'stand by your woman?' It's a two-way street." A hard knot formed in her gut, and she gripped the phone until her knuckles turned white. "This is the dream I've had since I was a little girl. I'm going to see it through." *Or die trying.* "I think it might be best if you didn't call again. We both need to get on with our lives. I do wish you the very best." She whispered the word "Bye" and cradled the phone.

***

After another sleepless, nightmare-filled night and no word from the animal warden, Sam called the Custer County Sheriff's office and asked to speak to Madison. He finally called her back late in the afternoon.

"Now, ma'am. I don't know why you're so concerned about this case." He snapped his gum as he talked.

"Because there's a horse starving to death—" Sam tried to interject.

"Listen, ma'am. It's not a problem. Just a simple case of misunderstanding. The owner said he's been gone a few weeks, and his nephew was supposed to be coming out from Miles to feed the horse, but he didn't get the message, 'cause he's been gone too. So, everything's been taken care of."

"A few weeks?" Sam was incredulous. "It takes longer than that to look like that horse does."

"Ma'am. I said, everything's been taken care of. You don't need to worry about it anymore." The officer hung up before Sam could say another word.

She slumped in a chair. *Don't need to worry, huh? Well, we'll see about that.*

When the phone rang later, Sam's shoulders tensed, expecting Kenny and more pressure. Just what she needed, another argumentative male. But when she heard her neighbor Horace's deep, soft voice, she released her pent-up breath.

"Hey, little gal. Haven't seen ya in a montha Tuesdays. Thought I better check up on ya."

"I know, Horace. I've missed you too. Working over at Clyde's, you know."

"Yeah, that's great. Clyde's good people. Still enjoyin' wranglin' dudes?"

Sam laughed. "For the most part. I like the kids best. Probably could do without most of the parents."

"Yeah, I hear ya." Horace cleared his throat. "Say, you had any strangers visit lately?"

"No, not since that guy I saw with a camera a couple weeks ago."

"Well, I had me a visit from some Reel-a-tor, from back east some'eres, wantin' me to sell my place."

"Really?" Sam frowned. "What for?"

Horace gave a derisive snort. "Says he wants t' build a wild game preserve."

"Huh?"

"Yeah, that's what I said. Told 'im we got all the wild game we'd ever want, and we preserve the meat just fine."

Sam stared out the window at the deepening dusty shadows. "Strange things going on around here. Clyde said he ran some photographer off his place a few days ago too."

"Yup. Yup indeed. Offered me five hundred an acre."

"Wow. A hundred's about the highest I've ever heard for land around here."

Sam heard Horace shuffling on the other end. "Yeah, it's too strange. Well, I'm agonna call around, find out if anybody else has had this visitor. I'll let ya know what I find out."

"Yes, do." Sam paused. "Listen, I know a woman real estate agent from Forsyth—she called me about an abandoned horse. I could call her and see if she's heard what's going on."

"Good idea. But... say what? Abandoned horse?"

Sam sighed. Her voice choking, she told him about the gelding she'd dubbed Apache. "I'm on pins and needles here, so afraid he's going to die before somebody starts taking care of him. I just can't stand it."

Horace made a growling sound and muttered what should be done about "people who mistreat their animals."

Sam bit her lower lip. *I couldn't agree more.*

"Well, little gal. You're gonna have to do what you gotta do. An' you can count on my help."

Sam thanked the old man, nearly in tears. Maybe it wasn't impossible to save Apache.

CHAPTER ELEVEN

The new dudes arrived the next day, three women with their daughters—five girls, ranging from seven to fifteen. Sam viewed the group with skepticism. The three younger children were rambunctious, giggling over who-knew-what and given to periodic ear-splitting shrieks. Sam saw Clyde wince every time that happened. Another girl appeared to be about twelve, quiet but poised. The fifth, a young teenager, dressed in Goth black down to her fingernail polish, hung back sullenly, her shoulders hunched and a blank look on her face. Two of the mothers acted a bit like silly teens themselves, talking about their "girls' vacation" and "bonding time."

Sam rolled her eyes at Clyde. "They get better every time, don't they," she muttered into his ear as she strode past to greet the women, a smile pasted on her face.

That afternoon, Sam introduced the group to the horses they'd be riding. The younger girls approached with wide eyes and soon were brushing and braiding and talking to their mounts like old friends. The two mothers, who Sam silently dubbed Blondie and Blonder, chattered away with their daughters and each other, giggling and joking.

"Do you think riding will make my butt smaller?" Blondie quipped.

"I don't know about that but think of the inner thigh strength you'll develop—I'll bet Reginald will like that." More giggles.

The third mother, dark-haired Alberta Lucci, stood quietly rubbing her horse's face and neck and running her fingers through the soft mane. Her daughter, Goth-Girl, hunched against the corral fence, picking at her black nail polish.

Sam approached her. "Would you like to try getting to know Ginger? She's a really nice, gentle horse, nothing to be afraid of."

The girl snorted, turned, and slouched toward the barn.

Sam tensed but then slow-counted to five. *Well, all right, then.* This was going to be fun. She walked back to the group to give instructions on how to put on the bridle, saddle blanket, and saddle.

Alberta came up to her later. "I'm sorry about Electra. I was hoping this would help. But ever since her father—" Her voice choked, and she walked away.

Sam fluffed her hair with her fingers and pulled it back in a ponytail. Did she have to teach them to ride and be their shrink too? This was a lot more babysitting than she'd bargained for when she took the job.

That evening, she called Teresa Knudsen, the real estate woman who'd told her about Apache.

"Oh, Sam, I was just sitting here thinking of calling you. What did you find out about that poor horse?"

Sam sighed. "There seems to be a slight problem with the animal control officer." She told Teresa what had happened. "And he basically told me to go away and mind my own business."

Teresa made a sharp sound. "That's not right, that's just not right at all." She rustled some papers at the other end. "Let me see if my Miles City contacts have any clout with the sheriff himself."

"That might help," Sam said. "I really feel like I need to drive back over there and check on Apa... uh... the horse. Make sure somebody has been coming to feed him. I think I'll call Clyde and see if he can get along without me tomorrow."

Teresa suggested meeting there and Sam agreed. "One more thing—I wanted to ask you if you've heard of a Realtor from out of the area looking to buy up property for a wild game preserve."

"What?" Teresa's voice rose a notch. "No, I haven't. This is weird. Another thing to look into. Listen, I'm going to make some calls right now. I'll meet you tomorrow, and let you know what I've found out, okay?"

When Sam called Clyde, he hemmed and hawed a bit. "Well, I was hopin' to take the ladies on a ride tomorrow, and I need your help with that."

"I know. I'm sorry. But you said you'd back me on this. I have a really bad feeling about this horse. I think I need to go right away."

Clyde chuckled a bit. "You have a big ol' soft heart when it comes to horses, don't you? All right then. I'll figure something for 'em to do tomorrow, and we'll take that ride the next day."

Sam breathed a sigh of relief. "Thank you, Clyde. I won't let you down."

**

The next morning, Sam loaded cake pellets and several hay bales into her pickup and took off for Miles City with trepidation. What would she find? Would Apache be dead? Her stomach twisted with the thought. *I should have gone back sooner. I'll never forgive myself if he is.*

As she drove the dusty road toward the highway, she caught sight of a dark figure trudging up ahead. Sam frowned. Hitchhikers were pretty rare out here. As she came closer, she recognized the slouched stance, the black clothing. Goth-Girl.

Sam came to a stop beside her, leaned over and opened the passenger door. "Going somewhere?"

The girl scowled into the pickup. "You."

"Yup, it's me. Hop in."

"I'm not going back there."

"Why not? Your mother's going to be worried."

A snort was the only response.

Sam forced herself to speak calmly. "Listen. Get in. I'm in a bit of a hurry to get to Miles City. I don't have time to take you back right now. I'll call and let them know you're with me, and you can come along. Okay?"

Finally, Electra nodded and climbed in.

They rode in silence for awhile. Sam glanced at the girl hunched against the door. "You ever been around horses before?"

A head shake.

"So, this wasn't your idea of a fun vacation then."

The signature snort again.

"What do you like to do—for fun?"

Electra shrugged.

Sam rolled her eyes. Oh, this was good. "Well, I happen to love horses. I adopted a racehorse that was going to be put down, and I want to breed her and raise Thoroughbreds on my ranch."

Goth-Girl turned slightly and peered at her from half-closed, black-rimmed eyelids.

"Right now, I'm going to check on a horse outside Miles that's been abandoned and starving. I'm really worried about him, and I want to at least get him some feed until I figure out what I can do."

Electra nodded, but turned back to stare out the side window.

By the time Sam reached the ranch, her shoulders were in knots, her knuckles white around the steering wheel.

She approached the windmill but didn't see him. Parking beside the big plastic tub she'd bought the other day for water, she got out. Only a pool of scummy water left in the bottom. No feed that she could see. Sam scanned the grassless pasture. Then she saw him—lying on the ground. *Oh no, oh no.* Barely able to breathe, she tiptoed toward the brown horse. She knelt beside him, feeling for a pulse in his neck.

A faint mewling sound came from over her shoulder. The teen had followed. Her eyes were big and glassy-bright, her black-nailed hands over her mouth. She knelt beside Sam. "Is he…?"

Then the horse peered at them from an eye crusted half-shut. Sam gave a sigh of relief. "Oh, thank goodness, he's alive." She crooned to him as she stroked his face and neck. "Oh baby, howya doing, boy? Are you all right?"

Electra reached a tentative hand out to touch his soft nose.

He lifted his head and nuzzled her hand. A tear tracked through the thick makeup on the girl's cheek.

Sam bit her lip. So, she's capable of feelings after all.

The horse gathered his legs beneath him and struggled to stand, like an old man rising from a chair. Sam and Electra stood, brushed the dust from their knees, and patted his neck.

"Good boy." Sam kept talking to him. "Oh, I'm so glad you're not dead. You can even get up. C'mon, baby. I brought you some food."

The horse blew and gave himself a weak shake to loosen some of the dust. On wobbly legs, he followed them back to the fence, where Sam grabbed the pail of cake and unloaded a bale of hay. While Apache munched and Electra stood close, caressing his neck, she turned the windmill on to fill the tub.

In the distance, she saw a cloud of dust approaching, with another not too far behind. A red sports car pulled up beside her beat-up pickup, bass rhythm rattling the chassis. A young man in his late teens got out. His sandy hair stood up in spikes, several earrings glinted from his ears, and he sported the low-slung baggy jeans of his urban peers.

Teresa drove up behind in her SUV, nodded to Sam, and raised an eyebrow toward Electra.

"Hey, that's my uncle's horse." The kid swaggered toward Sam. "Whatchu doin' here?"

Sam stepped forward. "What's it look like? I'm feeding your starving animal, the one you've been neglecting."

"Naw, naw, lady. You got it all wrong. That old nag's always looked like he's about to die. I been out here. He already had feed and water. He's doin' fine."

"That's because I left it for him." She swallowed the rage that rose from her core. "He's almost dead. He was on the ground when I got here, could barely get up. I don't call that being taken care of."

"I don't think it's any of your business." The kid smirked, reached into a side pocket on his voluminous pants, and pulled out a pack of cigarettes. He tapped one out, flicked a silver lighter, and took a deep drag, all the while eyeing her from half-closed lids.

Sam had to put her hand in her pockets to keep from punching that look off his face. She ground her teeth. What could she do or say to get through to this punk?

Teresa spoke up. "Now, look. There's no need for attitude here. We're simply concerned for this horse's welfare, that's all. I spoke to the sheriff on the phone, and he said you had promised you were taking care of him while your uncle is in Europe." She glanced at the bay. "But he doesn't look too good."

Sam let Teresa's calm tone wash over her. She leaned against a fence post. "Say, what's your uncle's name? Do you think he'd be willing to sell the horse?"

The kid shrugged as he blew a cloud of smoke. He pulled a cell phone from his pocket and punched in some numbers as he walked out of earshot.

Teresa made a face behind his back and shook her head at Sam. "Piece of work," she muttered. "Who's your friend?"

Sam introduced Electra who barely looked up from the horse. She was now combing her fingers through his mane, trying to untangle the dirty knots.

The young man sauntered back to where they stood. "Just talked to my uncle. Yeah. He'll sell."

She took an eager step forward, hope rising inside. "That's great! ...ah... how much?"

"Two grand."

Sam's hope wilted. Way out of her league. "That horse is not worth two thousand dollars. You'd have to pay to have him hauled to the rendering plant."

Teresa spoke up, her eyes narrowed. "Give us your uncle's number. We want to negotiate with him directly."

The kid shuffled his feet. "Naw, no need. He says I do what I want with the horse."

"Listen, friend." Teresa had a no-nonsense look on her face now. "I'm supposed to report back to the sheriff on the condition of this horse. As bad as it looks to me, we can easily get a lawyer to draw up papers..."

"Okay, okay." The kid wiped his palms on his baggy pants. "A grand, then."

"I'll give you five hundred," Sam said. "Take it or we'll begin legal proceedings." She swallowed hard, not sure if they could indeed do that. *It's all I've got. Please take it.*

The young man looked down at his feet. He fumbled for another cigarette.

"What's it going to be?" Teresa prompted.

He crumpled the unlit cigarette in his hand. "Okay. I'll take it."

Sam smiled. "You made the right decision. We need to write up a bill of sale right now. Teresa, do you have some paper?"

Sam grabbed her checkbook from the glove box. Teresa supplied a notebook and pen and Sam wrote out "I, _____, acting on behalf of my uncle, ___, hereby sell one bay horse, brand R hanging S, to Samantha Moser for the sum of Five Hundred Dollars." She signed her name and dated it, then handed it to him to fill in the blanks and sign.

As Sam signed the check, she had a momentary twinge. *The money I saved toward Sugar's stud fee. Oh well.* This was more important right now. "All right, then. Our business is finished. Teresa will notarize this, and I'll send you a copy." She offered him her check.

He stared down at it. "How do I know it's good?"

Sam leaned closer, her face inches from his. "Because I say it is. This is my signature. Take it or leave it. Either way, we're taking the horse."

"Okay, okay. Don't get your panties in a bunch." The kid grinned again, swaggered to his car, and spun a cloud of dust as he peeled out.

Teresa smiled at Sam. "We did it!"

Sam gave her a high-five and twirled in the dirt. "Woohoo. We make a good team. Thanks for your help. I gotta call Horace now, see if I can get him to bring his horse trailer." She turned to the horse. "Mister, you're coming home with me."

Electra looked up at her with a little-girlish, half-grin. "Can I come along?"

Sam gazed at the girl for a moment. That smile softened the hard edges of her face and her eyes were wide with expectation. *She's fallen in love with Apache.* Sam grinned back. "Of course. I'm going to need some help getting this guy healthy."

Teresa left, and while waiting for Horace to arrive with his horse trailer, Sam dug out a currycomb and brush.

Electra looked at the tools and at the horse. "Can I help?"

"Of course." Sam showed her what to do, and the teen set about detangling the mane, while Sam brushed the caked dirt from Apache's bedraggled coat. He stood without moving, occasionally turning his head toward them, as if he couldn't believe he was being cared for. Sam bit her lip as she ran her hand over his sharply defined ribs. The poor guy.

Electra paused in her ministrations. "Have you named him?"

Sam nodded. "I guess... I've been calling him Apache, after a horse that died when I was a kid."

"Oh. That's a good name." The girl worked on a stubborn tangle. "Do you... Will he... Will this Apache die?"

"Oh gosh." Sam blinked against a rise of emotion. "No, I think he'll be all right once we get him on regular feed and water. I'm going to take him by the vet's in Miles City before we bring him home, get him checked over."

Tension seemed to flow from Electra's stance. She threw her arms around Apache's neck and buried her face in his mane.

After about an hour, Horace came roaring up in his pickup, pulling a horse trailer. He eased out of the cab and stretched. "Hey there, little gal. So, you've rescued yourself a horse, huh?"

Sam grinned. "Yup. We did it." She glanced at the girl, still busy with Apache's mane. "Electra, come meet my friend and neighbor, Horace. Electra's with the group at Clyde's."

Horace raised one eyebrow but stuck out his hand. "Pleased to meetcha, Miss Electra."

The girl turned. Looking down at the ground, she took a couple of steps forward and inched her hand up toward Horace's. "Hi," she said in a small voice.

Horace smiled. "I'm sure glad Sam here had somebody along to help her today. Looks like you've got that ol' boy spiffed up pretty good."

Electra's face took on a pinkish hue under her pale makeup. "Yeah, you should've seen him before..."

"Yes, Electra's been great, and she's going to help me take care of Apache for awhile before she has to go back to New York."

"Terrific. Well, let's get this guy loaded." Horace opened the trailer gate, retrieved a halter and a pail of cake pellets. With just a little enticement from the food, and too weak to protest, Apache lumbered slowly up the ramp into the trailer.

A saddle-sized load lifted from Sam's shoulders. *I did it! I saved him!* It may have cost her the last five hundred she had, but that didn't matter right now.

CHAPTER TWELVE

The vet looked Apache over from head to tail, checked his temperature, pulse and respiration, peered into his eyes, looked into his mouth, and ran his hands over every joint. After drawing blood to check for diseases, he turned to Sam. "There's no question he's malnourished, and he's going to need a lot of care, but I think he'll come out of this with little damage."

"Oh, thank God." Surprised to find her hand shaking, she reached out to touch Apache's neck. Then she glanced at Electra who nodded with a big smile on her pale face.

The vet slapped the horse gently on the rump. "Do you have hay and oats available?"

Sam said she did.

"I'd suggest adding a good protein, vitamin, mineral, and fat supplement to the oats until he gets back to a healthy weight. Have a salt block available, and make sure he's drinking at least eight to ten gallons of water daily."

"Okay. Thank you, Doctor." Sam paid the vet, counting on payday to cover the check. She helped Horace and the vet reload Apache and they headed home.

On the way, she called Electra's mom to let her know how the day had gone. When they arrived at Sam's, Alberta was waiting. Electra jumped out of the truck almost before Sam came to a stop.

"Oh, Mom, come look at this horse, he was starving and we thought he was dead, but I petted his head and then he got up, and then Sam bought him from this nasty punker, and we took him to the vet, and his name is Apache, and I'm going to help Sam take care of him. Is that okay?" The girl finally paused to take a breath.

Her mother cocked an eyebrow, smiled, and put an arm around her daughter. "That's wonderful, honey. I'm so glad. Show me the horse." As they headed toward the barn where

Horace unloaded Apache, Alberta turned to Sam, blinking rapidly. "Thanks," she mouthed.

Later, after they'd all shared a bowl of venison stew, Horace went home, and Electra excused herself to go check on Apache again.

"Sam." Alberta's voice was choked. "She hasn't talked this much or smiled since..." She swallowed, "... since her brother was killed."

Sam stopped in the midst of stacking the bowls. "Oh my gosh. Killed?"

The woman nodded. "Car accident."

Sam swallowed hard. For a moment, her friend and a mass of crumpled blue metal flashed before her eyes. She shook her head, remembering her aunt Lizzie had died in a terrible accident too. "What happened?"

Alberta bit her lip. "A little over a year ago. My husband was driving. It was icy." Her lips trembled. "He blamed himself, couldn't deal with it, couldn't be around us anymore. He had to leave us." Her voice quavered. "And Electra turned to this Goth thing. I've been at my wits' end."

"I'm so sorry." Sam reached for the bowls again. *What can I say?* The man left his family. Kenny left... The bowls rattled in her hand as she walked to the sink, trying to hide her face. Was that what men did when things got tough?

"But today... seeing her like an eager little girl again... oh, I wish I could afford to stay at the ranch all summer." Alberta ran her hand over her eyes. Then she stood. "Oh well, one day at a time, as they say, huh? Let's go check on Electra and the horse. We'll need to be getting back to the bunkhouse."

Sam followed Alberta to the barn. She kept thinking of Electra's sullen face and hunched shoulders of a few days ago, and then today, the smile that transformed her. Aunt

Lizzie was a troubled teen back then—about Electra's age. Maybe if someone had rescued her…

In the barn, the black-clad girl stood inside the gelding's stall, her face buried in his mane and her arms encircling his neck. He looked content, occasionally turning his head to nuzzle her. Sugar arched her neck over the divider as if wondering who these strangers were and what was going on.

"Time to go, dear."

"Aw, Mom."

Sam grinned. "I'll see you tomorrow. Be ready to ride." Seeing a tremble in the girl's lower lip, she added, "And you can come back tomorrow evening to help me with Apache."

Turning slowly, her hand still reaching toward him, Electra left the horse, and the three said good night.

***

Sam lay awake a long time. It would be a shame to send Electra back to her old life in the city, before she had a chance to discover the good things about herself and what ranch life had to teach her. Not only had she seen the change in the girl's face and body language, but she'd also seen how Apache responded to her. His ears had perked up and a light came into his eyes when he saw Electra. *He's in love with her too.*

But how can she help? She didn't know anything about troubled teens. She plumped up her pillow and turned onto her side. Aunt Lizzie grew up on a ranch, with horses. What had happened to her? Aunt Monica said she'd changed when she went to high school in town and got into drugs. *I wish I could've known her.*

Sam turned over again. What if Electra went back to New York and got involved in drugs? Or a gang? Or witchcraft or whatever these Goth kids were into?

She sighed. *I may be an idiot for thinking this, but I have to help somehow.*

***

The next morning Sam met Alberta on her way to the barn at Clyde's. "Say, I have an idea. What would you think about Electra staying through the summer, with me?"

Alberta stopped and stared at Sam. "Oh. Well… oh my gosh. Leave her?" Her face contorted.

Sam was afraid the woman was about to cry. "I know you'll be alone, but I think it'll do Electra some good. There's something about horses that heal, and I see a huge change in her attitude already."

Alberta nodded. "Yes, but…"

"And I think she's good for Apache too. He seems to be the most responsive to her—even more than to me."

"Really?" Alberta raised her eyebrows. "That's not going to be a lot of trouble for you?"

Sam paused. What was she getting herself into, taking on a messed-up teenager? "I think Clyde and I can keep her busy enough that she won't be any bother." She smiled. "I assume Clyde has your phone number, just in case…"

Alberta managed a smile. "Yeah. Well, I guess so. If… Let's go ask Electra if she'd like to stay."

They went into the barn, where the girl was brushing Ginger. Sam rubbed the mare's face and ears while Alberta stopped beside her daughter. "Honey, Sam has invited you to stay with her for the summer and help her here at the dude ranch and with Apache. Is that something you'd like to try?"

Electra raised her head in a sharp, swift movement. "Really?" She looked from her mother to Sam, one pierced eyebrow raised. "I can? You don't mind?"

Sam grinned. "You're going to be working awful hard."

Pale lips curved upward. "I don't care. I'll do whatever you want." She looked back at her mom. "But you'll be all alone…"

Alberta hugged her daughter. "I know. I'll miss you like crazy. But I think this will be good for you."

The day passed quickly, the group of women and their daughters getting into the spirit of the ride, laughing and teasing each other. Even Electra seemed more animated. She rode close to Sam and asked non-stop questions about horses and riding.

That evening, as Sam finished putting away the tack, Electra came back into the barn. "Can I help?"

"Sure." Sam did a double take. Although the make-up was the same, Electra's red-streaked jet-black hair no longer stuck up in spikes but was combed in a style that Sam thought complemented the young girl's oval face. And she wore a pair of cowboy boots!

"I like your hair." Sam handed her an armload of bridles. "You can hang these up over there. Thanks."

Electra brushed a hand over her head in a self-conscious gesture and shrugged. "Ran outta gel." She busied herself, hanging each bridle up precisely, the reins looped over the hook. "Is it...?" She glanced at Sam and hesitated. "Can I...?"

"Come home with me and see Apache?" Sam finished the sentence. "Of course. Let's go see if your mom wants to come with us."

Electra glowed. She hurried to finish her task, and walked over to Sam, bouncing on the heels of her boots.

***

Teresa called that evening to check on Apache's prognosis and Electra's progress. Sam filled her in on the latest. "Wow, what you're doing is so cool, my friend. That takes a lot of guts. My hat's off to you."

Sam huffed into the phone. "Well, thanks, but we'll see how it goes. It may not work. I'm not sure but what I've bit off more than I can chew. I mean, what am I thinking—I'm trying to get a Thoroughbred farm going, I'm taking care of somebody else's livestock, working for Clyde, then I take in this poor old nag and a fatherless Goth girl. Am I crazy?"

"No, I don't think so. I think you are a very caring young woman, and I think it will be fine. Want me to drop by and see how you're doing in a couple of days?"

"Thanks. That'd be great. Why don't you come over for supper Saturday?" Sam switched the receiver to her other ear. "Oh, by the way, did you ever find out anything about that real estate agent who tried to buy Horace's place?"

"Oh, for heaven sakes. Almost forgot. That's one of the reasons I called." Teresa's voice took on an exasperated note. "The Multiple Listing Service has received several phone calls similar to what Horace told you, but nobody seems to know who this guy is. I'll keep my ear to the ground, though. Let you know anything I find out."

CHAPTER THIRTEEN

On Saturday, Sam awoke gratefully to a day at home. Electra would be there in the afternoon, but until then, she had the morning to herself. Pouring a steaming mug of coffee, she ambled down to the barn, where both horses greeted her with rumbling whickers.

"Hi, guys." She set down her coffee, scratched Sugar's warm, smooth head with her left hand and Apache's scarred, bumpy face with her right as they hung their heads over their stall gates. "Don't want you to be jealous. Good thing I only have two of you, I'd run out of hands."

Sam fed the horses and gave Apache his extra vitamins. Then she saddled Sugar for a short ride. Although she'd been riding with the dudes all week, it felt good to be on her own horse, by herself. The spring sun warmed her back, birds chirped, and little ground dwellers scampered out of the way of Sugar's hooves.

She smiled. A sense of freedom lifted her spirits, made her responsibilities seem as miniscule as the cactus buds about to bloom. This was why she wanted to be here. How could Kenny not understand?

Letting Sugar have her head, Sam leaned forward on the mare's neck, relishing the speed of the gallop over the prairie. For a few minutes she imagined herself on the racetrack, fighting to gain the lead, the crowd cheering. They topped a rise and Sam reined the horse in, laughing with sheer joy and abandonment. Sugar blew and bobbed her head. She'd enjoyed the run too.

Her gaze wandered the golden, green-tinged prairie. Peace flowed over her like a cool river—not a house, not a person within miles... What? She blinked. A white pickup down by the fence. Looked like the same one as before, impenetrable windows, some kind of logo on the door.

This time the man stood outside, a short distance from the truck.

She urged Sugar forward. Dressed in light khaki pants and hiking boots, the man bent over a video camera on a tripod. He trained it on her as she approached, then straightened and waved. "Hello."

Cute guy, but what was he doing? Sam frowned. "Are you lost?"

The young man pushed back a white straw hat, exposing deep brown eyes in a tanned face. He grinned, his teeth white and even behind full lips. "Are you?"

She furrowed her brow. "I live here. And I repeat, are you lost?"

Still grinning, he shook his head. "No, not exactly. Although I seem to have wandered out to the middle of nowhere."

Sam couldn't help herself. "Well, this might not be the end of the earth, but you can see it from here," she quipped. Then she sobered. "Can I help you?"

"Depends on what kind of help you had in mind."

Smart aleck. She stared, steeling herself against his attempt at humor. "I saw you here a couple weeks ago. You're trespassing on private property."

"Oh, Mr. Murdock knows I'm here." He winked. "And now, so do you."

Her face warmed, but she pinched her mouth into a scowl. "Did you just film me?" Sugar shifted her weight, stepped sideways, and Sam turned her head to peer at the man.

"You're going to be a star." He fished a notebook from his back pocket. "May I get your name and permission to use the footage?"

Anger boiled like lava. "How dare you? How dare you come onto my property? How dare you film me?" Reining her horse around, Sam headed back toward home.

"It's only a documentary," he called.

Documentary? *Some people have strange ideas.* She looked back over her shoulder and narrowed her gaze. "Watch out for rattlesnakes," she called and then smirked.

When Sam and Sugar trotted into the barnyard, she saw Jack Murdock leaning against his shiny black SUV, smoking a cigarette. Odd. He didn't often venture out to the ranch.

"Hi, Jack." She dismounted, tied the reins around a corral post, and loosened the cinch. "What brings you out here today?"

He took a last drag from the cigarette, dropped it, and ground it out with his black patent loafer. "Well, Samantha, I need to talk to you about something." He glanced up at the house.

"Go ahead and talk. I need to unsaddle and brush Sugar down before I can offer you a cup of coffee though."

He shrugged. "Guess I'll get to the point. I'm seriously thinking of selling the ranch."

The earth threatened to drop from beneath Sam's feet. "What?" She put a hand on Sugar's back to steady herself. "Why?"

"Got a heckuva good offer. More than the place is worth, really. I figure might as well take what I can get—nobody's wanted to buy land out here for years."

Sam swallowed. "But Jack, you can't do this. We have a written lease for five years, and I have the right of first refusal." Her armpits grew sweaty.

Murdock nodded, looking somewhat sheepish. "I know. But I was hoping we could come to some kind of agreement about that. I have another piece of land near Colstrip I'd be happy to lease you instead."

Her heart pounded. "By the coal mines? Does anything even grow there yet? No, Jack, you know this was my great-grandparents' place. It's important to me. This is where I want to stay."

He fished for his cigarettes, took one out and tapped it on the pack. "I was really hoping you'd be open to a deal."

Sam watched him strike his match, chewing her lower lip. "What is going on around here? Horace said he had an offer on his place, too. And I just ran into a guy out in the pasture who said he was filming a documentary, with your permission." She put her hands on her hips, her insides shaking. "I'd really appreciate it if you'd let me know about things like this."

Her landlord inhaled deeply, then blew out a cloud of smoke. "Sorry. I was about to tell you. Didn't know he'd be out so soon."

Sam frowned. *Yeah, right.* "I saw him out here two weeks ago already."

He shrugged and reached for the door handle of the SUV. "Didn't know about that. Give my offer some thought, that's all I ask. Any time you want, I'll take you out to look at that other property. It's not as bad as it sounds."

With that, Murdock got in his vehicle and drove away.

Sam stood staring at the cloud of dust in his wake. *Now what am I going to do?*

***

Her hands still shaky, Sam unsaddled Sugar, stowed the tack in the barn, and was brushing her when Alberta drove up with Electra.

The girl jumped from the car and ran toward Sam. "Hey, you didn't start without me, did you?"

Sam glanced at her and nearly dropped the brush. Electra's face was fresh-scrubbed—no black rimmed eyes or pancake makeup—and a big smile transformed her. She looked like a normal young girl, excited and enthusiastic. *Oh, my goodness. All this because of one old broken-down horse.*

She smiled at the teen. "No, I saved Apache for you. You can walk him around the corral awhile, then brush him down."

"Oh good." Electra took off toward the barn at a skip, then apparently remembering her age and new responsibility, abruptly slowed to a more sedate saunter.

Sam raised her eyebrows at Alberta who got out of the car, chuckling. "She's a whole different girl. I haven't seen her like this in months." Tears welled up in her eyes. "Thank you, Sam."

"Oh, I haven't done anything," Sam protested, secretly pleased. "It was the horse."

"Whatever it was, it's a miracle." Alberta patted Sugar's neck. "I don't feel quite as bad about leaving next week. I know she's in good hands."

The afternoon passed quickly, with Electra taking over many of the grooming and feeding chores. Finally, Sam hung up her feed bucket. "C'mon, let's go up to the house. I have some chicken marinating, and I'll fire up the barbecue."

Sam poured a glass of wine for her and Alberta and a Coke for Electra. They sat on the big wrap-around porch, waiting for the charcoal to heat.

Electra chattered away. "Apache looks so much better already, doesn't he? I think he was walking smoother today, not quite so stove up." She grinned like the proverbial cat who swallowed the canary.

Sam grinned. The girl had picked up some of Clyde's lingo already. "I think you're right. He seems happier."

"Yeah, I can see a light in his eyes. Did you notice, Mom?"

"Um..." Alberta looked a bit puzzled, but before she had to answer, a red sports car roared up the drive.

"It's Teresa." Sam stood. "Good, we can put the chicken on."

The four women ate with gusto, Alberta sharing stories of the city, Teresa telling about strange real estate clients, and Electra chiming in with comments about Apache. Sam sipped her wine, basking in the warm glow of camaraderie.

She hadn't thought about Murdock's shocking proposition or the hunky but brash photographer all afternoon. He did have a nice smile and a sense of humor. She rolled her eyes. *Stop it, Sam. You don't need to be thinking about that right now.*

The sun hovered above the low horizon, painting the sky with gold and crimson.

"Ah, this is the life." Alberta leaned back in the wicker chair and put her feet up on the porch railing. "I envy you this, Sam."

Teresa held her glass up in a toast. "Here's to the good life." They clinked glasses and drank.

As Sam poured more wine, she heard a truck grinding its way up the road toward the house. She laughed. "Lots of company out here today."

A pea-green pickup with a light-bar on top came to a stop in front them. *Now what?* Worry flickering in her chest, Sam stepped off the porch to meet the uniformed man as he disembarked. "Hello, Sheriff O'Conner. What brings you out this way?" The sheriff was a family friend, but...

He touched the brim of his hat. "Howdy, Sam." He waved at the group on the porch. "Ladies."

Sam waited while he hitched up his pants with the heavy gun belt and shuffled his booted feet. "Well, Sam. I got a call from the Custer County Sheriff this afternoon. Something about a stolen horse."

"Huh?" Sam's stomach swooped like a bad rollercoaster ride. "No. There must be some mistake."

"Did you remove a horse from a pasture outside Miles City a few days ago?"

"Yes." Sam swallowed. *That slimy little snake took my money and turned in a stolen report.* "Yes, I did, but I bought that horse."

O'Conner nodded. "The owner, a Mr...." He consulted his notebook. "Mr. Smythe said he'd been traveling in Europe and when he came home, the horse was gone."

Sam stood, her arms akimbo. "Why, that..." This was incredible. Her mouth was open, but she couldn't find the words.

"I know you, Sam. I knew your great-grandparents when I was a bitty kid. What's your story?" The sheriff leaned against the railing in a soft stance. His voice was calm, soothing, his expression kindly.

Letting out her breath in a whoosh, Sam licked dry lips. "That horse was nearly dead from neglect. Did the sheriff tell you about the complaints Teresa and I filed?"

O'Conner shook his head. "Guess he forgot about that."

Sam ground her teeth and turned to her friends. "Teresa, come here and tell the sheriff what happened with Apache."

Together she and Sam related the story to Sheriff O'Conner.

"And, I have a bill of sale," Sam remembered. She ran inside to retrieve it.

He looked over the handwritten note for long minutes, then scrubbed a hand over his face. "Well, ladies, this is a bit unorthodox, but it is signed by both parties and it is notarized." He twisted his weathered face into a frown. "If you don't mind, I guess I'll have to take this with me and fax a copy to the Miles City office."

With a sigh, Sam handed it to him, glad she'd made a copy. "Let me know what you find out right away, in case I need to get a lawyer."

"You bet." The sheriff touched his hat, got into his truck and drove away.

Sam's buoyant evening had deflated like a month-old helium balloon. Teresa tried to reassure her. "All the signatures are there. It's perfectly legal. Don't worry about it."

"I hope you're right." She picked up the dishes. "I'm going to clean up—no need to help. If you guys don't mind, I'd just like some time to myself now."

The women departed with hugs and words of encouragement.

But Sam couldn't just wave this latest trouble aside. She reached up into the cupboard for the vodka, and leaving the dirty dishes in the sink, went back to the porch. The evening darkness settled on her shoulders, heavy and suffocating.

Before she could really get settled into her funk, she heard a truck engine making its way up her road. She stood and stomped her boot. "Who is it now?" Somebody with more bad news? "Just go away and leave me alone."

The battered old pickup chugged to a stop, and out stepped a familiar figure.

"Horace!"

"Hey there, little gal. Ain't talked to ya in awhile. How's it going?"

Sam slumped into her chair. "Oh, Horace, it's not…"

Horace eased himself into one of the other chairs, a frown on his weathered face. "What's up? Yer not acting your usual chipper self."

"Ah, it's nothing, really. Just a bad ending to a good day." She sighed.

"Well, you're sittin' here drinkin' alone. That ain't right." He grinned at her. "Pour me one and tell me about it."

"I dunno. Nothing is going right." Sam poured him a drink. "First Kenny leaves me high and dry with no money."

"Hey. Yer better off without 'im."

She tightened her mouth. "Then I find Apache and use the money I saved for breeding Sugar to buy him."

"That was a good thing." Horace tipped his chair back on two legs. "You'll save up again for your Thoroughbreds."

A long sigh escaped Sam's lips. "But now Jack Murdock wants to sell this place, and on top of that, I'm a horse thief!" Sam's eyes stung. She pounded her fist against her thigh.

"What?"

Sam told him what had happened earlier in the day.

"No-no-no." Horace let his chair down with a thunk. "You're no horse thief. That bill-o-sale will hold up. Mark my words." He stood up and paced the length of the porch. "But Murdock cain't sell this place out from under you. Say, that reminds me—the reason I stopped by." He took a folded-up piece of paper from his shirt pocket and handed it to her.

Town Meeting
Jersey Lilly, 6 p.m. Tuesday
Come hear the exciting opportunities
to make money with your properties!

"Aha." Sam wrinkled her forehead. "Something's not right here. Murdock getting a big offer, those photographers snooping around. My real estate friend, Teresa, said she's heard some similar things, but didn't know any of the details." Was it a coincidence that both Horace and Murdock had generous offers? "What about the offer on your place? Have you heard any more about that?"

The old man shook his head and chuckled. "Well, he did call me back a couple times, but I purty much told him to get lost. I ain't leaving my place till they carry me out in a pine box." He snorted. "Game preserve. Huh."

"Sounds like we'd better go to this meeting."

Horace picked up his hat. "Yup. Time to get to the bottom of this. I'll pick ya up Tuesday." He headed to his pickup. "Don't be frettin' about things, little gal. They'll work out."

CHAPTER FOURTEEN

The room buzzed with questions and speculation as Sam and Horace entered the Jersey Lilly. The tables were pushed back and chairs set up in the bar area, with a podium and a projection screen at the far end.

"Looks like we're gonna see a movie." Horace took off his hat and fished in his pocket for his glasses.

Sam saw Jack Murdock at the front of the room talking to a couple of men. One half-turned toward the growing audience, and she recognized him as the guy from her pasture. She nudged Horace. "That's the man I saw filming the other day."

"Bet he ain't doin' no doc-u-mentary," Horace muttered.

They took seats next to Clyde and his wife, Irene. "What's going on? Do you know anything about this?" Sam asked her boss.

"Just rumors. Somethin' about wanting to set up a wildlife refuge out here." He shook his head. "Easterners and their darn fool ideas. Bad enough having to deal with 'em on the ranch."

"No kidding." Sam nodded. The dudes came to have a "true west" experience and then proceeded to tell the natives how they should be running their ranches in a more "eco-friendly" manner.

"Ladies and gentlemen, if I could have your attention, please." Murdock rapped on the podium. The murmurs died down as attention riveted on the men up front. "I know you all have a lot of questions about the strangers in the area the past week, and they're here to explain. Let me turn the meeting over to Mr. Scott Roberts from the National Institute of Environmental Conservation."

"Good evening, folks." Roberts smiled at the audience.

Sam studied the men. Dressed in new cowboy boots, jeans, and a Garth Brooks style western shirt, Roberts looked about thirty-five or forty. The younger photographer guy had a better build, nice-looking, in a city boy way. She laughed to herself. *Here I am, recently from the city myself, judging everyone against these crusty old cowboys.* But they were the "real" men of this country, the ones who made a living out of nothing, who survived the unsurvivable.

"Ladies and gentlemen, I've run into a few of you in the last few days while Brad and I have been taking pictures and exploring the area. Naturally, you're curious about what we're doing."

"Yeah, we run 'em off our property," said a man behind Sam.

Roberts gestured toward his companion. "Brad Ashton here is doing a documentary for the Montana Public Broadcasting System on eastern Montana, truly the 'last best place'."

He referred to a book by the same name. Sam sighed. It had generated a controversial influx of Californians to western Montana, wanting to grab up a last piece of that best place and raising real estate prices beyond what the natives could afford. But who'd want to do that out here, where ranchers were lucky to get $50 an acre—if they could find anybody to buy?

The man leaned against the podium and motioned for Ashton to start a PowerPoint show. "This part of the country is a commodity of beauty, of wide-open spaces."

Sam gasped. There on the screen, bigger than life—it was her, riding Sugar down the hill. She sat upright. *That dirty, low-down snake. I told him...*

Hardly able to believe what she was seeing, Sam stared at the screen. She clenched her fists, anger boiling up.

"You all know the assets you have in the land here," Roberts intoned. "The pristine beauty, the serene lifestyle you've chosen..."

Rescuing Samantha

She stood abruptly, nearly knocking over her chair. "Excuse me!"

Roberts jerked his head in her direction.

"I did NOT give you permission to use that footage of me."

Ashton stood. "Ah... I... ah... I thought it would be okay, since we're only using it for this presentation. I thought you might enjoy seeing yourself onscreen, and... maybe change your mind about letting me use it in the documentary."

"What makes you think blatant disregard for my wishes would make me do that?" Sam was vaguely aware of everyone in the room turning to look at her. She took a step forward. "Get that off there. NOW."

Roberts strode forward to meet her in the aisle. "Now, ma'am, this is just a misunderstanding. We will remove it right after the meeting." He turned to Ashton. "Forward to the next segment, please." Then back to Sam. "Will that be all right, ma'am? Please, just bear with us. Let us show you why we are here."

Sam expelled a puff of air. "You guys are the intruders here. We don't have to put up with your trespassing." She turned back to her seat. "All right. Give us your spiel. But you'd better watch yourselves."

Still seething, Sam sat and glared at the screen up front.

"Good for you, little gal." Horace reached over and patted her arm.

On her other side, Clyde nodded and winked at her.

Scenic photos depicted the graceful hills, the sweeping grasslands, the rocky buttes that Sam loved so much. *What are these guys trying to do?* She didn't want to share that with these foreigners.

Roberts continued his narration. "This is the area that early-day photographer L.A. Huffman coined 'the Big Open' with its native antelope and deer and buffalo and prairie dogs." More photos showed the animals, as well as herds of cattle and horses.

"This is the land you love... we all love. Granted, I'm from New York, but I've been spending summers in Montana since I was knee-high to a horse." Roberts was obviously trying for a bit of levity.

Good luck, thought Sam, when nobody laughed. His harsh New York accent grated on her nerves. She gazed around the room. Some men leaned forward as if trying to grasp what Roberts had in mind. One older fellow had leaned back in his chair, hat down over his eyes. A soft snore emanated from his lips. Sam put a hand over her mouth to stifle a giggle.

"But we're in danger of losing it... losing it to erosion... bankruptcy... coal plants... nuclear waste dumps."

Sam and Horace exchanged glances. *What's this guy saying?*

"I believe this is the time and place to bring attention to these naturally wonderful things we have in our wide, open spaces in Montana. And unless we take it into our own hands to market this commodity to people who will pay to see such splendor, we *will* lose it."

A murmuring wave spread through the room. "What're you talkin' about?" someone yelled.

"We're already doin' that," Clyde muttered.

"Who's this 'we' stuff?" somebody else spoke up.

"Yeah, what *is* he talking about?" Sam shifted in her chair. Utter nonsense, as far as she could understand.

Roberts held up a hand. "Now, just hear me out. This region was once wide-open range for thousands of wild animals. It was an immensely successful ecosystem—native deer and antelope, bison, elk, bighorns all existed here before being rather dramatically displaced by agricultural activities."

A man stood. "What're you proposing—gettin' rid of all us farmers and ranchers and lettin' it go back to wildlands?"

"Yeah, what business is it of yours? I ain't listenin' to no more of this fool nonsense. Get on back to New York. Leave us alone," a deep voice shouted.

Another man got up, put on his hat, and left.

"Me neither." Someone else walked out, then others followed suit.

Sam, Horace and Clyde stayed as if rooted to their chairs.

Roberts' jaw clenched.

Finally, Horace stood. "What *are* you proposing, sir? Will you explain, please?"

The man's face was flushed, but he smiled. "Thanks for staying. I would like to explain. If my idea is implemented, the landowners will maintain control of their land and still have the remoteness you all treasure. As you know, ranching is in economic danger—from drought, low prices, and foreign importation. And many of you are—against your instincts, I'd wager—beholden to the federal government for subsidies to stay alive."

"Yeah, he's right 'bout that." Horace shuffled his feet.

The young man waved toward the screen that pictured a lone graceful antelope standing atop a hillock. "Wouldn't you rather be making money from easterners like myself coming to catch a glimpse of splendor such as this, or paying you hundreds of dollars a day to hunt on your land?" He stepped forward and spoke with an earnest tone. "This could potentially result in about ten million dollars more a year in income to the area and a thousand new jobs. You have a treasure here. Why not use it to your advantage?"

Jack Murdock got up from his chair, clapping. No one else joined his applause. He turned toward the group that remained in the room. "Well, folks, Mr. Roberts has given us some good food for thought. I think this is something we need to chew on a bit. So, why don't we get ourselves a drink, and we can form a committee and … go from there." He shook the man's hand. "Thanks, Scott. I'll talk to you tomorrow."

Horace stood again. "No, sir. We need to know more. Why don't you stay, have a drink with us and let us ask you some questions?"

The small group of half a dozen headed for the bar, then settled around a table Jack moved back from the wall.

"You said this plan would generate several million dollars and provide jobs," Clyde said. "I just don't see how that's gonna work. We don't have our farmin' and ranchin', we ain't gonna need more workers."

Roberts took a sip of his whiskey. "That's the beauty of it. Tourism and recreation bring in large revenues—just look at Yellowstone Park. And you know, Mr. Bruckner, you're already providing that type of service with your dude ranch."

"Yeah, but not that many people're wantin' to come to this lonesome, dried-up part of the country." Clyde squirmed in his chair. "I'm barely stayin' alive with the dudes I get and a few hunters in the fall. They'd rather go to western Montana, to the mountains and lakes, where it's green, and there's people and shopping…"

Sam nodded. "Especially for the wives. What's there to do here? It's ninety miles to Miles City and not much shopping there, if you're used to big city malls." She glanced at Ashton. *Wonder how well he'd do trying to eke out a living here?*

"Besides, who's gonna pay us if we get rid of our livestock?" Maury Johnson, who had a ranch on the other side of town, spoke up.

Roberts leaned forward with an earnest expression. "It would be a cooperative between private owners and public entities who are interested in investing in the future, to recapture a bit of the original American heart, to offer something brave and wild to those who've never experienced it."

Sam rolled her eyes. *Gobbedlygook.* "Nice turns of phrases, Mr. Roberts, but that doesn't put food on the table for those of us who live here. We all love this land." She gestured around at the group. "I'm a relative newcomer to Ingomar myself, but I was raised in this state. I understand. These people have survived all their lives by sheer independent will and the hope that next year will bring rain and better prices."

Horace gave her a big grin. "Well said. We'd rather tough out a few lean years than be herded by the government or some such 'public entity.'"

"Hear, hear." A chorus of voices gave approval.

Roberts shook his head. "But look at the possibilities. According to my research, a ten thousand-acre ranch could net at least $48,000 a year from hunting licenses alone. You get exotic animals in here—bison, elk, even elephants—you're going to have the easterners, heck, Europeans, flocking in to see them, to bag that big game trophy. I can see a thousand new jobs—outfitters, taxidermists, gas station workers—new construction for restaurants, motels." His voice rose with excitement. "Ingomar and other dying little towns could thrive again—just like in the heyday of the railroad."

"Elephants?" Sam screwed up her face, perplexed. "That's not a native animal. Do you realize it gets thirty below zero or more here in the winter? Not to mention the wind chill factor."

"Well." Roberts huffed and shuffled his boots under the table. "There used to be woolly mammoths and mastodons here."

"Elephants ain't no wooly mammoth." Horace set his beer glass down with a resolute thump. "You bring an elephant over here from Africa, and he'll be dead in a matter of months. That's just stupidity."

"No, no. We wouldn't just dump them here." Roberts tried to backtrack. "We'd have to climatize them, help the species adapt. This all won't happen overnight."

"Durn right it won't." Clyde stood up and put on his hat. "It ain't gonna happen atall."

**

Sam and Horace drove back home in silence. Her thoughts whirled. Anger bubbled up with the image of her riding on the big screen, embarrassment heated her neck at having felt any attraction toward that... that underhanded scoundrel.

Now and again Horace shook his head and mumbled to himself. She finally turned to the old rancher. "What do you make of all this, Horace? Do you understand what's going on here?"

"Naw. I been mullin' it over ever' which way to Sunday and I can't make no sense of it." He hit the steering wheel with the flat of his hand. "Ya know, I've been squeakin' by in this Froze to Death district my entire life. Worked hard. The wife worked herself to death." He paused and wiped his mouth with the back of his hand. "My son didn't want nothin' more to do with this country. So now, it's just me. And sometimes I wonder... is it worth all the trouble?" He glanced at her. "Maybe I oughta sell out. Retire. Move in to town. Live a little easier."

No! Not Horace. He's the epitome of what this country is all about. Her shoulders drooped.

"Oh my," she said finally. "I guess I can understand how you'd get discouraged after all these hard years. And it is a big opportunity for you to sell out, make some money and live the rest of your years more comfortably." She turned her body square to him. His face had sunk into its weather-beaten years of wrinkles. "But would you be happy?"

Horace shook his head. "I dunno, little gal. I dunno."

CHAPTER FIFTEEN

The next day, working at Clyde's, Sam could hardly keep her mind on her tasks. She found herself reacting sharply to Alberta and the other women who wanted to get in one last ride before leaving.

Electra trotted up to her. "Well, tomorrow I get to come home with you and be with Apache."

I wonder if I'll have Apache much longer. Smythe may be able to take him back. Sam grimaced. And what about Electra then? She would be heartbroken and might revert back to Goth-Girl.

The teen gazed at Sam for a minute when she didn't answer. "Don't I? Did you change your mind?"

"Oh. No. No, I haven't changed my mind." Sam shook her head. "I was just... preoccupied." She forced a grin. "We still have a deal."

The girl's brilliant smile rewarded her, and Sam felt a flash of guilt for neglecting the group. "Okay, ladies, let's go for one last hoorah before you have to go back to the concrete jungle."

That evening she said her good-byes to the women and promised to see Electra in the morning. "Be ready to work. We've got lots to do before the next bunch of dudes show up."

"You bet." The girl put on a swagger as she walked away.

On her way through Ingomar, Sam slowed at the Jersey Lilly. Tomorrow she'd have a teenager living with her. Might as well stop for a drink while still free. The bar was relatively empty, a couple of old-timers sitting in a corner. Sam sat at the big mahogany bar.

"Hey there, Sam. Can I pour ya a cold one?" Billy greeted her.

"Sure. And I guess I'll have a burger too."

"Ya got it." Billy set the frosty glass of beer in front of her and walked back to the kitchen to put in her order.

Sam took a long draught. Ah, that tasted good after a long dusty ride. She drained the glass and motioned for a refill.

Billy brought her another. "So, what was that meeting all about last night? Did you get what these guys are tryin' to do?"

"It boggles my mind, Billy. Doesn't make any sense. Why would they spend a lot of money buying up worthless land to develop a big game reserve?"

"Because they can?" He dipped his bar rag into soapy water. "I dunno. I suppose if it'd really bring in the tourists, it would be a boon to this poor, dying little berg. I live for the summer when we get a handful through here for the rodeo, or to hang out at Clyde's, or go dinosaur fossil hunting. If it weren't for that…" He paused and wrung out the rag. "There ain't that many locals left no more. Probably just a matter of time before we have to close this place."

"Oh my gosh, Billy." Sam stared at the man. "This has been an icon in eastern Montana since before my grandparents lived here. That would be a tragedy."

"Yup." Billy walked to the window and grabbed her burger. "Well, don't worry about it. Ain't gonna happen right away. Enjoy your supper." He left to check on his other customers.

Sam took a bite of the thick, juicy burger. Was this a dying place? Maybe it was a mistake for her to move here. Nothing seemed to be going right since she came. She sighed and drank some more beer. The alcohol seemed her only respite these days. *Darn that Kenny. Why didn't he have the guts to stick it out with me?*

"Excuse me, ma'am. Mind if I join you?"

Sam jerked her head around to peer at the owner of the voice beside her.

"You."

Brad Ashton grinned and slid onto the bar stool. "Yeah, it's me. Just like a bad penny." He waved to Billy. "Two beers."

"I don't remember giving you permission to join me." Sam squinted at the young man. "Not that it stopped you before."

He shook his head. "I apologize for that, really, I do, Miss Moser. That was out of line. I'm not used to a woman who doesn't just gobble up the chance to be on television. I made an assumption, and we all know what that means." He grinned boyishly and ducked his head. "Will you forgive me?"

Sam blinked. He did have a nice smile. Then she frowned. All the better to cover the lies. She shook her head and turned back to her burger. "Well, don't be ASSuming anything when it comes to me."

Ashton laughed, a rich baritone that came from deep within. "You *are* a breath of fresh air."

Sam studiously attacked her food, taking small bites and chewing thoroughly. Maybe if she ignored him, he'd go away.

"So, what's a pretty girl like you doing in a place like this?"

Sam rolled her eyes. *Oh criminy, what a lame old line. Can't he do better than that?* She glared at him. "What exactly are YOU doing here?"

Taking a sip of his beer, he set the glass down. "Just a film. Roberts approached PBS about doing a documentary about the last, undiscovered bastion of the West. You know, how the strong moral work ethic has kept the spirit of the land alive through drought and failed crops."

Sam snorted and waved his words away. *This guy and his stupid clichés.* "Yada, yada. Walking billboards. Would you just go and leave me alone?"

Brad leaned a little closer. "All right. But I honestly don't know any more about what Mr. Roberts is doing than you. I got this freelance assignment, and I thought the station was working with him to help me make contacts for the film. That's all."

Ashton's words rattled around in Sam's head as she drove home. He irritated the heck out of her with his silly one-liners. But maybe he *didn't* know what was behind Roberts's plans. Pulling up in front of her house, she rested her forehead on the steering wheel. *What next?* Her head hurt and she was too tired to mull all this stuff over anymore.

***

Electra left the truck door open and sprinted ahead of Sam to the barn, yelling, "Apache, Apache, I'm here!"

Sam chuckled as she entered the dim, musty stalls. The gaunt horse pricked its ears forward at the sound of the girl's voice. He stepped to the gate and greeted her with a low rumbling whicker. Sam almost thought she could see his eyes light up. She smiled. A girl and her horse. There was nothing like it in the world. She went outside, where Sugar paced the small pasture, to get her own greeting of love. Rubbing the mare's face, she fed her a cake pellet. "How ya doin', girl? Ready for a little ride?"

She slipped a halter over Sugar's head and led her back into the barn where Electra brushed Apache. "What do you think? Is he strong enough for a short ride?"

The girl widened her eyes. "Oh, do you think so? I'd love it."

"Let's try. We won't go too far." They saddled their horses and walked them out into the prairie, littered now with a riot of wildflowers. The evening sun burnished the horizon, and Sam let out a long sigh. She'd needed this. Too bad she couldn't just give Sugar her head and gallop over the hills. She glanced at Apache, plodding slowly along. He looked a lot better. Still pretty thin, but his ribs weren't showing so prominently, and his coat was getting sleeker.

"He's happy to be out here." Electra turned her grin toward Sam. "So am I. Thanks…"

"Well, it's obvious you've been good for him. He's a one-woman horse now."

They settled into a companionable silence, listening to the crunch of the horses' hooves on the grass, the trill of meadowlark, the ratcheting of an insect. She felt her shoulders relax. *This is good.*

As they rounded the corner back home, Sam gasped and drew up her reins sharply. Sheriff O'Conner's rig was parked by the house, and down by the barn was another vehicle with a horse trailer. "Oh no." She nudged Sugar forward.

"What? What's going on?" Electra's quavery voice came from behind.

Sam dismounted in front of O'Conner, dread turning her knees to water. "It's…?" She couldn't get the words out.

The big officer scrunched his face into a rueful frown. "I'm sorry, Sam." He withdrew a piece of paper from his breast pocket and handed it to her.

Her hands shook as she took it, and the letters blurred. Her worst fears were coming true. She looked up at him.

"I'm afraid Smythe got a court order to return the horse. The nephew had no legal rights to sell it, and Smythe wants him back."

"N-o-o!" The young girl's anguished cry caused Sam to drop the paper and turn to her, reaching for her hand.

"Sheriff… this is terrible. Isn't there anything we can do… contest it? Keep him until…?"

O'Conner shook his head. "I'm sorry. The Custer County animal warden has instructions to take the horse back immediately."

Sam looked toward the barn, where the pudgy warden leaned against his truck, chomping on his gum, and studying his fingernails like they were the most fascinating things in the world. Then he looked up and sauntered toward them.

"You saw the order. I gotta take 'im." He reached for Apache's bridle.

Electra threw her arms around the horse's neck. "No. Please! Please don't take him. He was near-dead. I helped... He's better now... Please..."

The animal control officer merely huffed, pulled on the reins, and led Apache toward the horse trailer, Electra hanging on for dear life, sobbing and pleading. Sam's heart splintered. She covered her mouth with her hand to keep from crying out too.

She strode to Electra and put her hands on the girl's shoulders. "Honey, we have to let them take him... for now." She swallowed. "But we'll get him back. We're going to fight this, I promise."

Electra collapsed in her arms. She rocked the girl and patted her back as the men loaded Apache, tossed the saddle and bridle on the ground, and then drove away. Slowly the two slid to the ground, holding onto each other, their tears mingling in the dust.

CHAPTER SIXTEEN

With shaking hands, Sam poured coffee for Horace and Clyde, one hunched over the kitchen table, the other leaning back in his chair. Electra's face was puffy and blotchy, and she still hiccupped a sob now and then.

Horace cupped his hands around the cup. "Well, there's no doubt about it. You're gonna have to get yourself a lawyer."

Sam sat heavily. "I have no money for a lawyer. I spent the five hundred I had saved, to buy Apache from that... that conniving little scoundrel. And now it looks like I won't even get that back."

Clyde shook his head. "This is outrageous. The owner obviously didn't care a whit about his horse, leaving him for months like that and not even checking to see if the nephew was caring for it." He sipped his coffee. "Seems to me, you have a clear-cut case of animal abuse."

Sam sighed. "Yeah, you'd think so. But that Custer County warden didn't seem to care one way or the other that Apache was almost dead."

Electra sniffled. "We have to get him back. He's going to die."

"Listen." Clyde set his cup down with a thump. "Let me give my lawyer a call—see how much he'll charge to take this on. I'm willing to give you an advance on your wages. I don't want to see you gals lose this horse."

"Oh, Clyde." Sam's tears welled up again. "I can't let you do that. I'll be in debt to you for the rest of my life!"

Horace made a growling sound. "Don't worry about it, little gal. I've got some set aside—I'll chip in. We're gonna get this thing solved."

Teresa called Sam on her cell the next morning at Clyde's. "I just heard from Horace. My gosh, girl, this is terrible!"

Sam set down the bridle she was polishing and switched her cell phone to her other ear. She still felt like she'd been kicked by a ton of bull. "Yeah. Electra is just devastated. I couldn't get her out of bed this morning to come work with me at Clyde's. I'm worried about her."

"What about you?" Teresa's voice held a note of concern. "Are you all right?"

"No, not really. But I'll get there." She told her friend about the men's offer to pay for an attorney.

"Oh hey, I'll contribute to the cause, too. And, I'm a witness. We'll take this to court—we'll get Apache back."

Sam thanked the real estate agent and disconnected. She sat in the barn for the longest time, trying to get her mind around what had happened the night before. She had really thought she was doing the right thing, rescuing Apache. *Am I doomed to fail at everything I try?* Angry tears stung her lids.

What would Gramma Nettie do? Sam pictured her great-grandmother's strong, resolute face, her confident stance. Everything had conspired against her, too. Nettie wanted to be a rodeo star. And one thing after another had come between her and her dream. But she didn't just lie down and give up. She kept fighting. Standing, she planted her fists firmly on her hips. *I'm going to fight, too. I'm not giving up!*

Electra was still holed up in her room when Sam got home. She knocked on the bedroom door. No answer. "Electra, are you all right?"

Finally, a small, muffled voice. "C'min."

Sam opened the door, startled by the darkness. The blinds and curtains were drawn, and she saw Electra's outline under a mound of bedclothes. She walked in and sat on the edge of the bed. "Honey, are you sick?"

"No."

"Then why are you still in bed?"

No answer.

She pulled the blankets back. Electra's black hair stuck out in disarray. Her eyes were swollen.

"You're upset about Apache, aren't you?"

The girl nodded and turned her face into the pillow.

"Electra. We can't give up on him. We're going to fight this. You heard Horace and Clyde last night—they're going to help us. And Teresa too."

"No use." Electra sobbed.

"That's not true." Sam desperately cast about for the right things to say. It was so hard when she had the same doubts herself.

"Wanna go home."

Sam hung her head toward her knees, then she straightened and gripped Electra's shoulder. "We can't just let them do this. I'm not going to. I'm going to fight this... And I need your help."

The shoulder twitched.

"I can't do this without you." She prodded the girl's side. "C'mon. You've got to get up. Let's do this—together." She stood, threw open the curtains and blinds.

"I'm going to fix supper and then we'll strategize. Okay?" Sam made her way downstairs to the kitchen, hoping against hope that she'd gotten through with some of her words.

Soup and sandwiches were on the table when Electra finally came out. She'd reverted to her black clothes, and white makeup covered her blotchy face. Sam turned to the stove and winced. How could she deal with this kid *and* the horse *and* maybe losing the place and... She forced a smile and sat down. "Now, what we're going to do..."

***

Sam and Electra stopped at the Dairy Queen in Forsyth for lunch before their appointment with Clyde's attorney. Sitting outside on the picnic bench, Sam tried to let the warm sun soak the tension out of her back. Electra looked a little better today—she was still dressed in black but had foregone the pancake makeup for a fresh-scrubbed look.

The girl took a sip of her Coke. "Do you really think we'll be able to get Apache back?"

"Well, that's what we're here to see this lawyer about. I have hopes—I honestly do. We're going to do whatever we have to, to get him back."

"Ah, if it isn't Samantha Moser." A deep voice spoke from behind her. She turned to see Jack Murdock. *Oh no. Just what I don't need today.* "Hi Jack, are you slumming?" She indicated his burger and fries.

He chuckled and sat next to Electra on the bench. "Oh, I enjoy my quota of grease now and then." He turned to the girl. "How are you, young lady?"

Sam introduced them. "We're here to see a man about a horse."

"Oh yes, the allegedly stolen horse."

Sam bristled and braced her hands on the table to stand.

"Now, now." Jack held up his hand, palm out. "Just ribbing you a little. I know you like to rescue abandoned ..." he glanced at Electra, "...things. I'm not making any judgments."

She ground her teeth. Why was he such an adversary? She couldn't think of a thing she'd done to deserve that.

Jack put a couple of fries into his mouth and chewed. "In fact, I might be able to help you with that little problem."

Sam cocked her head. "You might?"

The man wiped his lips with a napkin. "Yes, I might. Why don't you let me put you in touch with my attorney?" He reached into his pocket for his wallet.

"We already have an appointment with one, in just a few minutes." Sam checked her watch. "But thanks anyway."

"No, no. This guy's the best. If you've got him working on your side, you're assured success." He handed her a card.

She stood. "Well, thanks, Jack. Let me go ahead and meet with my guy, and if he doesn't think he can take the case, I'll give yours a call." She took the card and stuck it into her purse. "C'mon, Electra. We don't want to be late. See you, Jack."

The grease from her lunch congealed in her stomach. Murdock wasn't just making this offer out of the goodness of his heart. He wanted something in return—like the ranch.

***

Clyde's attorney had a one-man office on the second floor of an old brick office building just off the main street in Forsyth. He greeted them with a handshake and ushered them into his dimly-lit office—forest green walls, dark walnut desk, and brown upholstered chairs. Sam blinked, letting her eyes adjust.

"Clyde filled me in a bit on what's happened. "The gray-haired man steepled his fingers. "Why don't you tell me in your own words."

She related the story, with additions from Electra.

The lawyer nodded occasionally and jotted a few notes. "Did you happen to take any pictures of the horse in his original condition?'

Sam grimaced. "Gosh, no. I sure wish I had. But I do have some I took not too long after we brought him home and some more recently that show how much improvement he's made." She reached into her purse. "I also have the vet and feed bills. And a copy of the bill of sale I made out."

The attorney looked the papers over and nodded again. "Um-hmm. Well, let me do a little research. I'll let you know if I think you have a case." He stood and held his arm out toward the door. Sam and Electra left.

"I don't know. He didn't sound very encouraging, did he?" Electra squinted at Sam through the bright sunlight outside.

Sam shrugged. "I don't have any experience with lawyers. Maybe that's normal. I suppose they have to look into similar cases, see if we have a leg to stand on." She patted Electra's shoulder. "I'm sure it'll be okay." At least he didn't ask for money up front.

In the pickup, Sam picked up her cell phone, called Teresa, and recounted their experience. She needed someone to talk to besides Electra.

"Oh! Idiot." Sam heard a slapping sound, as if Teresa had experienced a coulda-had-a-V-8 moment. "I was taking pictures of property that day, and I snapped a couple of the horse. I forgot all about that. I'll print them out for you."

Sam laughed. "Teresa, you're a life-saver. I'm sure that will help." She paused. "Will you... if it comes to court or something like that, would you consider...?"

"Testifying?" Teresa finished her sentence. "You bet I will. Hey, don't you worry a thing about this. It's gonna turn out fine."

Sam hung up and sighed. She wished she could feel some of Teresa's optimism, that she even believed some of the positive things she'd tried to reassure Electra with. The trip home was quiet, Electra sitting hunched against the door, staring out at the passing prairie. When they got home, she immediately went up the stairs to her room and shut the door.

After checking on Sugar and feeding her, Sam retrieved the vodka bottle from the cupboard and went out on the porch to watch the sun set into a liquid pool of dark blue velvet. *Gramma Nettie, I wish you were here to talk to. What am I going to do?* Retaining a lawyer was going to cost a lot of money. Despite her friends' assurances of help, she intended to pay them back, every cent. *Sure, I will, if I get a couple more jobs and keep working till I'm fifty, maybe.* She let down her ponytail and ran her fingers through her hair. *I'm doomed to failure... again. Who can I ask for help this time?* Not her folks. Not Aunt Monica. *They've already bailed me out enough.* She curled herself into the wicker rocker as if it could enfold her into its comforting arms.

CHAPTER SEVENTEEN

"I've got ten kids from a group home in Billings coming this weekend," Clyde told Sam the next day. "They're teens who've been in some kinda trouble or were homeless, and the leaders want to expose them to horses and the ranching lifestyle." He rolled his eyes. "D'you think Electra will be up to coming back and helping? I think we're gonna need more than just you and me."

Sam stubbed the toe of her boot into the dirt. "I hope so. She's retreated into the dark again herself. I don't know what to do with her. I keep trying to get her to show some fight, to help me get Apache back, but she seems to have given up."

Clyde shrugged. "I can't figure out kids these days. When I was a kid, my dad kept me so busy I never had time to get depressed."

"Times have changed." She let her gaze flow over the rolling prairie. "Life is so fast-paced, with today's technology. People want immediate gratification. Kids have short attention spans. They don't have to work, like ranch kids did."

"I don't get it. Hard work never hurt anybody." Her boss lifted a saddle out of the back of his pickup. "Speaking of that, we'd better get to it. Would you check to make sure we have enough working saddles and bridles? And then we need to ride the string, make sure none of the horses have gotten too feisty for dudes."

Sam smiled, glad for work to take her mind off her worries. "Sure thing. Let me take that newest gelding out on a ride right now—he might be the one to watch. Then I'll work on the tack."

***

The light blinked in staccato on Sam's answering machine. The house was quiet, Electra's door closed. She sighed and hit the button. The first message was from

Clyde's attorney. "I'm sorry, Miss Moser, but I just can't take on this case at this time."

What? Sam dropped into the chair. The machine beeped, and another voice came on, introducing himself as Gerard Waterston, Murdock's attorney. "Jack has informed me of your plight, and I would be most happy to look over your case."

She dropped her elbows to her knees and stared at the floor. *Something smells like horse manure.* She chewed on the inside of her lip. One attorney drops the case, and immediately another one steps in. Murdock. It had to be him. He wanted her to give up this place so he could sell. Sam stood and paced into the living room and back to the kitchen. *But why? Why is this such a big deal?* Finally, she picked up the phone and called Teresa.

"Hmm. That doesn't seem quite right." Her friend paused. "What's your gut feeling? Do you think Jack's attorney can help you get the horse back?"

"Oh, I think he's probably high-powered enough. But I'm sure he would charge an arm and a leg. Plus, there's got to be a catch." Sam told Teresa what she thought.

"Aha. That sounds exactly like what Murdock has in mind. You know what? I'll bet we can pursue this on our own."

Sam's stomach knotted. "By ourselves? Oh gosh. There's no way I can get up in front of a judge and talk."

"But I think we have the evidence on our side. I'll bring the pictures over tomorrow evening, and let's talk about our strategy." Teresa hung up before Sam could come up with any more protests. She shook her head. This was crazy. No way it would work.

She tried to get Electra to come out for dinner, but the girl refused. "We're going to get Apache back. Teresa's going to help us." No answer. Sam leaned her forehead against the bedroom door. "Oh, dear God, help me deal with this..."

Finally, Sam gave up and went to bed, thoughts of lawyers and judges, horses and Murdock skittering through her thoughts.

The next morning, she pounded on Electra's door. "C'mon, girl. You gotta get out of that bed and help me today. We've got a bunch of people coming to Clyde's."

A groan. Sam pounded again. "Electra. Come on out. Now."

Pretty soon the girl opened the door and slouched out, hair askew, eyes smeared with mascara, creases in her cheek from the wrinkled bedclothes. "I don't want to."

Sam swallowed. "Electra. You've got to snap out of this. Clyde and I need your help today."

"No, you don't. You can't make me."

"Yes, we do. We have ten kids coming today, and we need you to be there."

Electra glared. "No."

She fought the urge to slap the girl. "You are coming to work with me today."

Another sullen glare and Electra stomped back into her room.

Now what am I going to do? She yanked on her own braid. *I can't very well drag her along.* With a sigh, she poured a travel mug of coffee, and prepared to leave. Just as she headed out, Electra slammed her bedroom door and stomped down the stairs. Sam turned, startled.

"Okay, I'll come. But you can't make me like it." The teen's black-rimmed eyes stared out of her white face, her hair spiked up like nails from her head.

Sam stopped an exasperated sigh and tried to smile. "Great. Hop in the truck."

***

About 11 o'clock two minivans arrived, loaded with jostling, scuffling teens. Four adults disembarked and herded the ten kids into the yard, where Clyde had set up picnic tables. Baggy-panted boys with shaved heads sauntered from the vehicle; others with long hair or dreadlocks slouched behind. Sam watched the girls from beneath her hat brim—some with too much makeup, some unkempt, some tattooed and pierced.

Clyde stopped in mid-stride and stared openly at the low-rider, crack-of-dawn pants one boy sported.

Sam smirked. *Ah, Electra will fit right in, with her looks anyway.* But at least the girl hadn't gotten into trouble like these kids—yet.

She went into the house to help Irene Bruckner bring out lunch for the group. "Where's Electra?" the older woman asked. "I thought I saw her arrive with you."

"I don't know." She sighed. "I suppose she's down at the barn. She's pretty depressed about losing Apache."

Irene patted Sam's arm. "I can imagine."

During lunch, Clyde talked to the group, explaining how ranch life worked and what they'd be doing over their weekend stay. "Today, we'll introduce you to the horses, let you get acquainted, maybe feed or brush them. And tomorrow, if you want to, we'll go on a little ride. It's not mandatory, so you do what you're comfortable with."

"Aw-right, just for you, Tex. Ride 'em, cowboy." One boy sporting a black leather jacket elbowed the one next to him, wearing Levis and a western-style shirt. The second kid glared and moved away. The rest of the group tittered and made scoffing noises.

"Settle down, kids." The man in charge sent them a warning look.

When they'd finished eating, the counselors made sure the kids cleaned up the tables, put their paper plates in the garbage and soda cans into a recycling bin. Then Sam, Clyde, and Irene led the group to the corrals where the horses stood, some dozing, some hanging their heads over the fence.

Clyde grabbed a halter and demonstrated how to catch one of the horses. Sam and Irene did the same, then led their charges out of the corral to the group. Some of the kids leaned against the fence, too cool to care. Others walked right up to a horse and put out a hand. A few hung back, watching cautiously.

Out of the corner of her eye, Sam saw Electra leading Ginger from the barn. *Oh good. She's going to help after all.* Sam talked to the girls clustered around her and showed them how to approach the horse, quietly from the front or side and not from behind. "You could startle him, and he might kick, in self-defense."

She glanced over at Electra, standing with Ginger off to the side by herself. Sam shook her head. She certainly didn't look real inviting. No wonder nobody was going over.

Then a younger version of the teen stepped toward Ginger, face down, eyes on the ground. She stopped and looked around as if to see who might be watching her, then came forward again.

Electra didn't say a word, just stood combing the mare's mane with her fingers. The girl put out a hand, then quickly withdrew it as the horse fluttered her nostrils.

Sam stopped what she was doing. *C'mon, Electra, say something to her.* She started to take a step toward the pair but stopped when Electra took the girl's hand and guided it toward the horse's face. Her hand trembled, but when she touched Ginger's velvety nose, her black-rimmed eyes opened wide. She raised her head and looked at Electra who put out her hand, flat-palmed, with a carrot. Ginger ate the treat and nuzzled Electra's pocket for more. Electra handed the girl a carrot. She copied the open-handed offering and gave a little gasp when Ginger lipped it into her mouth.

Smiling, she slowly, deliberately stroked the contours of the mare's face, as if she were a blind person memorizing someone's features.

Sam blinked to clear her vision and turned back to her charges. Looked like Electra had it handled.

***

Sam and the Bruckners spent the rest of the day showing the kids who were interested how to brush and currycomb the horses. The group home counselors took those who were too shy or too cool to deal with horses around to show them the chickens, the kittens, and the collection of old farm machinery Clyde had set up.

"This is LeRoy." Sam introduced the horse. "He's a chestnut—you can tell by his reddish-brown color. I'm going to show you how to take care of him."

The group of girls who'd flocked around her earlier giggled and jostled each other for a turn, their tough bravado momentarily forgotten.

"Let me brush him now."

"Can I braid his mane?"

"Ooh, wouldn't he look cool with dreds?"

Sam smiled. A summer of working hard on a ranch would turn this bunch around. Too bad they were only there for the weekend.

"Okay, let me show you." She patiently explained to the next girl how to approach the horse and what to do. "Stand back a little, so you can lean into each stroke." She demonstrated, then handed the brush to the heavy-set girl with multiple rings in her eyebrows and nose. "Now you try it."

The girl took the brush and awkwardly started at the belly, stroking toward the horse's neck.

Sam placed a hand over the girl's. "Work front to back, like this. That's the way the hair grows. Good." She stepped back and nodded. "Good job."

It seemed like hours of repeating the instructions over and over and letting each girl try her hand at brushing or braiding or simply how to gently stroke the horse's face and neck. Her group had gradually changed from boisterous showing-off to a quiet, near-reverence toward the horses. A couple had actually attempted putting on the bridle.

As the afternoon sun sank into the roofline of the barn, Sam finally turned to the girls. "Well, it's getting close to suppertime, so let's take this equipment back to the barn. Then you can help us feed and water the horses."

Again, with enthusiastic whoops and giggles, the girls picked up the brushes and blankets and bridles and ran for the barn.

Sam rested her forehead against LeRoy's neck and breathed out a long, tired sigh. This was harder work than rounding up cattle all day. She allowed herself a small grin. But she could see some progress already.

"Hey there, Ms. Moser."

She jumped at the voice behind her. She turned to see Brad Ashton smiling. "I'm impressed."

Her face heated. "What are you doing here?"

"Watching a pro at work."

Sam gave a dismissive wave. "Just introducing city kids to the country." She grabbed LeRoy's halter to lead him to the corral.

Ashton followed.

She led the horse to the water tank and let him drink. Ashton stood nearby and watched. Half annoyed now, she asked again, "What *are* you doing here? You didn't come to watch me water a horse."

He chuckled. "No. But I did want to talk to you a bit more. I heard what happened with the horse you rescued, and—"

With an exasperated sigh, Sam shook her head. "Yeah, by now everybody in the county's heard I'm a horse thief," she mumbled and strode away to meet her group of girls. "Okay, you can lead him over there where Mr. Bruckner and the boys are putting out feed."

When she turned to head back toward the barn, she nearly collided with Ashton. "You still here? What part of 'leave me alone' don't you get?"

He threw up his hands in mock surrender. "Sorry. I really didn't mean to hit on a sore spot. I thought I might be able to help you get the horse back."

Sam stepped back, stunned. Before she could think of a single word to say, Irene Bruckner rang an old cowbell to signal the kids for barbecued burgers, and they ran toward the house, laughing and chattering.

Clyde sauntered by. "C'mon up t'the house, Brad, and have a bite."

"Don't mind if I do." Ashton swept a hand toward the house. "After you, ma'am."

Sam glanced at the man from the corner of her eye as they walked toward the house, but studiously avoided eye contact. At the house, she chose a seat on the picnic bench near the girls she'd been working with. She munched her burger, smiling at the girls' teasing and giggles, watching Electra and the other Goth girl huddled off to one side. Yet, she kept glancing over at Ashton's table. What was he up to? She was curious but didn't know if she wanted to trust him. After all, he'd lied to her about using that film footage.

He looked in her direction, and Sam averted her gaze, breaking into a laugh as if she'd been joking with the girls all along. Her neck felt hot.

She was just about to get up and collect Electra to take her home when she felt a light touch on her shoulder. She jumped as Ashton sat beside her.

He grinned and shook his head. "Quite a bunch of JDs you have here, huh?"

Sam shrugged. "So, what did you mean about helping get Apache back?"

"Oh. Well…" He tipped his hat back. "I thought you could tell me what happened and maybe I could come up with some ideas. You know, as an objective observer."

"Hmmph." Sam's shoulders fell. "I thought you might have a more concrete plan." She stood and called out, "C'mon, Electra, let's go home."

"Wait. Can't you talk a minute?" Ashton's voice held an exasperated tone. "I really do want to help."

"We gotta get home, do our chores. If you have an idea, leave a message on my machine." Sam did an about-face and walked toward her pickup.

CHAPTER EIGHTEEN

The next day, after a successful ride, the group home kids unsaddled and brushed their horses before heading back to Billings. After just two days Sam could see a difference of demeanor in several.

Electra and her charge tended to Ginger. The girl smiled as she caressed the soft nose and ran her hands up the horse's face. Then she took the golden mane in her hands, and buried her face. Sam met Electra's gaze. Her young friend beamed.

As the group boarded the vans, one girl came back to Sam. She stopped short and looked up shyly. "Miss Sam... uh... thanks." Then she ran to the vehicle.

A twinge of regret shot through Sam. If only these kids could stay longer...

On the drive home, Electra quietly gazed out the passenger side window.

Sam glanced at her. "You did a really good job with that girl this weekend."

The girl looked back at Sam, her eyes glistening. "Yeah. I think I helped her a little." She bit her lower lip. "She lost both her parents. Ended up on the street, stealing, an'..." Her voice broke, and she stared out the window again.

Sam squeezed Electra's arm. There, but for the grace of God... She blinked a tear from her own eyes.

When they drove up the rise toward the house, a white pickup was parked out front. She pulled up beside the logoed truck door and sighed. Ashton.

"Who's that?" Electra asked. "I saw him yesterday."

Sam huffed another sigh. "He's a film-maker. I wish he'd just go home." She opened her door and walked around the front of her pickup to meet Brad Ashton who already stood outside, smiling broadly.

"Now what?" She stopped, her fists on her hips.

Ashton chuckled. "Just like a bad penny, huh?" He reached into his shirt pocket and drew out a sheet of paper. "A release form for the documentary." He offered it to her. "That is, if you want to. If you don't, then I will take your scene out."

Sam hesitated. Hmm. Maybe she'd misjudged him.

"But I'd really like to keep the footage in. You sit a horse so pretty." Ashton continued to hold the paper out. "You don't have to decide right now. Think about it if you want."

"Well, it's about time." Grinning, Sam took the form and put it in her pocket. "Nice to meet a man who can admit he was wrong."

Brad quirked an eyebrow. "Wrong? Me? Never."

Sam snorted. "Yeah, right."

Behind her, Electra cleared her throat. "Want me to start the chores?"

Sam turned. "Chores. Yeah." Then to Brad. "We have to feed my horse and exercise her a bit. You wanna come along?"

"Sure." Ashton touched two fingers to his hat brim.

At the barn, Sugar trotted up to the fence and whickered when she saw them approaching. Electra rushed forward and threw her arms around the horse's neck. Sugar nuzzled the girl's pocket looking for a treat.

Ashton walked slowly forward, holding his hand out for the mare to sniff, then rubbed her face, talking in a quiet voice. "Easy there, girl. Do I smell all right? Huh? Okay then." He reached out his other hand to Electra for another cake pellet and let Sugar eat from his open palm.

Sam watched open-mouthed. "You don't act like a city boy," she blurted, then winced. *Why don't I think before I talk? Just because he has a city job and dresses impeccably.*

"I've rode a green horse or two." He exaggerated a bow-legged stance.

117

Sam felt her eyes grow big. "Where?"

"Livingston."

"Ah, wind country."

Brad chuckled. "You could say that. All our cows were shorter on one side, from leaning into the wind."

"What? Really?" Electra popped her head from around Sugar's neck, then rolled her eyes as she saw his wink.

Sam snorted a laugh. "So, why did you leave?"

"Dad lost the place." He stared at the horizon, a faraway look in his eyes.

"Oh. I'm sorry." Sam chewed on her lower lip. A familiar refrain. Drought, poor stock prices—so many had lost everything.

Electra dragged a saddle from the barn. "Okay if I take her for a short ride?"

"Sure. But don't run her too hard." Sam watched with a measure of pride as the young girl bridled and saddled Sugar, swung easily aboard, and trotted off.

"Your niece?" Ashton asked.

"No, just a young friend I met at Clyde's." Sam gazed off at the horse and rider as they grew smaller against the vast prairie. *Electra's changed so much.* Then she turned back to Ashton. "You want to stay for supper?"

"Depends… Whatcha cookin'?"

Sam gave him a mock glare. "Leftover spaghetti. Take it or leave it." She spun around to head to the house.

"Spaghetti—always better the next day."

The ridiculousness of this conversation suddenly made Sam laugh. "All right then. Here comes Electra. Let's go on up, and I'll put it on the stove."

In the house, she glanced in the mirror and smoothed the fly-away strands of her hair. This Brad Ashton was quite the character. A ranch-kid. Hmm. She patted the paper in her pocket. Being featured in a film might not be so bad. And he said she looked pretty on a horse. She grinned. But she wouldn't sign it just yet. Let him sweat a little.

Electra tromped in, giving Brad dark sidelong glances. *Now what?* Sam set the steaming bowl of spaghetti on the table. "Wash up, sit down, and eat." She pointed to the bathroom.

"Yes, ma'am." Ashton saluted and headed for the hallway. Sam started dishing up plates.

"Why'd you ask him to stay?" Electra sat at the table with a sullen pout.

Sam stopped in mid-ladle. "Well, he said he might be able to help us get—"

Brad appeared, wiping his hands on his pants. "Mmm, that smells good. Let me at it." He sat, tucked a napkin into his shirt front, and picked up his fork and knife, striking a comical expectant pose.

Sam set his plate in front of him.

"Ah, a woman who serves." Brad twitched his eyebrows.

Sam laughed. "Oh no. Don't you be getting used to it."

"So you're just being nice 'cause I'm company."

"Something like that." Sam ignored Electra's glare and sat down to eat.

He raised a forkful of spaghetti high in the air, leaned his head back, and slurped down a long strand. He winked at Electra. "Bet you can't do that."

She curled her lip and hunched back over her plate, deliberately cutting her noodles into small pieces.

"Sorry." Brad looked at Sam. "I should mind my manners when I'm with ladies."

The teen snorted.

Sam grinned. "So, do a lot of riding on your dad's ranch?"

"Fair amount. Helped with branding, fall roundup, stuff like that."

She twirled her spaghetti around her fork. "Ever do any rodeoing?"

"Naw. Not really. Just around home when a horse suddenly decided to get feisty. Did my share of hittin' the dust."

"Didn't need to do it in front of a crowd, huh?"

He chuckled. "That's right. How 'bout you? I'll bet you'da looked cute running the barrels."

Heat rose up her neck. "Don't know about that. Did a little when I was about ten."

"You oughta try it again. You got the build."

With a long, exaggerated sigh, Electra pushed back her plate, got up and stomped upstairs to her room.

The heat spread into Sam's face. *What's with that girl?* Turning back to Brad, she said, "No barrel horse." She took a sip of water. "Anyway, enough about me. When did you get into making documentaries?"

"College. Took a broadcast journalism course at UM."

As they mopped up the last of the sauce with French bread, she heard a car pull up, and went to the door to welcome Teresa. Her friend carried a manila envelope and a bottle of wine.

"Oh dear, you should have been here fifteen minutes ago," Sam apologized. "We just finished off supper."

"No, that's fine. I ate in town." Teresa handed Sam the bottle. "But crack this open and I'll have a glass." She stepped into the kitchen, where Sam introduced her to Ashton. He stood and held out a hand for her to shake. "Pleased to meet you. I understand you've been helping Sam try to rescue a horse."

"Yeah, that's right." Teresa glanced at her with raised eyebrows. "And that's why I stopped by tonight. I have those pictures of Apache when I first found him." She opened the envelope and spread them on the table.

Electra slouched down the stairs, but gasped as she looked at the photos, and choked back a sob. "We've got to get him back."

Sam sighed. She could only hope he was being cared for, and not dead by now.

"I talked briefly to our real estate attorney this afternoon, and he suggested we look into civil court. We have the signed notarized bill of sale, and these pictures. Maybe we'll get lucky and draw a sympathetic judge."

"Oh man, getting up to present a legal case in front of a judge." Sam's knees felt like jelly thinking about it. "I don't know if I can do that."

"Sure, you can. I'll be there with you, and I'll testify too." Teresa peered earnestly into her face.

With a grimace, Brad put down the photos. "Before you do that, why don't you let me nose around a little. I've been filming all over this country and people are pretty used to seeing me by now."

Teresa met Sam's glance. "Really? That'd be great."

"What's the owner's name?" he asked.

"Richard Smythe." Teresa picked up the photos and put them back into the envelope.

"Okay. I'll see what I can find out." He stood and reached for his hat. "Well, I better be going. Thanks for supper, Sam. Day-old spaghetti. Very tasty." He winked.

She shook her head.

After he left, she found a notepad and pen. "Let's make a list."

"Okay." Teresa grinned broadly. "Number one. He's cute."

Sam hmphed a little snort and bent over the paper to cover for the rising blush. "Okay, we have the photos, we have the bill of sale."

"Number two. He's willing to help you out," Teresa persisted.

Electra scowled. "He's just trying to hit on her."

Teresa cuffed her shoulder playfully. "Number three. He's got a nice butt."

Sam rolled her eyes. "Come on, you two. Knock it off and help me out. I don't have a lot to go on here. And if I do have to present my case to a judge, I'd better have more than this."

It was close to midnight when Teresa got up to leave. They'd mulled and discussed and made lists and drafts of speeches until her brain felt like a cache of dust bunnies from under the bed. But they were no closer to a solution than before.

"I think we're going to have to wait and see what Brad comes up with," Teresa said on her way out the door.

Sam waved goodnight to her friend. *She's right. Maybe Brad isn't such a bad guy after all.* She yawned. "I'm going to bed. I'm fried."

Electra didn't say anything but stayed hunched over the wads of paper littering the table.

Sam frowned. "What's the matter?"

Electra shrugged. "Nothin'."

"C'mon, I know you better than that by now. There's something bugging you." She stopped a tired sigh from escaping. All she wanted to do was crawl into her soft bed and sleep.

Hands flattened, then re-crumpled paper. Electra's black nail polish was chipped and scratched now, her cuticles bitten.

"Is it Apache?" Sam persisted. "We'll get him back. I'm even willing to get up in front of the judge and talk him into believing our side of the story."

"It's not that." The girl stood, gathered the litter, and threw it into the garbage. She headed toward the stairs, stopped on the first step, and looked back. "Why d'you need *him* to help anyway?" Before Sam could comprehend what she meant, Electra ran up the stairs and slammed her door shut.

Sam drooped in her chair. *She's jealous of Brad.*

CHAPTER NINETEEN

The next morning, Electra didn't come down for breakfast. Sam went to the corral to take care of Sugar, then took a short ride.

Brad Ashton. He really did seem genuinely interested in helping. His mischievous grin flashed in her mind. *He is cute. Wonder how he kisses.* Despite a lack of sleep, the blue sky seemed clearer, the wildflowers more colorful. She giggled.

But images of Apache lying in that dusty pasture kept interfering with Brad's smile and playful teasing. And Electra's black glare haunted her. Sam batted at a fly.

Back at the barn, she was no more at peace than before she'd left. After brushing down Sugar, she made her way to the house. She sighed. *Might as well talk to her. Can't avoid it forever.*

"I'm leaving." Electra's snarl greeted her in the kitchen.

"Electra!" Sam leaned wearily into the doorjamb. "What's gotten into you?"

The teen slumped in her chair, mute.

"C'mon, girl. Tell me what's eating at you." Sam sat next to her.

The sullen teen glared from under mascara-caked eyelashes.

"I'll let you ride LeRoy today." She put on what she hoped was a cheerful expression.

"I want to go home." The girl's lip quivered.

Sam felt a catch in her chest. "Oh, sweetie. Tell me what's wrong. Then, if we can't make it right, you can go home."

"I always sat next to you." The face was defiant now.

She bit her lip. "You don't like Brad?"

Electra rose from her chair. "I thought *you* didn't like him."

"But why? He may be our only hope of getting Apache back." Sam was incredulous.

"Not *him*." Her voice rose to a shout. "I'm packing." She strode toward the stairs. "And you can't stop me!"

The door slam reverberated through Sam's teeth. *Oh, dear Lord, help me.* She went upstairs. "Please don't do this, Electra. Come out and talk to me."

"You don't like me anymore," came the muffled reply.

"That's not true! Where did you get that idea?" Sam leaned her forehead against the door.

"You ignored me."

"When?"

"All the time *he* was here."

Sam breathed in deeply, then turned the doorknob and went in. She sat on the bed where Electra lay. "If I did, I didn't mean to."

"Just like Dad." Electra buried her face in the pillow.

Sam swallowed hard. *Ah, her father.* She rubbed the girl's thin back. "Because he left you?"

A slight nod.

"I'm not leaving you, Electra. You're my friend. I like you, and I want you to stay for the rest of the summer." She blinked, surprised at the truth of her statement.

Electra lay still, her shoulders rigid.

She tried again. "I need you to help me. I can't do this without you."

An eye peeked out from the pillow.

"Honest, I can't. You're my right-hand girl. You and me together—we'll come up with the ideas and if we need some muscle, then *maybe* we'll let Brad or Clyde help us."

The teen turned her head to look at Sam. "Can we go see him?"

"See Apache?" Fear skittered through her body. "Sure. Why not? Let's drive by there and see if he's being cared for."

"Yeah." Electra sat and wiped black-stained eyes. "Bring your camera. If he's not, then we'll have evidence."

Sam smiled. "Good idea. Why don't you take a quick shower, and we'll go."

***

Leaving the rough dirt road outside Ingomar, Sam shifted into high gear and sped down the highway. Beside her, Electra was silent but leaned forward slightly, peering out the windshield. Sam rolled down the side window a bit to create a breeze.

"Do you think he's all right?" The teen turned her fresh-scrubbed face toward her.

"I sure hope so." Goosebumps prickled her arms. "We may have to be prepared for anything, though."

Electra slumped against the back of the seat, her mouth downturned.

Sam swerved to avoid a road-killed rabbit. Teenagers were so hard to read. *And it wasn't that long ago, I was one.* She smiled. *Ironic.* "You mentioned your dad this morning. He ignored you?"

Her young friend snorted. "Like, ye-ah. Jimmy was the only one who mattered."

"Your brother."

The girl nodded.

"And," Sam spoke hesitantly, "Jimmy was killed. In an accident?"

"Yeah." The reply came as a hoarse whisper. Then she sat up straighter. Her words came with force. "And Dad was driving."

Her heart felt like a bass drum in a brass band. The image of a mangled blue vehicle flashed before her. "So he blamed himself."

"I guess." Electra shrugged. "Didn't take him long to leave."

Like Kenny, when the going got tough. The empty miles swallowed the long ribbon of highway ahead. Sam clenched the wheel. What could she say to Electra? What could she do to fix things for this girl? She watched a dust devil whirl through the barrow pit up ahead. Fix things? *I can't even fix them for myself.*

Stopping at a drive-through on the edge of Miles City, Sam bought a soft drink for Electra, a cup of coffee for herself, and a giant home-made cinnamon roll to share. *To fortify us for whatever we find.*

The late morning sun bore down. Low on the horizon, thunderheads gathered. Dust swirled in a long tail behind them on the country road as they drove closer to the ranch where Apache's fate lay hidden.

Up ahead, the windmill blades churned in the increasing wind. Sam's chest tightened. What would they find?

"There he is!" Electra's words came in an explosive breath, and she pushed her face closer to the windshield.

Apache stood by a gleaming new water tank, his tail switching in the breeze. "Oh, thank God." Sam released her own pent-up air and parked the pickup.

Electra was out the moment the truck came to a stop, leaving the door wide open. She took a couple of running steps, then slowed to approach the horse cautiously. Apache lifted his head. His ears pricked toward her. He whinnied, trotted to the fence, and stretched over the wire. With a half-cry, half-giggle, Electra flung her arms around Apache's neck.

Sam blinked against the tears rising. Feeling a bit like a Cheshire cat, she got out of the pickup and joined the girl and horse, rubbing his face and murmuring, "You're still alive. You're okay. Oh, I'm so glad."

Apache fluttered his nostrils and nuzzled them both. Electra stepped back, reached into her pocket and offered him a handful of cake pellets. "He's still awfully thin."

Sam nodded. "Yes, but he's got water and a feed trough." She glanced around, spotting an open gate. "Looks like access to a grassier pasture too. Oh, I'm so glad."

Electra sniffled and hugged the horse again. "But I miss you so much."

The roar of a diesel engine brought Sam's attention to the road. A big black 4x4 pulled up beside hers. A tall, muscular man stepped out, leaving his door open to the view of a shotgun on a rack in the cab. He stood within reach, arms crossed over his barrel-chest. "What are you ladies doing here?"

"We're just check—"

Sam cut Electra off before she could say any more. "We were just driving by and stopped to pet the horse. My young friend here loves horses."

"Hmm." The big man didn't look convinced. His forehead furrowed. "Say, aren't you the two who stole this horse a couple weeks ago?"

"No!" Electra's denial was a shout.

Sam put an arm around her. Her insides quaked. "It was just a misunderstanding, sir."

Glowering, he took a step forward. "Well, that's not what I heard. You gals can just get off this property right now."

"Who are you?" Sam wasn't about to give in so easily.

"Let's just say, I been hired to keep the likes o' you away from this horse." He puffed out his chest, uncurled his arms and reached inside his pickup toward the shotgun.

"We're leaving. No need for threats." She grabbed Electra's arm and propelled her into their vehicle. Gravel spun under the tires as she punched the accelerator.

Her heart beat nearly out of her chest and her mouth was so dry she could barely swallow. As she sped down the dirt road, she kept glancing into her rearview mirror to see if they were being followed. Finally, when they reached the highway, she stopped the car. Her hands shook when she unclamped them from the steering wheel.

She heard a gulping sob from beside her and turned to Electra. Tears streamed down the girl's cheeks. She took short, hiccupping breaths and her face was red and distorted.

Sam took Electra's hand. "It's okay. Take a deep breath now. You're hyperventilating."

Her young friend wheezed and collapsed into sobs again. "No... use... never... get... Apache... back... now."

Sam put her arm around the girl. "No. We are NOT giving up. We're going to get him back, I promise!" She closed her eyes in a grimace. Who was she trying to kid? It sure looked impossible.

Once home, Electra stormed into her room and slammed the door. Sam grabbed the bottle of vodka and went back to the porch, weariness pressing her into the chair. *How could I promise something I don't believe will happen? Another failure.* If she had an old-time gunslinger's belt, it would be so full of notches it would probably fall apart. She took another drink that burned away the bile in her throat. And how in the world was she going to deal with Electra's moodiness? If only she could just sink into oblivion and not have to deal with all of this anymore.

***

Sam fought the blankets binding her, punched lumps in her pillow. Images ran in a continuous reel: the first Apache lying dead; her best friend Jace in a mangled blue Fiat; a skeleton of the second Apache standing by a dry reservoir; Kenny boarding the plane back to Phoenix; Electra, eyes black holes in a blank white face; Sam, alone in the midst of a thundering herd of buffalo, lions and elephants, powerless to stop any of it.

She sat up, gasping, and swiped sweat-damp hair from her eyes. The clock's face glowed a red 3:34 a.m. Two and a half hours and she had to get up to go to work. She couldn't stop her mind, couldn't stop the moving pictures, the litany of failure and sadness of her life. Great-Grandma Nettie wouldn't have let this defeat her, nor would Grandma Anna—after all, she learned how to live in a totally new country, AND she defeated leukemia.

A sob caught in her throat. *I miss Grandma and Grandpa.*

Swinging her feet out of bed, she padded to the window to stare at the black prairie. Maybe another vodka would help. No, she'd just be hung-over and drunk at the same time going to work. She paced the floor and took deep, slow breaths, trying to calm her racing heart.

A quote Aunt Monica had sent her once flashed into Sam's mind. "Give your troubles to God; He's up all night anyway."

She gave a wry smile and sat on the bed. It had been a long time since she'd talked to God. She'd been raised in the church but fell away after Jace's accident. Bad things happened to good people and where was God in all that?

A sigh slumped her shoulders. She looked out toward the sliver of moon. "Okay, God. If you're still up there... And if you still recognize me... It's me, Samantha. I got troubles and they're keeping me awake. If it's true—about you carrying our burdens—then can I give them to you? Just for tonight anyway. So I can get some sleep and figure things out in the morning..."

"Okay, God, good-night." She lay down and curled onto her side. "Amen."

CHAPTER TWENTY

The alarm shrilled at 6:00. Sam hit the off button and stared at the rays of sunshine slanting in through the window, a cool breeze ruffling the curtains. A strange peace lifted her as she got up and grabbed her robe. She felt rested—after only a couple hours of sleep. Coffee soon burbled in the pot as she fried eggs and made toast.

Upstairs, she knocked on Electra's door. "Time to rise and shine, sunshine!"

An immediate "Okay" startled her, and the door opened. Electra stood there, fresh-scrubbed and fully dressed.

"Wow. Look at you." Sam tucked her own wayward tendrils behind her ears. "C'mon and sit down, breakfast is ready."

They sat and Electra attacked her eggs and toast. "Y'know what," she said with a mouthful, "it might be okay to have Brad on our side. He's been all over the country, talking to people. Maybe he knows somebody who can help us get Apache back."

She opened her mouth but couldn't speak for a moment. "Uh… Yeah! I mean… yeah, he said he'd do some nosing around, see if he could get any information for us." She blinked. What had caused that about-face? Well, never look a gift-horse in the mouth, as the old-timers said.

"Okay then. Let's get over to Clyde's and see what he has for us to do today." She smiled and squeezed Electra's arm. "Thanks."

The girl ducked her head and grinned back. "Sure."

To take her mind off Apache, Sam kept busy oiling and repairing tack, cleaning stalls, riding the friskier horses, preparing for the next group of dudes.

"You're just a whirlwind of busyness today." Clyde startled her as she unsaddled Ginger.

"Yeah." She gave him a lopsided smile. "I keep mulling over the situation with Apache. I don't know what to do." She told him what had happened the day before.

He raised bushy eyebrows. "Dang. That sounds serious. Why in the world would Smythe hire a thug to protect that broken-down old horse? Against two little gals?" He reached into his shirt pocket for a snoose can. "And my attorney not wanting to take your case. That don't make any sense. Somethin' stinks."

Electra came up behind them, leading LeRoy. "Yeah, but Brad said he'd find out what's going on. He'll help us get Apache back."

"Oh yeah? Well, it's good to have people on your side." Clyde smiled at her and turned back to Sam. "I've tried calling my lawyer, but he hasn't returned my calls. But ya know, that punk nephew took your money. You oughta at least be able to get that back."

"We don't want the money." Electra's voice rose. "We want Apache!"

Sam nodded. "They've bonded and I can't see either one without the other."

"Well, what the kid did was illegal. Maybe you oughta at least write Smythe a letter, see if that'll get him to talk to you about the whole mess." Clyde spat a stream of tobacco at a dirt clod.

"Yeah! Can we, Sam, huh? Will that help?" The teen hopped from one foot to the other.

"Well, we can try it." Sam sighed. *But I don't see that it'll do any good.*

That evening after chores were done and supper dishes washed, Electra sat at the table with a tablet and pen. "Dear Mr. Smythe... Is that the right way to start?" She looked up.

"Well, I think it should be a little more formal. Here's how you'd do a business header." She showed the girl the format.

Electra leaned over the paper, wrote, scribbled out words, and chewed on the pen. "How does this sound?"

Sam read what she'd written.

> *Mr. Smythe:*
>
> *We found your horse—almost dead—laying in the dirt in 90-degree heat with no water and no food. Miss Samantha Moser bought a tub and gave him water and hay. We met your nephew, Todd Smythe, and he said he called you to get permission to sell Apache to us.* ~~*Sam Samantha*~~ *Miss Moser wrote him a check for $500 and wrote out a bill of sale and he signed it. We took your horse to the vet, gave him medicine and special food, and we loved him. He was getting better, but you took him away. Please, can we have him back?*
>
> *Sincerely,*
>
> *Electra Lucci*

Sam's chest tightened and she fought the sting in her eyes. She took a breath to keep her voice from trembling when she spoke. "You've written a very impassioned plea. I'm proud of you." She corrected a couple of grammatical errors. "Do you want to type this up on my computer? I'll print it out, and we'll send it off." She closed her eyes for a moment. *With a prayer.*

Electra's eyes glistened. She nodded. "You think it's okay? Really? Thanks. Yes, let's do it."

The next day they mailed the letter, Electra pushing the envelope through the slot herself with a determined exhale. She turned to Sam. "So, if it takes two days to get there and maybe he thinks about it for a day, and then two days to get an answer back..." She ticked off the days on her fingers. "Maybe we should give it a week, just to be sure."

Sam gave her a bemused smile. "We can hope for that anyway."

Before the week had passed, Electra badgered her to stop at the post office every day after working at Clyde's. But no letter came. One week became two, then three, and four.

One evening Sam sat in the living room after supper, Electra brooding on the sofa with defeated shoulders. "He's not going to answer, is he?"

"Who?" She looked up from her book.

"Mr. Smythe."

Sam sighed. "It doesn't look like it."

When the phone rang, she jumped. "Wonder who that could be."

"Maybe it's him." Electra leaped up from the sofa, her eyes wide with expectation.

Sam answered, to hear Brad's voice. "Hey there, cowgirl, how's it going?"

"Oh, hi, Brad." She steeled herself against the thumps in her chest.

Electra slumped back on the couch.

"I just wanted to touch base with you. Sorry I haven't been by earlier. Boss is keeping me busy. Anything new on the horse?"

"No, we're just sitting and waiting." She told him about the letter.

"Good idea, but I wouldn't hold my breath." Brad paused. "I've been looking into Mr. Smythe a little. He's from back east and is a foreign investor, apparently quite wealthy. He's a big landowner over there in Custer County, and apparently, he is in the process of stocking his ranch with buffalo. He's a big proponent of 'economic viability with ecological sustainability,' to quote his website, and talks about returning the land to the wild."

Her lip curled. "Hmm. I wonder if he knows Jack Murdock and Scott Roberts."

"I'd bet they probably do run in the same circles."

Sam frowned. "Well, thanks for the information, Brad." She hung up.

"We're not getting Apache back." A tear rolled down the teen's cheek.

"Well, I don't think we should give up." Sam tried to sound reassuring, while inside she had a dark, heavy feeling of dread. This was not going to end without a fight. Maybe she could try to contact him through his website. But what could two "little gals," as Clyde said, do against powerful men like Smythe, Roberts, and Murdock?

***

The following weekend, two counselors brought a small vanload of kids from the group home in Billings—some who had been there before plus a couple of new faces. "They had such a good time here before, we thought we'd try it again," one leader said.

This time the kids approached with much more enthusiasm. "Can we ride?" "Let me brush the horse." "What can I do?"

The little Goth-girl look-alike approached Sam shyly. "Hi. My name is Sapphire." She asked Electra, "Can I pet Ginger again?"

The teen nodded. "C'mon, we'll go get her."

Sam smiled, her heart proud. This was good—keep Electra's mind off Apache. *And mine.*

The kids were mostly well-behaved—if a little clumsy and over-enthusiastic—and after lunch, Clyde and Sam saddled the horses and took the counselors and their charges for a short ride.

The woman counselor, Robin Johnson, rode up next to Sam. "This is so good for these kids. I couldn't believe the difference in this group after last time. They've all been clamoring after us to come back."

Sam nodded. "That's great. I'm really glad."

"I'm especially encouraged by the bonding Sapphire and Electra have done. Sapphire is such a broken little girl." The counselor sighed. "I wish there was a place in Billings these kids could go to regularly."

"Well, it's only about a two-hour drive here. Maybe we could work something out on a more regular basis," Sam offered. "Let's talk it over with Clyde when we get back."

"That would be great." Robin patted her horse's neck. "Have you lived here all your life?"

"I grew up in Montana, but only about a year at this place." Sam told her about Great-Grandma Nettie, about rescuing Sugar, and her dream to raise Thoroughbreds.

"What a wonderful story about your horse. I love a happy ending like that. I know this is tough country, but I hope you can achieve your dream."

Excitement caught in her throat, and before she knew it, she told Robin about Apache, Electra, and their dilemma.

"Oh my!" Robin's eyes were wide. "That's just awful. You need to file a complaint against those men."

"I know. Electra loves that horse so much, she is heartbroken over losing him. I'd really like to get him back for her."

The group approached the corrals. "Well, I wish you luck. I hope you can get the horse back." Robin smiled at Sam. "Thanks so much for working with us again." She rode off to round up her charges.

Before they left, the counselors met with Clyde and Sam and worked out a schedule to bring kids to the ranch once a month.

Clyde grinned at Sam later. "A steady gig! Should work out fine, except maybe during hunting season, when I'll need all—or most anyway—of the horses. But we'll figure somethin' out."

Sam and Electra checked the mail on the way home. No letter from Smythe. "What should we do?" The girl turned to Sam, a tear trickling down her cheek. "Brad sure hasn't come through for us either." Her mouth turned down at one corner.

"I know. I hoped he'd have some ideas. Other than how 'big and powerful' Smythe is. I think I do need to pursue charges against his nephew though. We can't let him get away with what he did." She patted the girl's knee and changed the subject. "You did such a good job with Sapphire both times the kids visited. I'm really proud of you."

Electra wiped her cheek and allowed a small smile. "I like her. She reminds me…"

"Of you?" Sam grinned.

"Yeah, a little. But she had a really bad life. She lost both parents, and the uncle she went to live with didn't want her, treated her really mean. She got in some trouble and when she got out of juvie, he wouldn't take her back." The teen stared out the window for a moment. "She needs an Apache."

An ache grew in Sam's throat. *I need to do something. Now.*

CHAPTER TWENTY-ONE

The message light blinked on the answering machine. Sam hit "play" as she sat to take off her boots.

"Hey, babe, it's me."

Sam squeezed her eyes shut. *Kenny.*

"Just wanted to hear your voice again. You're still welcome here in Phoenix—any time." A pause. "Ran into Jace the other day. She's doing pretty good. Asked about you. Here's her phone number, if you want to call her..."

The message ended. She froze, one boot off, hanging from her hand. Jace. Her best friend, a paraplegic. All because of their stupid argument at a stupid party. Her mind flashed back to that night—Jace so drunk, so angry, storming out the door, getting into her blue Fiat, tires screeching. Sam angry too. *Why didn't I stop her? Why didn't I grab her keys, run after her?* She *had* followed, minutes later. Cresting a hill, she saw the taillights swerving ahead. And a one-ton truck approaching from the side. Her heart exploded. *NO!* Sam could only watch, powerless to stop it.

Tears trickled from her eyes. Weeks in the hospital, months in rehab. Sam visited, but it wasn't the same. Her friend was a stranger. *It was my fault. She'll never forgive me.*

Electra banged in through the kitchen door. "You okay?"

She jumped and dropped the boot. "Sure. I'm fine." She forced a grin. "Did you get Sugar fed?"

"Yeah, and I gathered the eggs." Electra set the hatful on the counter. "What's for supper?"

"Supper." Sam looked around the kitchen, still half-dazed. "Yeah, we should eat something." She opened the refrigerator. "We need to go grocery shopping. Well, there's lots of eggs. How about scrambled eggs and bacon?"

"Okay. I'll make toast." Electra grabbed the loaf of bread.

As she cracked the eggs into a bowl, the images of the accident kept replaying: the mangled mess, her friend trapped inside. Like her aunt Lizzie must have been. She swallowed a sob. She couldn't help Jace. Who was there to help Lizzie? No one.

The sound of a car pulling up to the house broke the dark spell.

"It's Brad," Electra announced with a sneer in her voice. "Nice of him to show up now. Just in time for supper."

Her heartbeat tripped a little. She opened the door. There he stood, grinning, a dark wayward lock curling over his forehead. Her breath hitched. "Hi. Haven't seen you in weeks. What are you doing here?"

Brad stepped inside. "Hi, Sam. Hi, Electra."

The girl ignored him.

"Well, I had some more work to do on the documentary, so I was in the neighborhood." He handed Sam a grocery sack with pre-made salad and tomatoes. "Since I seem to be crashing your supper, maybe I can contribute something."

She snorted a little laugh. "Well, thanks. All we're having is scrambled eggs, so if you want to fix the salad, you can join us."

Electra gave him sidelong glances as they sat down to eat.

Brad grinned at her. "Am I still on your 'list'?"

She rolled her eyes. "I thought you were going to help us get Apache back. Where have you been?"

He shook his head. "I'm really sorry. I've been running all around the state with work, and I haven't been back here at all. It's been crazy." He turned to Sam. "Anything more on the horse?"

She shook her head. "No. But everybody keeps telling me I need to file charges against the nephew."

Brad nodded. "I agree."

"Where do we go, and how do we go about that? Do we have to go to a judge?" The grasshoppers in Sam's stomach reminded her how much she hated public speaking.

"But I don't want the money back," Electra wailed. "I want Apache."

"Tell you what." Brad nodded at the girl. "I'll go with you. Let's go talk to Sheriff O'Conner in Forsyth tomorrow. He should be able to tell us what steps we need to take."

Sam inhaled deeply. "Okay. Thanks. I'd appreciate your company." She squeezed Electra's shoulder. "We'll work on this. Together. Okay?"

***

The next morning Brad roared up to the house, and Sam and Electra piled into his pickup.

"So, this Smythe is a big money mogul, huh?" Sam asked.

Brad curled his lip and nodded.

"Is he part of this 'Big Open' movement?"

"I've only dealt with Roberts, doing this documentary. Hadn't heard Smythe's name before this. But he sure sounds like he'd fit right in, with his buffalo herd."

Electra leaned over the seat back. "Well, if he's such a big ranch owner, why did he abandon Apache, and why does he care if we wanted to buy him?"

Brad shook his head. "That's a really good question. I'd like to know the answer myself."

"Me too." Sam watched the prairie roll by. "Me too."

In Forsyth, Brad turned down 13th Street and pulled up in front of a low, brown-stucco building that stated: "Rosebud County Law Enforcement." A narrow strip of lawn wilted in the summer heat and a couple of cottonwoods provided meager shade.

After checking in with the receptionist, they sat for a few minutes on cracked plastic-cushioned chairs before the tall, broad-shouldered sheriff strolled out to the lobby. "Howdy, folks. C'mon back to my office." A kind smile crinkled his weathered face.

As they stepped into the musty room, Sam introduced Brad and reminded him who Electra was.

O'Connor shook hands with his powerful, rancher grip and sat behind his paper-cluttered desk. "So, what can I do for you?"

"Well, you remember the horse I rescued, and you and the Custer County animal warden came to take him back..." Sam spoke hesitantly.

He nodded. "Oh. Yeah, yeah, I do."

She filled him in on what had happened since. "And I understand what the nephew did was illegal, so I guess we want to know what we can do to get the money back—"

"We really want Apache back," Electra interrupted.

"Yes, well, that would be the ultimate outcome," Sam said, "but..."

The sheriff stroked his gray-stubbled chin with his thumb and forefinger, a frown creasing his forehead. "But..." he finally spoke, "the horse does belong to Mr. Smythe, and if he doesn't want to sell, I'm afraid there's not much we can do about that."

Electra sniffed. Sam put a gentle hand on her arm.

"But..." the sheriff said again, in his slow, contemplative way, "you can charge this kid with fraud."

"How do I do that?" She asked. "I don't have money for an attorney. I gave my last five hundred to him."

"Yes, what is her recourse here?" Brad spoke up.

O'Connor picked up a pen and tapped it on his desk. "This took place in Custer County, right?"

Sam nodded.

"So, what I'd advise you to do, is go to justice court in Miles City and file a small claims complaint. It's a civil court, with no lawyers, just a judge, and there's a minimal fee to file—fifteen or twenty dollars, I think." The sheriff nodded. "Yeah, that'd be your best bet."

Brad looked at Sam. "I'm guessing they'll need to serve papers on Smythe. Do you know his address?"

She shook her head. "I only know the pasture where Apache is."

O'Connor reached into his desk drawer and withdrew a phone book. He riffled through the pages. "Hmm. Uh-huh."

She held her breath, waiting on the edge of her chair while he shuffled and passed a thick finger down the columns.

"Okay. Here it is," the sheriff said at last. He picked up his pen and a notepad and wrote down the information. "Good luck to you." He smiled.

"Thank you, Sheriff." Sam stood and turned to her companions. "Well, wanna go on in to Miles City?"

***

Sam put one foot on the bottom concrete step and gazed up at the gray, two-story Custer County Courthouse. She glanced at Brad and Electra and squared her shoulders. "Okay, let's go see what we can do about getting Apache or the money back."

Their boot heels echoed on the stone floor as they walked through the lobby, and then following the sign downstairs, the group approached the window for Justice Court. A woman greeted Sam at the counter. "Good afternoon. Can I help you?"

"Yes. I'd like to file a small claims complaint against this man." She handed the clerk the paper with Smythe's name and address.

The woman turned to a file cabinet and withdrew some papers. "Here you go. Fill out these forms. You can have a seat over there."

Sam joined Brad and Electra in the hallway where they sat on chrome and rust-cushioned chairs. Electra peered over her shoulder as she filled out her name, address, and phone number, along with Smythe's information, the five hundred-dollar amount, and a description of what had happened with the "sale" of Apache.

She also filled out an "Order and Notice to Defendant" form and another which stated copies would be delivered to Smythe.

The clerk skimmed the papers. "Okay, that'll be fifteen dollars."

Sam took out her checkbook. "Is a check okay?"

"Sure." The woman nodded. "And you'll need to go to the sheriff's office and ask someone to deliver the summons."

After they left the courthouse, Sam exhaled a sigh. "Whew. I'm glad that's done."

"What happens now?" Electra asked.

Sam shrugged. "We wait. The clerk said Smythe can decide to settle out of court or show up at on the court date, and we'll go from there."

Brad reached out his hand to shake hers. "Good job. The first step taken. Let's go to the 600 Café to celebrate. I'm buying."

Electra's face lit up, and Sam smiled. "Sounds good to me." *First step accomplished.*

CHAPTER TWENTY-TWO

Sam and Electra settled back into their routine at home and working at Clyde's, preparing for the next visitors. They were kept so busy neither had much energy at the end of the day to talk, much less think about what might happen with the court and Apache.

The next weekend, they were expecting the group home kids. "I think we'll take Sugar along today. We might need an extra gentle horse." She backed up Horace's trailer to the chute and loaded the Thoroughbred.

Sapphire was the first out of the group home van and ran toward Electra. "Where's Ginger? Can I ride her?"

"Sure. C'mon. We have a new horse for you to meet too." Electra led the girl to the corral.

One small victory. Sam shook her head, allowing a warm rush of pleasure. Actually two—Electra *and* Sapphire.

While Clyde took charge of the returning clients, she turned her attention to Robin and a couple of new kids.

"Good to be back," the woman said. "This is Justin and Wendy. They'd like to meet your horses."

Justin, like several of the other boys from the home had on their first visit, stood with a defiant stance, thumbs hooked in the waist of low-riding pants, eyes mere slits, slowly chewing a wad of gum. Wendy was a tiny, fair-haired waif who stood behind Robin, head down, shoulders hunched.

Sam's heart wrenched at the little girl's defeated posture. She made eye contact with Robin, who lifted one corner of a smile and gave a small shrug.

"Well, Justin, Wendy, I'm glad you've come to visit us. Do you want to go see the horses?" Sam gestured toward the corral.

The boy merely shrugged, but Wendy's gaze lifted for a fleeting moment.

"C'mon then. Let's go." She led them to where Electra and Sapphire were grooming Sugar.

Sapphire stopped in mid-brush and turned. "C'mere, Wendy. Come help us." She walked to the gate and put out a hand. The little girl glanced quickly at Robin who nodded, and then scuffed over to Sapphire. Electra joined them and the two older girls flanked Wendy as she hesitantly approached Sugar. Her head rose in tiny, halting movements until she came face to face with the mare. Sugar's liquid brown eyes held hers and time seemed to stop. Sam dared not breathe, waiting for a sudden movement to startle either one.

A small hand reached up. Sugar lowered her head to meet the touch. For long moments Wendy stroked the velvet muzzle. Then she suddenly darted forward to wrap her arms around Sugar's foreleg.

Sam gasped and stepped forward, but Sugar stood perfectly still. The mare curved her head back around Wendy. *She's giving her a hug!*

Robin stood, eyes wide, and Electra and Sapphire were also frozen in place as they witnessed a tiny miracle. Even Justin had abandoned his nonchalant pose and stood with an open mouth.

At lunch Robin sat down next to Sam, her eyes still misty. "*That* was awesome. I've never seen anything like it."

"Yes, it was." She too still held on to the wonder of that moment. "Horses and kids. Who knew?" She crunched a potato chip. But then, she'd always felt that freedom and the healing power of horses.

Robin chuckled as she gazed at the other table where the boys sat. "Even Justin got into it. He's almost a different kid." She turned back to Sam. "Say, any news on that horse you tried to rescue?"

145

Sam shook her head and told her she'd filed a complaint. "We're just waiting now."

"Hurry up and wait, huh?" The counselor bit into her sandwich. "I sure hope you can get him back—or at least your money."

"I hope so too," she said, "but I'm not holding my breath. This is one powerful bigwig, and he has lots of money and resources. What can one broke woman do against all that?"

"Well…" Robin paused and peered into Sam's eyes. "The Lord does work in mysterious ways. You just never know."

For a moment, a glint of hope flickered through her chest. *Oh, for another miracle.*

***

Sam braked as they approached her neighbor's driveway. "Let's stop and visit Horace for a minute. We haven't seen him in a while."

"Yeah, let's. He's a cool old guy." Electra jiggled on the seat.

The gray-haired man opened his screen door with a flourish. "Come in, come in. So nice to see you! I have some iced tea if you'd like to wet your whistles."

Sam gave him a hug. "Sounds great. How you been, Horace? You haven't been by lately."

"I'm a doin'. Every day I wake up on the right side of the sod, I figure that's a blessin'."

Sam and Electra laughed.

"How's the dude-bustin' goin'?"

"Good." She looked at Electra. "You want to tell him about today?"

"Ohm'gosh yes!" The girl's eyes lit up. "You aren't going to believe this. We took Sugar over to Clyde's and there was this shy little girl who would hardly look at anybody and then she petted Sugar and ohm'gosh…!" She paused her rush of words and a tear trickled from the corner of her eye. "It was awesome," she whispered.

Horace's leathery face beamed with his grin. "Now, that's what I like to hear. You're doin' good things there." He nodded. "Yup. Good things."

A flood of satisfaction washed over Sam. Yes, it was good.

They talked a little more about horses and Apache, and then Sam asked if he'd heard any more about the offer on his ranch.

"Oh yeah, I had a coupla calls and a letter or three. When the last guy showed up, I told 'im if they didn't 'cease and desist' they'd be hearin' from ol' Bertha." He glanced over at the rifle hanging on the wall. "I think maybe they got the message."

"Well, good." Sam smiled. "I hated the thought that you'd be moving away."

"Naw. The fancy life of leisure ain't for me. I'll be here till I die."

***

After chores and supper were finished, Sam settled into her rocking chair to relax and read.

"Can I use your phone and call my mom?" Electra leaned against the living room doorway. "I gotta tell her about Wendy and Sapphire."

"Sure. Go ahead. Tell your mom hello for me."

"Okay." The girl spun and ran into the kitchen. "Mom, hi, it's me, you'll never guess what we did today!"

Sam chuckled and opened her book. She couldn't help but hear the note of excitement in Electra's voice as she talked to her mother, blurting out the story in a flash flood of words. Finally, she was quiet for a few minutes.

"…'kay, Mom. Love you too." She came back into the living room and plopped on the couch. "Oh, Sam, I don't want this summer to end. That was just too cool today!"

"It was, wasn't it?" Sam set down her book. "I couldn't believe Sugar was so quiet and so patient. I knew she was a sweet, loving horse, but I had no idea she had such a compassionate heart."

"I know." Electra's eyes were luminous. "It was like she knew how sad and lonely Wendy was... Like with Apache and me." She swiped at a tear on her cheek.

Sam couldn't speak for the sudden thickness in her throat. She nodded, studying the fresh-faced teenager. What a difference that horse had made in Electra's personality. She *had* to get him back. But there were only weeks left in the summer, and Electra would soon be going back to her mom in New York. A dark cloud settled on her shoulders. She would miss the girl.

And what then? After hunting season in the fall, Clyde probably wouldn't need her again until spring. She would be all alone to go through the winter, feeding Murdock's cattle and fighting snowdrifts. Uncertainty added its weight and directed her thoughts to the bottle in the top cupboard. She bit her lip. No, that wasn't the answer. Drinking hadn't helped before, just made her feel worse.

Sam smiled at Electra. "One day at a time, huh? Well, I'm beat. Shall we call it a day?"

***

Several days later, when Sam and Electra got home, the answering machine blinked furiously in the kitchen. The first message was from the clerk of justice court in Miles City. "We have set a court date for July 21 at 10 a.m. If you have any questions, please call..."

Her stomach flip-flopped. *I'm really going to have to do this!* She swallowed and punched the button for the next message.

"This is Sheriff O'Connor. The Custer County Sheriff's office has given us a heads up that Mr. Smythe is trying to file charges that you took his horse without permission..."

"What?" Sam slammed a fist on the counter. "He can't do that!"

The message continued, "...but I've advised them of the circumstances and that I was there personally when the horse was returned. Give me a call..."

Charges? Theft? Angry bees buzzed in her tummy. What was going on? She looked up to see Electra staring with moon-sized eyes.

"What does that mean?"

Sam shook her head. "I don't know for sure. I'll have to call tomorrow and see if I can find out more." She hit the button for the next message with more force than she intended. "I can't believe that man!"

"Hey, Sam, it's Robin. I have an interesting proposition for you. Give me a call."

She dialed the counselor's number, putting the phone on speaker as she opened the cupboard to take out noodles and a can of tuna for a casserole.

"I'm glad you called back this evening. Listen. My daughter has a neighbor, an older woman who is going to be moving to an assisted living facility."

"Okay?" Sam frowned.

"Turns out the lady was a trick rider up until just a few years ago, and she has a horse she would like to rehome. My daughter says it's a sweet, older mare, and I thought of you and how well the kids respond to your horses at Clyde's. I know he's going to need all his stock during hunting season, so I thought maybe..."

"Oh!" Sam's thoughts jittered through her mind. Horses, kids, hunting season. Money. "Uh... that sounds really great... but I don't have any money to buy the horse. I dunno, maybe Clyde would, but if it's an older horse, he probably won't want her for his string. He's been very generous with me, but I don't want to owe him money either."

"I thought about that," Robin said, "but I think it might be kind of a rescue situation. This lady has no relatives to take the horse, and she told my daughter she might have to send her to auction. She is heartbroken at the thought."

Sam's own heart contracted. "Oh dear. I'll bet she is."

"Well, why don't you do this—can you come to town sometime this week and meet her and the horse? Maybe we can work something out."

"Okay, yeah. I'll talk to Clyde tomorrow and see if I can get a day off. I'll let you know... And, thanks."

Electra hovered nearby. "A new horse, maybe? We can't let it go to auction. That means...?" Her forehead pinched.

"Probably would be used for dog food." Sam winced.

"No! That can't happen."

"Well, I'll see if Clyde will let me off tomorrow, and we'll drive to Billings and take a look at the situation. I can't make any promises though." She shook her head, already knowing the fight she'd have on her hands if they couldn't take the horse. Where on earth would she get the money for another horse and for the feed?

CHAPTER TWENTY-THREE

Sam's hands shook as she dialed Sheriff O'Connor's office the next morning.

After a brief hold, he came on the line. "Hi, Sam. Guess you got my message."

"Uh… y-yeah. What…? Can he do that?"

"Naw, I don't see that he can. The horse was returned, plus he's still got your five hundred." The sheriff's mellow baritone soothed her jitters somewhat.

She gulped. "I guess he got the summons for small claims court." She told him the date. "C-could you come as a witness for me?"

"Ah, let me check my calendar." Paper rustled. "July 21? Yeah. Yeah, I can be there."

Sam swallowed. "Thank you, Sheriff. I really appreciate this."

"Sure." He paused for a beat. "Say, might not hurt to get that animal warden to come too. He's another witness."

"Well, he was there at the beginning when we found Apache, and he picked up the horse to return it. But he wasn't very cooperative. I don't think he'd be a willing witness."

O'Connor chuckled. "Yeah, I gathered that. Let me make a call, see what I can do."

"Thanks again, Sheriff." Sam hung up. *Oh my gosh, I'm going to have to prepare for this court thing in two weeks!* What else did she need? She tried to think back on the strategizing she and Teresa had done. Teresa. She would be another witness. Sam dialed her friend and filled her in.

"Of course, I will," she said immediately. "You want to get together again soon and go over some more plans?"

"Oh, could we?" Sam swallowed. "I'm so nervous already, I don't know what I'm going to do."

"It'll be fine. You've got at least three witnesses, maybe four if the warden cooperates, plus the photos and bill of sale." Her friend's cheerful voice sang over the line.

"Thanks, Teresa." Sam hung up from the call, weak, as if all the blood had drained from her body. *I wish I felt that confident.*

"Are we going to Billings today to see that horse?" Electra's voice came from the doorway.

Sam jumped. "Oh. I didn't know you were up. Almost forgot! I'll call Clyde right now."

Clyde didn't hesitate. "Of course. Take the day. We've got the fourth of July rodeo coming up in a week, but we're moving along well with those plans. And... if you need a loan to get this horse..."

"Oh gosh, Clyde, I really don't want to borrow money if I don't have to. That's very generous of you, though. Thanks. We'll see you tomorrow."

Sam and Electra piled into the pickup and headed down I-94 toward Billings, Electra chattering away about the "new horse we're getting."

This seemed an impossible task. She had no idea how she would be able to buy the horse, or even feed and care for it. The "to-do" list of her life cascaded through her mind—this horse, Apache, the court appearance, the rodeo. Her breath locked in her chest, her heart beat faster, and her hands seemed frozen to the wheel. A wave of dizziness swirled over her. Her vision blurred and the road undulated. She slowed the truck and pulled to the side of the road.

"What's the matter?" Electra paused her endless, one-sided conversation and peered at her. "Why are we stopping?"

Sam stepped out of the vehicle and bent over, taking deep gulps of the warm, fresh air. *What is happening to me?* She straightened and looked up into the blue-washed sky. *Lord, if you're there, this is a time I might need some help.* Taking another long, slow inhale, she allowed the breeze to waft gently over her. Her wavering vision gradually cleared.

Electra ran around the truck. "Sam? Sam, are you okay?"

She forced a smile. "Yeah. I am now. Just got a little dizzy, that's all." Air whooshed from between her lips. "All right then. Let's get back on our way and go see a lady about a horse."

As they picked up speed again, her cell phone rang. Electra looked at the display. "It's Bra-a-d."

"Answer and put it on speaker, please."

Electra punched the buttons. "Hi, Bra-a-d. We're in the truck, but you're on speaker. Talk to Sam."

"Hey there, how are my favorite cowgirls today?"

Electra rolled her eyes.

"Hi, Brad," Sam said. "We're okay, on our way to Billings. What's up?"

"Oh, you are? That's great. I'm working in town today. Are you coming in for supplies?"

"No, we're going to look at a possible horse rescue situation." She told him the story.

"Cool! Can I meet you there? I'd like to meet this horse too."

"Um, sure, why not." She gave him the address. "We'll be there in about forty-five minutes."

At the outskirts of Billings, Sam turned onto a secondary road that led out into a more rural area with small ranches and homes with acreage. She pulled into the driveway at the address Robin had given her.

The counselor was already there and stepped out of her SUV as they drove in. "Hi there. Ready to meet Miss Ellie and her horse?"

Electra gave her a huge smile. "Yeah!"

Sam grinned and followed Robin to the house. A snowy-haired woman, possibly in her seventies or even eighty, opened the door. "Hello, dear. I see you brought your friends. Come in, come in." She maneuvered her walker to the side to let them by.

The women entered a tidy living room where the walls were covered with pictures of Ellie as a young woman in various poses—standing atop her horse, hanging sideways, and over the horse's rump, even one under the belly of the horse.

"That's me with my Trixi." Ellie's voice held a note of pride as she pointed to a more recent photo. "I've had her for twenty years, since she was a foal."

Sam glanced from the pictures to the woman. *Life has taken its toll on this lady. She's not as old as she looks.*

The woman continued. "Named her after Trixi McCormick, Montana's own famous trick rider from the 1940s and '50s."

"Cool." Electra's voice was breathy. "How did you learn to do all that?"

Ellie chuckled. "Lots and lots of practice and many, many falls."

The doorbell rang. "I'll get it for you," Robin offered.

Brad entered, holding a camera. Sam grinned. *Always the newsman.*

"Hello, ladies." He took off his hat. Robin introduced him to Ellie.

He shook her hand. "Do you mind if I do some filming?"

"That would be just fine, young man."

He glanced at Sam, one eyebrow raised. She shrugged and gave him a slight nod.

"Would you folks like to meet Trixi?" Ellie gestured toward the picture window in the back of the house, which overlooked a nearby red and white barn and a green

154

pasture. Standing by the fence was a light tannish-brown mare with lighter mane and tail.

"Oooh." Electra pressed against the window. "Is she a palomino?"

"No, she's a light-colored chestnut. But she's beautiful, isn't she? We made a good pair back in the day." Ellie opened the back door and stepped her walker out onto a porch. "I can't trek all the way out there anymore with this thing, but you folks go ahead and meet her. She's very friendly."

"She is gorgeous." Sam could almost picture herself on Trixi's back, executing some exotic trick. She shook her head. *What am I thinking? I don't know how to do that!*

Electra was the first to the fence and held out a hand for the mare to sniff. She ran her palm up the horse's face and rubbed behind her ears. Sam joined her and stroked Trixi's neck and combed her fingers through the almost-blonde mane. The horse nuzzled her arm. She took a cake pellet from her pocket and fed her the treat.

"Go on in the pasture with her," called Ellie. "I'll show you something."

When she and Electra stood by the mare's side, Ellie gave a couple of sharp whistles and motioned with her arm. Sam startled when the horse bowed, then folded her front legs under, followed by her back legs. Trixi turned her head and looked at Electra as if expecting something.

"Go ahead, climb on." Ellie had a big smile.

Electra raised her brows. "I can?"

"Yeah, you sure can," the older woman called from the edge of the porch.

The girl looked at Sam with wide, questioning eyes.

"Go ahead. I'm right here. It'll be okay."

Electra gently straddled the horse, and Trixi rose to her feet. With heel pressure from Electra, she walked along the fence.

"Wow!" Brad spoke from behind Sam. "That's awesome." He had his camera trained on the pair.

She shook her head. "Isn't it?" She could hardly believe what she had seen. What a great horse. No saddle or bridle and yet she responded to Electra as if she was tacked up.

"You try it, Miss Samantha," Ellie called.

When Trixi returned, Electra slid off. Once again Ellie whistled and made her hand gesture. Trixi kneeled and Sam mounted. In a smooth motion, the horse got up and walked toward the barn. When Sam used slight pressure with her left knee, the mare turned to the right. Pressure from the right and she turned left. They rode back to the group. Ellie whistled again and Trixi lay down so Sam could get off.

She returned to the porch. "This is one amazing horse, Miss Ellie."

"Isn't she?" Ellie's face was lit with a proud glow. "We had a good long ride together, but now…" Her blue eyes misted, and she stared off at the rolling hills in the distance.

Sam blinked back tears, swallowing with difficulty. "Miss Ellie, I—"

"Yup. I can't get around anymore without this thing." The older woman smacked her hand on the walker. "Can't take care of my baby anymore. Dadgummed stroke." She shook her head and smiled again. "You and your girl there would be perfect for her."

Sam opened her mouth and closed it again. *Oh yes. Trixi would be perfect for us.* She took a shaky breath. "I would love to own her, but…"

"Only five hundred." A determined look came over Ellie's face. "She's worth a lot more, but I want her to have a good home. I had one guy interested, but she's too old and not trained to work cows. The second family had a troop of hellion kids. Not letting Trixi go to them! I could use the money, and if I can't sell her to someone worthy, she'll have to go to auction."

Sam caught a glimpse of Electra's horrified face and steeled herself. *I shouldn't have done this. I shouldn't have come here.* "Miss Ellie, I don't have any money." She looked down at her boots. "I'm sorry I got your hopes up," she turned to Electra, "and yours too, honey. I don't think this is going to work out." She turned and strode around the side of the house to the pickup, fighting tears.

Electra's boots crunched on the gravel as she ran behind her. "Wait! No! Nooo." It came out in a wail. Her face scrunched into misery and tears cascaded down her cheeks.

Sam opened her arms and took her into a hug. They rocked together, their tears mingling. Finally, Sam disengaged and blew her nose. "I need to thank Miss Ellie and tell her good-bye. You can wait here if you want to."

Her young friend sniffled. "No, I'll come too."

They went back into the house, where Ellie sat in her recliner, her wrinkled face downturned. Brad and Robin sat nearby, concerned looks on their faces.

Sam knelt beside the chair and took the woman's hand. "I'm sorry, Miss Ellie. I'm not sure if I have any options, but let me think about this and see if there's anything I can come up with. I really like Trixi and would love to have her."

Ellie nodded. "You will be able to. I think you're the one."

"Bye, Miss Ellie." Electra gave her a hug. "We'll be back. I know we will."

They all said their goodbyes and headed out to their vehicles. Robin rolled down her window. "See you at Clyde's in a couple weeks. I'll be thinking about this too. Hang in there." She drove away.

Brad paused beside Sam's truck. "May I buy you ladies lunch?"

"Sure. That would be nice." she forced a smile.

They met at the Pays Café near the stockyards. The waitress offered them menus and poured coffee. Electra silently stared at her menu, her eyes red. Sam's own eyes felt puffy and sore. She pushed a strand of hair out of her face. *I must look a sight.*

Brad took a sip of his coffee. "You know what I'd like to do, with your permission?"

She shook her head. "What?"

"I did a bit of filming at Ellie's, and I got to thinking. She's a pretty well-known person in Montana. I'd like to do a feature on the fact she has to give up her horse, and that you would like to rescue Trixi, also bring in what you've done to try to rescue Apache."

"Me?" Sam raised her eyebrows. "I haven't done anything. I've failed at it all."

"No, you haven't. You did save Apache's life, and you're trying to save Trixi's too. I think it would be a dynamite story."

Electra's eyes were wide now too. "That'd be so cool, Sam."

"I dunno." She scrunched her mouth to one side. Butterflies batted tennis balls in her stomach. "I don't know what good it would do, and I... I don't think I want to be on TV for everybody to see." Her face heated, thinking of the old saying that television adds ten pounds. *What if I make weird faces or say something stupid?*

"I know you're basically a shy country girl." Brad grinned. "But I already have some awesome footage of the two of you on Trixi. Not to mention that scene of you riding down the hill when we first met. I'd like to show the before and after pictures of Apache. I think people would really like this story."

"Yes!" Electra bounced in her seat. "Please say yes, Sam! It would be so cool to be on TV!" Then she sobered. "And

158

maybe it would help get Apache back... and maybe save Trixi too."

Sam leaned back against her chair and exhaled. "I'm not sure... Let me think about it. There's so much to digest, and I'm going to have to make some decisions. If I get a loan from Clyde to buy Trixi, I'm going to be in debt, and I really hate that. I saw what that did to my folks."

On the way home, Electra sat quiet for a while then she turned to Sam. "You know what? I have about seventy-five dollars saved from my allowance. And maybe my mom would pitch in something too, and that would be a start toward buying Trixi."

Her heart lurched. She glanced over at the eager teenager. "Oh, honey, that is such a generous offer. I appreciate it, I really do. But I can't take your money. I have to figure this out on my own."

"If I did, then I'd be a part-owner of a horse." Electra grinned. "Hey, I could call Mom tonight—maybe she would buy Trixi!"

"But even if your mom could come up with the money, where would you keep a horse in New York City?" Sam cocked an eyebrow.

"Well, there are some stables not too far away where I learned to ride."

"That costs quite a lot though."

The teen shrugged. "Okay, but if you need it, I want to contribute."

Sam blinked away the mist in her eyes. "Thanks." She glanced at her watch. "It's early enough yet. Let's stop at Clyde's and see if he needs us to help with anything this afternoon."

CHAPTER TWENTY-FOUR

When they drove up, the wiry rancher was at the chute, prying off a rotten board that had been kicked one too many times. He straightened and tipped his hat back. "Howdy. How was the horse?"

Sam shook her head. "It's a beautiful mare, well-trained, really perfect, but the lady wants five hundred for her." She sighed. "I just don't have it."

Clyde spat tobacco off to the side. "Well, I know you don't want it, but my offer stands…" He picked up the pieces of broken board and tossed them into the bed of his pickup. "We could take a little out of your wages every week until it's paid off."

"I don't know, Clyde. I have so much on my mind right now, with the court date coming up, this horse, and the rodeo next week. I'll have to sleep on it—for a couple of nights at least." She smiled. "Speaking of the rodeo, is there something we can do to help?"

The rancher grabbed a new board from the back of the truck. "You can hold onto this while I get it fastened."

Sam took hold and guided it into place.

The rancher picked up his drill. "Electra, it'd be a big help if you'd walk around the corral and see if there are any other posts that are wobbly or rails about to break."

"Okay!" The girl danced off to make her rounds.

He took a bolt from the corner of his mouth. "She sure is a different kid from when her mother first brought her."

"Isn't she, though?" Sam reached into her pocket and took out a washer to hand him. "It's the horses, especially Apache. I never realized how healing it can be to broken kids. I guess I always took for granted how horses affect people, being around them most of my life."

Clyde drilled another hole. "Yup. I've been amazed at those kids from Billings. My wife calls it a miracle. You know, I could buy this Trixi, and keep her here for the kids."

Her breath hitched. At least the horse would be close by, and she could still work with her and Clyde's clients. *And if I win the lottery, I could buy her.* She quirked one side of her mouth up. *Well, I guess a person has to buy a ticket first.* "Another option to think about, Clyde. It could work, I suppose." She peered into his weathered face. "But I know she's really not a horse you want for your string. She would be good for the kids, but she's too old for strenuous work and not really trained for packing."

He shrugged. "Something t' put in your poke to think on. Let's go see what Electra has found for us to fix."

That evening, after Electra had gone to bed, Sam sat at the kitchen table, pen, paper and calculator in front of her. She wrote her income and assets in one short column and all her expenses in another. She sighed. Her wages from Clyde barely covered her lease, gas, and groceries, and an occasional burger in town. There was no way she could take anything out of her check to pay him back if he bought Trixi. Jack Murdock supplied hay and cake pellets to feed his cows, and she had permission to also feed Sugar from that supply, but he might not be so generous if she had more horses. She snorted a half-laugh. She hadn't even thought about that when she tried to rescue Apache.

She scribbled more notes, pros and cons, figured and refigured. No matter how many times she added up the numbers, it didn't come out any better. Her eyes burned. If she accepted Electra's offer of seventy-five and maybe if her mother matched that... *No. Good grief.* How could she even think about that? The girl would be going home in a few weeks, and even if she came back next summer, it wasn't right to take her money. She growled her exasperation and threw the pen on the table.

Her eyes went to the top cupboard. *Just one won't hurt. I need to relax.* She poured a double shot of vodka over ice and went out to the porch.

The moon hung full and bright in the night sky, illuminating the rolling prairie in a silver wash. Sam took a deep breath and let it out slowly, trying to relax the knots in her shoulders. *It's so beautiful here. So peaceful.* She didn't want to get into a position of losing this place. Murdock would use any excuse to try to break their contract.

For some inexplicable reason, she was drawn to these horses. She'd always been that way—rescuing injured birds and stray kittens as a child, and then Sugar. It seemed important to pursue… something. But what? What would she do with them? She couldn't even afford to board them at Clyde's to use with the group home kids. He had his own horses for his dude and hunting clients. And if he bought Trixi for the kids, it would be simply to help Sam out. It wouldn't be right. And it wouldn't be the same as if she owned her.

She went inside and poured another double.

CHAPTER TWENTY-FIVE

The rest of the week was a dust devil of activity for Sam and Electra, helping Clyde ready the corrals and dig a fire pit for the beef they would barbecue. Irene Bruckner even put them to work baking rolls. The rest of the food would be brought potluck by the neighbors.

The fourth of July dawned bright and warm with a tangerine wash outlining the horizon in a clear blue sky.

By 7 a.m. Sam and Electra were on the dusty road to the dude ranch. They were greeted by a cacophony of bawling calves, bellowing steers and bulls, and whinnying horses. A rancher from Miles City had arrived the night before with the bucking stock for the competition.

All morning, neighbor women arrived with cookies, cakes, and pies, salads, pickles, and condiments. Irene set up a tub of ice and an old-fashioned ice cream maker.

Cowboys and cowgirls stood in line to sign up for events, and more neighbors and tourists arrived to watch. Even the vans from the group home joined the crowd.

At 2 p.m. Clyde mounted a platform above the chutes with his bullhorn. "Ladies and gentlemen, welcome to the annual Ingomar July fourth rodeo!"

The Forsyth High School marching band stepped out into the arena, playing a rousing Sousa march. Then they stood back with the opening notes of "The Star Spangled Banner." The crowd rose from their lawn chairs and seats on vehicle hoods, hands over hearts as the Custer County Rodeo Queen rode out with the American flag. Her attendants carried the Montana flag and other colorful banners as they galloped around the arena. When they came to a stop in the center, all the horses bent one knee and bowed.

Sam stood and sang along with the audience. A lump formed in her throat, and her eyes stung. She shook her head. She could never get through this song without crying. That was one of the reasons she loved Montana—people still stood and respected the flag. Beside her, Electra sniffed and wiped the back of her hand over her cheek.

As the last notes died away, the crowd erupted in applause.

Clyde took up the bullhorn again and announced the first event. "Give our youngest cowpokes a hand as they try mutton-bustin'."

The first sheep lumbered out of the chute, a helmet-clad boy of about five clinging to its wool as the creature ran and swerved toward the center of the arena. In a couple of seconds, the little cowboy was picking himself out of the dirt. Several more girls and boys followed, some spitting out dirt, others rubbing their backsides, some bursting into tears. Only two stayed on their sheep's back for the six-second ride. The six-year-old girl and seven-year-old boy ran out to share the applause as Clyde announced a tie.

Sapphire and Wendy had joined Electra, and the three were hooting and giggling at the sheep and kids' antics. "That's looks so fun." Electra looked at Sam. "I wish I could've done that when I was little."

Sam laughed. "I tried it a couple of times. Never could get the hang of staying on. It's harder than it looks."

"I'll bet you were the cutest little mutton-buster though." Brad's voice came from behind them.

Sam rolled her eyes. "Oh yeah, sure, after I fell off and rolled around in the dust and manure. I was real cute. Uh-huh."

Electra laughed and punched Sam's arm.

"Lots of people seem to know about this little rodeo—got a big crowd here today." Brad swept one arm over the scene, his video camera in the other hand.

"You covering this?" Sam raised her eyebrows.

He nodded. "Yup. Always on the job, ya know. Besides, I'd like to do a little interview with you and Electra." He fixed his chocolate eyes on hers. "I'm still hoping you'll let me do the story."

Her heart turned to liquid. She blew out a breath.

"C'mon, Sam," Electra prodded. "It's for a good cause."

Brad nodded. "Yes, it is. If nothing else comes from my video, maybe someone will step up to rescue Trixi."

Sam pressed her lips into a thin line. *I want to be that someone.* She sighed again. "Well… okay. Let's do it."

"Yes!" Electra high-fived Brad. She squealed and turned to the other girls. "We're gonna be on TV! We'll be famous!"

"Yeah, you will." Brad chuckled. "And, if I can get permission from your group counselor, I'd like to talk to you young ladies too."

Wendy stood slightly behind the older girl, eyes downcast. Sapphire's eyes widened. "Really?" She grabbed Wendy's hand. "Let's go find Miss Robin!"

"Yeah!" Electra ran along behind.

Sam shook her head. "Kids."

Clyde announced the team roping segment and cowboys showed their finesse with a lariat.

Robin and the girls showed up just as the barrel racers began their competition. Again, Electra's mouth was gaped open. "Sam! Sam! Could I learn to do that? That is so cool!"

She grinned and tousled the girl's hair. "Well, first you need a good horse. And remember, they cost a lot of money. Then, you'd have to work really hard and practice every single day."

Electra's face clouded. "Oh. Yeah." But as quickly, the smile was back. "If we get Trixi I could at least start practicing, and when I go home, I'll go to the riding stables every chance I get, and when I come back here next summer you can help me some more."

Sam nodded, trying to suppress a laugh. "That's a good plan, honey. Let's wait and see what happens."

Sapphire joined in. "Yeah, me too! Can I learn barrel racing too? Will you teach us?"

"Hold on, hold on." Sam held up her hands in mock surrender. "You're ganging up on me here. One thing at a time, okay?"

Robin had turned away from the girls and her shoulders shook. Brad's mouth quirked up in one corner. He introduced himself to the counselor and talked to her about the interview with the girls.

She nodded. "Sure, why not. It'll be good publicity for what Sam and Clyde are doing here as well as the rescue horse aspect."

Now Electra and Sapphire were jumping up and down. "Yes! We're gonna be on TV!"

"All right, girls, calm down now," Sam admonished. "Act professional and answer Brad's questions politely."

They immediately sobered and stood straight. Brad lifted his hand-held camera and began asking questions. To their credit, Electra's and Sapphire's answers were thoughtful and articulate. Wendy remained glued to Robin's side and merely shook her head when the counselor asked if she'd like to talk to Brad.

He also interviewed Robin and then lowered the camera. "Thank you very much, ladies. I appreciate it."

"Thank you, Brad," the girls chorused and then ran off, giggling and squealing again.

Clyde announced saddle bronc riding next, and they watched the cowboys try to stay on the back of the bucking, kicking, sunfishing broncs. Several bit the dust and got to their feet, ruefully shaking their heads and slapping their jeans with their hats. Brad filmed the event.

"My great-grandma did this." Sam shook her head in awe.

"Really!" Brad swung the camera back to her. "Tell me about her."

"Well, Grandma Nettie mostly rode steers—in those days they weren't the little yearlings the kids ride now. They were big rangy, long-horned ones brought in off the prairie. Some were even full-grown older bulls that had been castrated."

"Did she win any competitions?" Brad prompted.

Sam nodded. "Yeah, she once beat Marie Gibson who was a world champion bronc rider."

"Pretty impressive." Brad asked more questions, and she warmed to the subject.

Finally, he lowered the camera. "That's great, Sam, thanks. Well, I think I'll go talk to the winners and the not-so-lucky." He winked. "Catch up with you later, and we'll do the rest of your interview."

Her heartbeat pounded. *Oh my gosh, I just talked in front of the camera, and I'm still alive.* Maybe it wouldn't be so bad after all.

After the last bull had been ridden—or cowboy bested—the winners of all the events rode a victory lap around the arena. Then the band came out, playing "God Bless America," and the rodeo royalty in their bright blue, red, and spangled costumes once again displayed the flags. When the applause died away, Clyde took up the bullhorn. "Ladies and gentlemen, thank you all for coming. Now please join us for the barbecue. I hope you enjoy yourselves."

Most of the spectators drifted over to the tables by the fire pit, where men and women cut and served melt-off-the-bone beef, and helped themselves to the bounty of food. Sam loaded a plate and looked for a place to sit. She spied Teresa at a picnic table and went to join her.

"This is the most fun I've had in years." The real estate agent grinned. "One of the reasons I came back. These old-fashioned neighborhood rodeos were part of my childhood."

"Me too. I think they're lots more fun than the big fancy productions in the cities."

They chatted for a while, then pushed their paper plates away. "Seconds?" Sam asked.

Teresa patted her stomach. "No way."

"Surely you saved room for homemade ice cream." Brad came up behind them and plopped bowls of the soft creamy dessert in front of them.

Teresa winked. "Of course, we did." She scooted down the bench to let him sit beside Sam.

The warmth of his thigh against hers brought heat to her face. "Thanks." That errant lock of dark hair fell over his forehead, and she caught her breath. Mentally chastising herself, she turned to her bowl and took a bite. "Mmm. This is better than Ben and Jerry's."

"That's cuz me and Sapphire were turning the handle for this batch." Electra bounded up and sat across from them.

Sam smiled. "That's what makes it so special."

All around, people sat in clusters visiting, while Horace led a horseshoe competition. As dusk gathered in shades of orange and purple, someone brought out a guitar. Soon a rancher joined in with a fiddle and his wife brought out her accordion. Couples stepped out onto the gravel driveway and danced to the old-time tunes.

"Before we go join them," Brad said, "let's do the rest of your interview."

Sam's toe stopped tapping. "Okay."

As soon as he brought his camera up to his shoulder and asked her the first question, she froze, her mind blank. "Uh…" *Oh no! What did he just ask?* This was exactly what she'd been afraid of! Her hands turned cold and clammy.

"It's okay, Sam. You'll be fine." His soothing voice broke through the fog. "Just take a deep breath."

She did and her shoulders lowered a notch. Brad's brown eyes twinkled. "Okay, Sam, tell me about the mare you rescued."

"Sugar?" She smiled as she thought back to the first time she'd seen the Thoroughbred who'd been injured on the racetrack and about to be put down. It was instant love. Before she realized it, she was simply having a conversation with Brad, telling him all about her beloved rescue horse.

They talked about her dream of raising Thoroughbreds and the obstacles she'd encountered, how she came to work with Clyde, and how Electra and the group home kids had been changed by the love of a horse. That segued into Apache's story, and a tear ran hot down her cheek as she said, "I'm afraid he may be a lost cause."

After they'd talked more about Miss Ellie and Trixi, Brad lowered the camera. "That was great," he said in a soft voice. "You did a wonderful job."

Sam unclasped her hands, aware now of clapping from around her. Teresa, Robin, Horace, the Bruckners, and the girls all beamed at her as they applauded. "Now *you're* famous too!" Electra gushed. Everyone laughed.

Brad set his camera on the picnic table. "May I have this dance?" He swept his arm toward the musicians as they played the first chords of "Tennessee Waltz."

She could only nod. He took her hand and led her to the improvised "dance floor"—gravel the men had raked and smoothed earlier. Light from the lanterns illuminated Brad's tanned and smiling face, the lock falling over his forehead. As he took her in his arms, she could barely breathe. Her feet seemed to act on their own and settled into the rhythm of the waltz, only stumbling a little over the gravel. At the end, he twirled her around, then bent her backward with a flourish.

"Thank you, *Madame*." He bowed and kissed the back of her hand.

169

She giggled. "That was fun. Thank *you*."

They danced almost every dance after that. She couldn't remember when she'd had so much fun. Laughing and hooting, they grabbed beers and made their way back to the table when Clyde announced it was dark enough for fireworks.

Brad draped an arm around her shoulders and pulled her closer as the shooting stars and miniature rocket explosions lit up the night sky in rainbow colors. With a tiny moan of contentment, Sam leaned into his embrace, and they oohed and aahed with every burst. Her heart threatened to explode with the wonder of it all.

After the applause died down for the last spectacular fireworks display, people headed for their vehicles, shouts of "Bye now, see you next year" and "Thanks, Clyde, for another great rodeo."

The proud cowboy sat back in a lawn chair with a beer and gave a huge, long sigh. "Whew. Glad that's over for another year." His wife joined him, nodding. Horace clinked his bottle with Clyde's.

Still encircled within Brad's arm, Sam smiled at her employer. "This has been such a fun day. I don't want it to end." She gave a little sigh. "But it's late, and if we are to get back here in the morning to help you guys clean up, I'd better take Electra home."

Clyde took a swig of his beer. "Don't need to be early. Anytime is fine. Thanks for your help in getting this ready."

Brad gave her shoulders a squeeze. "Let me walk you to your truck." He turned back to the Bruckners and Horace. "Great day. Thanks again." He stopped. "Oh, by the way, that "Big Open" documentary is going to be shown on PBS tomorrow night at seven."

Clyde groaned. "Spose we're gonna have to watch it, see what we're up against."

"Yup." Horace slapped his leg. "Guess the nearest place with a tee-vee is the Jersey Lilly."

"Okay, see you guys there." Sam gathered Electra who dozed, her head on her arms at the picnic table. "Let's go home, honey."

Brad opened the pickup door for Electra and then came around to do the same for Sam. "Sure enjoyed spending time with you." He gave the young girl a sidelong glance, then quickly pecked Sam on the cheek. "I'll be at the Jersey Lilly tomorrow too. See you then."

She started the engine, her cheek flaming. She put the truck in reverse and gave him a little wave before backing out.

Electra giggled sleepily. "I saw that."

"Saw what?" She stared straight ahead at the dark road.

The girl simply gave another soft giggle and leaned back against the seat.

Sam snuggled in her bed, images of the day flickering through her mind. The excitement of the bronc and bull rides, imagining Great-Grandma Nettie riding the big steers, the music, flags and colorful costumes. The interview with Brad—she had actually done it. His attentiveness and patience. Those dark brown eyes and the wayward lock of hair over his forehead. His kiss, fleeting as it was, and on the cheek. She dozed, dreaming of a kiss, full on the lips.

CHAPTER TWENTY-SIX

The next evening, after cleaning up the remains of the festivities, Sam and Electra, Clyde and Irene piled into their vehicles and drove to the Jersey Lilly. Horace was already seated at a big round table and waved them over. They ordered food and drinks and gradually a few more ranchers without TV at home gathered as the time approached for the documentary.

Sam raised her brow when Jack Murdock walked in and sat at their table. "Hello, Samantha."

She nodded. "Hi, Jack." What the heck was he doing here? She frowned. Probably trying to put more pressure on her to give up her lease. *Not gonna happen, Jack.*

Brad breezed in a few minutes before 7:00. Her cheeks warmed as he pulled out a chair next to her. "Hey. Sorry I'm a little late." He signaled Billy Cole for a beer. The proprietor nodded and picked up the TV remote to bring up the audio before he brought more drinks to their table.

Chattering ceased and the sounds of silverware on plates quieted as the narrator introduced the documentary. "We're here in Montana, Big Sky Country, where the wide-open spaces beckon, warm breezes blow, rich grasses grow, and the deer and the antelope literally play…"

Sam gave a sigh of relief to see that Brad had taken out the introduction with her riding down the hill. He'd said he'd save that for her interview. She nodded her thanks. He grinned back and flashed a thumbs-up.

The narrator continued speaking about the praises of "beautiful eastern Montana" and how few people actually inhabited the area. "Wouldn't you love to drive through a wildlife park and see buffalo as they used to roam…?" On the screen, a bison herd dotted the rolling hills. "…or even exotic animals like elephants or tigers…" Photos of these wild animals had been super-imposed into Montana scenes.

Sam opened her mouth in shock. "Did you do that?" she hissed at Brad.

He looked down at his beer. "Well…" He shook his head as more photos and more rhetoric filled the TV screen.

The ranchers mumbled and squirmed in their chairs. "Boo!" yelled someone. "Turn the dadgum thing off." Horace stood and gestured to Billy who hit the power button.

As one, the group turned toward Murdock. He held up his palms. "Gentlemen. Ladies. Let's try to have an open mind here."

Snorts and laughter greeted his comment.

"I know you love your land. But, in reality, you are barely subsisting. Wouldn't you like to live more comfortably, have a little financial cushion to ease your golden years…?"

Clyde stood, his palms on the table. "What do you know about our lives and what we want? What right do you, or this big-city Roberts guy, have to tell us what we need or want?"

"Yeah." Horace stood beside him. "This is our land, our lives, our decision to make, and we don't appreciate this high-falutin' pipe dream. 'Big Open,' my hind leg!"

The group chuckled, but sobered quickly, adding their opinions until Murdock finally stood. "Well, folks, sorry you feel that way. I was just trying to help make life a little better in this part of the state." He put on a phony smile. "Think about it a while. If any of you are interested, let me know." He tossed a handful of business cards on the table and turned to leave.

Near the door, he paused. "Mr. Roberts will be in town a week from today, and he'd like to set up a meeting. Maybe he can ease your fears, explain things a little better." He hurried out the door as shouts followed the slam.

Everyone talked at once. "Low-down, lyin' scum!" "What right do they have?" "This is OUR Montana!"

Sam turned to Brad whose face was crimson. "What did you do? Why?"

He put a hand out, palm up. "No. Wait. I didn't do the final edits on this piece. I took the footage for the area—"

"And the tigers and elephants?"

"The director ordered me to do that. I'm at their mercy. If I want to get paid—"

Sam snorted. "Paid, huh? Blood money. Is that all this country means to you, just a paycheck? 'Just doin' my job,'" she mimicked. "I really thought better of you." She grabbed Electra's arm. "Let's go."

The door slammed behind them, and Sam stomped to the pickup, muttering, "Turncoat. Traitor. I can't believe…"

Electra sat in the passenger seat, staring at her wide-eyed. "Did Brad really make that film?"

Sam stomped on the accelerator, and the pickup fishtailed on the dirt road. "Yeah. He did. He's as bad as Jack Murdock and that New York scum Roberts."

Her cell phone rang as she headed out of town. She glanced at the screen. Brad. She threw the phone on the floor where it bounced and vibrated and continued to ring.

By the time they reached home, her stomach was tied in knots, and her supper threatened to come back up. She slammed doors and rattled buckets as they did chores, anger surging like molten lava in hot waves.

Sam grabbed the vodka bottle and headed out to the porch, not caring that Electra was still up and watching, pale and frightened. She tossed back a shot. *I can't believe I fell for his line of bull.* Her cheek flamed again where he'd kissed her. She roughly swiped the back of her hand across her face, as if to erase the memory. *Ugh. Men!* First Kenny, now Brad. She couldn't trust a dang one of 'em.

***

The week that followed, Sam went to work, woodenly doing required chores at home and at Clyde's. She muted her phone whenever Brad called and deleted the voice mails without listening. Realizing she'd probably scared Electra, she tried to smile and treat the girl more gently, but she was an empty shell, an unfeeling robot. *Failure. Stupid. Failure.* The mantra punctuated her steps, followed her wherever she went. Vodka wouldn't dull the voices at night.

Horace stopped by Clyde's, and the men grumbled and cursed about the meeting and documentary. "Has anybody sold to this Roberts?" Clyde asked.

Horace shook his head. "Nobody around here. Well, one couple closer to Forsyth did, I guess. The husband had a stroke, and the wife couldn't handle the work."

"You'd think they'd get the message. We don't want no part of their fool scheme." Clyde spat a stream of tobacco, raising a tiny dust cloud.

The next Monday, toward the end of the day, Clyde approached Sam. "Why don't you knock off early and head home."

"Well, I planned to go to that meeting. Might as well go from here."

Clyde shook his head. "I think you should stay away tonight." He narrowed his eyes and his steely gaze bored into hers.

Sam stepped back. "Uh... well... I..."

"Go home," Clyde repeated.

She gathered Electra, and they headed down the road.

"Why doesn't he want us to go tonight?" Electra frowned.

"I'm not really sure. That was weird." She chewed on her lower lip. There was no way she would miss this meeting. She drove into Ingomar and parked out of sight behind the post office, but where she could still see the entrance to the

Jersey Lilly. "You stay inside." She stepped to the front of the truck.

They'd been there a few minutes when Clyde's truck parked in front of the bar. Horace's pickup pulled in beside him. The men stood talking as several more vehicles joined them. Clyde looked at his watch and then turned his gaze up the dirt road that led from the highway into Ingomar. A plume of dust rose in the distance.

As if choreographed, the men reached inside their trucks and retrieved rifles and shotguns. Sam gasped. They lined up on the boardwalk in front of the Jersey Lilly. Billy came out the door, also toting a long gun.

A sleek black SUV, now covered in dust, snaked its way down Main Street toward the saloon, and slowed as the driver apparently caught sight of the line of men. The vehicle stopped, and after a long minute, Murdock and Roberts stepped out.

Roberts held his arms out, palms up. "Gentlemen. Can we talk?"

The sound of a dozen rifles cocking snapped him to a halt.

"You ain't welcome here." Horace's voice was a ribbon of steel.

"C'mon, folks." Roberts took one tentative step forward. "This isn't the wild West. We're a civilized society now. Please hear me out."

The barrels raised, all pointed directly at him.

"You heard the man," Clyde said. "We're done talkin'. Get out."

Roberts' Adams apple bobbed, and his mouth opened and closed like a fish out of water. "All right. All right. Easy now." He backed toward his car. "I'm leaving now."

"And don't come back!" someone else hollered.

Roberts and Murdock jumped in and slammed their doors. Dirt and gravel flew as the vehicle spun and swerved away.

Sam stood beside her pickup, her mouth hanging open. She glanced at Electra. The girl's eyes were huge dark holes in her pale face. "Just like that TV show, the Wild, Wild West."

Then they both grinned at the same time. It *was* the wild West!

***

The next day, Sam heard a vehicle crunching up the driveway and peeked out of the Bruckners' barn. A large, black 4x4 pulled in and parked at the corral where Clyde worked. Sam drew in a sharp gasp. Sheriff McCollum.

The tall, muscular law officer stepped out of the truck, and Clyde met him at the gate. "Howdy, Sheriff. What can I do ya for?"

McCollum put out his hand to shake. "Nice day."

"Yup." Clyde nodded.

Sam stayed in the shadow of the barn door, her palms suddenly sweaty.

"Well…" The sheriff cleared his throat.

Sam wiped her hands on her jeans. *He sure does take his sweet time spitting it out.*

"I had a visit from a Scott Roberts and Jack Murdock this mornin'." McCollum leaned against the corral fence.

Clyde switched his chaw from one cheek to the other. "Oh, yeah?"

"They said somethin' about an 'armed stand-off' at the Jersey Lilly last night." His mouth twitched at one corner.

"They did, huh?" Clyde spat a stream of tobacco into the dust.

"Yup."

Was he going to arrest Clyde? Sam's stomach twisted into knots. *C'mon, guys, just say it!*

"Well… I guess that's true. We'd dis-invited Mr. Murdock and Mr. Roberts with their 'Big Open' scheme and told 'em we weren't sellin'. But they showed up anyway."

McCollum nodded. "Figured as much." He kicked at a dirt clod. "Told 'em I'd come talk to you, but they better fergit about that whole thing anyway. Nobody in the country is interested in lions and tigers." He grinned and gazed around the corral. After a long pause, "Hear you had a purty good turnout for your Fourth celebration."

Clyde nodded. "Yup. Real good this year."

"Well, gotta be goin'. Take care, now." The sheriff touched his hat and got in his truck.

Sam realized her mouth hung open once again. She stepped out of the barn. "Wow" was all she could say.

Clyde grinned. "Yeah. Guess he agrees with us."

Mrs. Bruckner came running from the house. "Oh, my gosh, I was so afraid he was going to be hauling you away." Her face was pale. "What did he say?"

"Nothin'." Clyde shrugged. "Roberts and Murdock complained, but he told 'em where ta stick it, I guess."

His wife shook her head. "You guys and your 'wild west' antics." She looked at Sam. "It'll be the death of me yet."

Sam nodded. "I know. I saw the whole thing."

Clyde jerked his head back. "You did? That was a foolhardy thing to do. It coulda gotten ugly. I told you to stay home."

"I couldn't. I needed to know what was going to happen. My ranch and my future are at stake." She held her palms out. "Don't worry. I was out of the line of fire, behind the post office."

Clyde huffed a sigh, but then his face crinkled in a grin. "All's well that ends well, I reckon. Dinner ready?"

Chuckling, Sam followed him inside.

CHAPTER TWENTY-SEVEN

While Electra called her mom for a lengthy visit, Sam went out to the corral to check Sugar and make sure she had water. Her mind was overloaded with a jumble of thoughts—the standoff at the Jersey Lilly, Fourth of July with Brad and his tender attention, then her rage at his sellout. At Kenny's betrayal. She ground her teeth. Why was she so bad at relationships? Next was this darn court thing coming up—five hundred dollars, Apache, Trixi, her ranch dreams—all at stake. What kind of future did she have? Every time she thought her path might be straightening, something or someone came along to throw in another curve, another steep hill.

The dream picture of her herd of Thoroughbreds had burst like a soap bubble, the vision vanished, her dream broken. The only Thoroughbred she was likely to ever own was the one in front of her right now. Even the poor, broken-down horses she was trying to rescue were just out of reach.

"Oh, Sugar, what are we supposed to do?" Tears flowed now. She threw her arms around her horse's neck and buried her face in the silky mane, breathing in the dusty, horsey scent. Sobs shook her body until her knees gave out, and she slumped to the ground. She pounded her fists into the dirt, punishing the clods with her anger and anguish.

Spent at last, she lay there, taking in gulps of air. Sugar turned her head toward her and blew softly through flared nostrils. Finally, Sam pushed herself to her knees, then to her feet, put a bridle on her horse, and slipped onto her bare back.

The lavender shadows grew long beside the silvery sage as dusk approached. Sugar's stride lengthened with a barely detectable hitch. Sam smiled. Her baby improved every day. She didn't want to overtax her though and reined her in to an easy lope. The warm July breeze loosened strands of chestnut hair around her face, and she inhaled in the scent of sunbaked grasses and clean, fresh air.

She topped a low hill and stopped Sugar. Below, white-faced Hereford cattle grazed near a small pond with several cottonwood trees growing beside it. Sam sat atop her mare, absorbing the idyllic scene. This country was her home, in her blood and the very beat of her heart. Whether she would ever have a herd of horses or not, she couldn't give up. She had to keep going, one step at a time. Grandma Nettie's image came to her mind, tiny, but strong and resolute in her dreams.

"If you can buck the system, I can too," Sam whispered.

The air had cooled, and the sun barely peeked over the undulating horizon, spreading its orange and gold fingers of light. She took a last cleansing breath. "Okay, baby, let's go home now."

Electra sat on the top rail of the corral when Sam rode in. "How's your mom?"

The girl shrugged. "Good." Her face brightened. "She's coming here the second week of August, so she can ride and visit with everybody again."

Sam smiled. "That's great! I'll be glad to see her."

Then Electra's shoulders slumped. "But then I have to go back with her. She says we have to go shopping and get ready for school."

Blinking her own swollen eyes, Sam removed Sugar's bridle and let her trot out into the enclosure near the barn. "Yes, I suppose you will need some new clothes."

Tears trickled down the teen's cheeks. "But I don't wanna go back to New York. I wanna stay here," she wailed.

Sam reached out a hand, and Electra jumped down from the fence. She buried her face in Sam's chest and sobbed. Sam patted her back. "I know. I'm going to miss you too." When Electra withdrew from her embrace, Sam looked into her tearful eyes. "We knew this day would come. It's been a great summer, and you've done such a good job, helping me here and at Clyde's. We can always look forward to next summer, if your mom says it's okay to come back then."

Electra nodded and sniffled. "She better."

"I'm sure she will, when she sees how much you've grown up." Sam put her arm around the girl's shoulders. It took every ounce of her energy to put on a positive front. "C'mon, let's go up to the house and have some supper. That always helps."

Electra nodded. "Oh yeah, Brad called."

Sam stiffened.

"He said he would really like to talk to you and apologize for the misunderstanding in person."

"You talked to him?" Sam stopped and stared at Electra.

"Sure. I thought it was Mom calling back." She held Sam's gaze. "Y'know, I thought he was a poopyhead when I first met him, but he's really not a bad guy. I don't think he meant to hurt you with that documentary. I think he really likes you."

Sam blinked. Where did that "older sister" kind of talk come from? Here was this kid, still wet behind the ears, as Grandpa used to say, giving her advice. "Oh, honey. Thank you for saying that. But I'm still really mad at him, and he's going to have some 'splainin' to do, when—if I decide to ever see him again."

She cuffed Electra's shoulder. "Quit meddling in my love life, okay? Let's go eat."

***

Over the next few days, whenever Brad called, Sam still ignored the messages. The trial loomed before her and occupied her mind every waking moment. She practiced a speech, then revised it, then scrapped it altogether. Tennis-playing butterflies kept up a marathon in her stomach. She found herself being short with Electra and Clyde, not wanting to be at work, but not wanting to be at home either. She paced, she mucked out stalls, she brushed horses. *Maybe I should just call it off.* Maybe getting her $500 back was not worth all this fear and anxiety. But Great-Grandma Nettie always came to mind, and she could almost hear her voice: *Follow your dream.* Besides, if there was any chance of getting Apache back for Electra…

The night before the 21st, Sam tried to ignore what the next day might bring. But she lay in bed, at first rigid and staring at the ceiling. She turned and curled into a fetal position. Then onto her back. She fluffed and reshaped her pillow, turned onto her other side. The red numbers on her clock blinked at her: 1:00 a.m., 2:00 a.m., 3:00 a.m. She sat up and turned on her light, grabbed her book, and tried to read. Her hands were clammy and shook as if the temperature was zero degrees.

Letting the book fall, Sam got up and gazed out the window at the star-glazed sky. "Hi God, it's me again. Sam. I know I don't talk to you very often, only when things are really bad." She sank to her knees and leaned on the windowsill. "But I need to sleep, and I think I'm going to need your help tomorrow. I still don't know what I'm going to say and how I'm going to convince the judge that I should get my money returned. I know it's probably a waste of time to hope that I might get to keep Apache too, but… I know you've done miracles before…" She sighed. "Okay, I'm going back to bed. I'll talk to you again… soon. G'night. And amen."

She crawled back in bed, feeling somewhat more relaxed, and before she knew it, the 6:00 a.m. alarm blared.

CHAPTER TWENTY-EIGHT

Teresa drove up in her SUV at 7:30, and Sam and Electra piled in with her. Sam peered at her friend through bleary eyes. "You look all chipper and cheery this morning."

Teresa smiled. "I think maybe I got a little more sleep than you did."

"Does it show that bad?" Sam pulled down the visor with the mirror and groaned. The mascara and eyeshadow had helped, but the whites of her eyes were still bloodshot. She grimaced. Nothing she could do about that.

She clenched her hands, which despite the promise of a 90-degree day, were cold and clammy. The coffee and three bites of toast sat in her stomach like a lump of coal. Electra and Teresa kept up a running chatter that Sam tuned out as her thoughts churned.

After about an hour, they arrived and parked in front of the tall, gray courthouse. "Well, here we are." Teresa reached over and patted her knee. "You'll do fine. We're here with you."

Sam nodded. She gathered her files, got out of the car, and walked up the steps, her legs heavy as if she were a felon about to meet a hangman's noose. Inside the lobby, she stopped short as Brad strode toward them.

"Good morning, ladies." His dark brown eyes crinkled at the corners with his smile.

Sam frowned. "What are you doing here?"

"I came to support you. Listen, I'm really sorry—"

"I can't talk about that right now, Brad. I'm headed into court, and I have more important things on my mind." Sam brushed past him to go down the stairs.

"Okay, but I think you might want to see these photos."

She turned back, and he handed her a manila envelope. Peering at him from beneath lowered brows, she took out several photos. Her breath caught. Apache.

"I stopped by the pasture yesterday. Thought they might help."

The pictures showed the horse standing next to a half-filled water tank with no evidence of feed in the same bare pasture where she'd found him. His head hung low and his ribs still showed through his dusty coat. Sam gulped.

Beside her, Electra gasped. "Oh no."

"Thank you, Brad." Sam gave him a quavery smile, the hard lump in her chest softening. *He really is trying to help.* "I appreciate this." She put the photos in her folder, and they headed down the gray-carpeted stairs. Stopping at the clerk's window, she gave her name and who was with her. The woman smiled at her and gestured. "I'll show you to the courtroom."

In the hallway, several men stood by the court's door. "Smythe," Teresa whispered, "and the nephew. I don't know the other guy."

The clerk stopped in front of the group. "Mr. Smythe, Todd, you checked in with me, but who is your friend here?"

"Oh, this is my attorney, Justin Bragg."

She shook her head. "I'm sorry, sir, but no attorneys are allowed in small claims court. You'll have to wait outside."

"But..." Smythe sputtered.

"Judge Pepperman will not allow it." She gestured toward the stairs.

Bragg shrugged. "Okay. Worth a try, Richard." He patted his client's shoulder. "Good luck."

The clerk unlocked the door, and they filed in. Sam and the Smythes took seats at folding tables in front on opposite sides. Teresa, Electra and Brad sat in chairs behind her. With shaking hands, she opened her file and laid everything out. She stared at the photos and papers, but her mind would not focus.

The door opened behind her, chairs creaked, and low male voices conversed. Sam didn't turn, simply sat like an ice sculpture, trying to control her jittering nerves.

After what seemed like an hour, a man entered from the judge's chambers, dressed in a dark suit and tie. He stood behind a tall, light-oak desk. Behind him, an American flag adorned the corner. He brushed a hand through salt-and-pepper hair and nodded at the group. "Good morning. I'm Judge Pepperman." He put on half-glasses, picked up a piece of paper and read off a number. "This is small claims court, and this is Moser vs Smythe." He looked up at them. "Is that correct?"

Sam nodded. Smythe rumbled, "Yes, sir."

The judge sat in his black leather chair. "All right then. We will proceed. I will be recording this session." He set a small handheld recorder on his desk. "The plaintiff—that's you, Ms. Moser, will present your case first. I ask you, Mr. Smythe, to remain silent until she is finished, and then we will hear your presentation. No attorneys are permitted." He nodded at Sam. "Ready, Ms. Moser?"

"Yes." Her voice came out with a squeak. She cleared her throat and rose, her knees like rubber. Teresa's whisper came from behind: "You'll be fine." And a low murmur echoed from Brad.

Sam swallowed. "Thank you, your honor." She stopped, frozen again, her heartrate accelerated and chest constricted.

The judge gave her a kindly smile. "It's okay. I don't bite. Go ahead when you're ready."

She took a breath and let it out slowly. *You can do this.* "I'm Samantha Moser. I was made aware of a starving horse by Teresa Knudson," she turned and pointed to her friend, "who knew I had a rescued mare. She thought maybe I could help this poor animal." Her voice grew stronger and the icy nerves calmed as she warmed to the story. She chronicled the events: seeing the horse nearly dead, talking to the animal warden with no results—heat rising as she remembered their confrontation—bringing feed and a tub for water, and then meeting Todd Smythe, the nephew, the offer to buy the horse and the subsequent "sale." With mixed hope and trepidation, she gave the judge the photos Teresa had taken, the copy of the hand-written bill-of-sale, and the pictures after she had taken care of the horse for several weeks, plus a copy of the vet bill.

Then she gestured toward Electra. "This young lady came to work with me this summer, very unhappy and troubled over the loss of a brother and her father." She showed the judge a picture of the Goth-Electra. "She was so moved by the plight of this horse I call Apache, and he immediately responded to her in such a... a marvelous way." She swallowed past a thickness rising in her throat. "Your honor, I have witnessed a couple of miracles with kids and horses recently that I never would have dreamed." Her voice caught, she paused, and looked at the judge. "Your honor. This claim is to get my five hundred dollars back, but I truly believe, I feel it—" she put a hand over her heart. "If I could get Apache back, that would be my wish come true. This horse... and this girl deserve happiness."

Sam laid Brad's photos on the judge's desk. "These were taken yesterday by Mr. Ashton there. As you can see, the horse is still not being well cared for."

Judge Pepperman leaned forward and studied the photos for several eternal moments, creases deepening in his forehead. Then he nodded at Smythe. "Mr. Smythe, your turn. I believe you are the owner of the horse and guardian of your nephew Todd, who is under age eighteen, is that correct?"

Fighting an urge to throw up, Sam steeled herself.

Smythe stood. "Yes, your honor. That is correct. This was my late wife's horse, so I didn't want to sell him, but I was out of the country on business for an extended period. My nephew was in charge of caring for Sebastian—who Ms.

Moser calls 'Apache'—but he did not have power of attorney to sell the horse. So as far as I'm concerned, the sale was null and void, and I enlisted the assistance of the Rosebud County Sheriff and Warden Madison to retrieve my property, which I considered stolen."

Sam clenched her fists but bit her lip to keep from protesting. *I paid that little punk.* She glanced at the men at the back of the room and did a double take to see Sheriff O'Connor, the Custer County Sheriff, and the animal warden. That's right, Sheriff O'Connor said he would see if Madison would be a witness. But what would he say? Bile rose in her throat. She swallowed and took slow, measured breaths.

Judge Pepperman scrutinized Smythe over his readers. "But you received a check and cashed it?"

"No, *I* didn't. I never saw a check." His eyes shifted momentarily toward his nephew.

"Did you cash the check, Todd?" the judge asked.

The teenager shifted in his chair and looked down at the floor.

"Answer the judge, Todd." His uncle prodded his shoulder.

"Um… no." He shook his head.

What? Sam put her hands on the table to rise. The judge turned to her. "Ms. Moser, do you have a bank statement that shows the check went through?"

Bank statement… Sam paused, trying to think. "Yes, your honor. I know I saw it on my statement." She riffled through her file folder. "Oh, wait." She opened her purse and dug out her wallet, where she had put the cancelled check weeks before. *How could I have forgotten that? Thank goodness for small town banks that still return cancelled checks.* "Here it is, your honor."

He took the document and turned it over to look at the back. Then he leveled his gaze at Todd. "Looks like your signature right here, young man."

The boy's face reddened, and he squirmed again.

Judge Pepperman continued to stare at the teen for several moments. Then he studied the photos and papers again. Looking toward the back of the room, he finally spoke. "Mr. Madison."

The animal warden stood. "Yes, your honor."

"I see you are listed as a witness. Ms. Moser called you about the condition of this horse, is that correct?"

"Yes, your honor."

"And you went to the pasture and saw him in this emaciated state?" The judge held up the photo of Apache Teresa had taken at the beginning.

The warden shuffled his feet. "Yes, your honor."

"And you did nothing?"

Madison's face flushed in red blotchy patches. "Uh... well, no, your honor. At the time I was there, the horse had water and feed, so I deducted that it was being cared for."

"That's because I bought the water tub and the feed!" Sam blurted out, unable to stop herself. Her neck and face burned.

The judge held up a hand. "And did you check with the owner or return at a later date to see if the horse was being cared for?"

Madison studied his fingernails. "Um, no, your honor. I came to Ms. Moser's with Sheriff O'Connor to return the horse to Mr. Smythe, and he appeared to be healthy at that time. Mr. Smythe was back home by then, so I assumed the care would continue."

Sam closed her eyes. Heat flushed through her body and her insides shook. *Incompetent jerk!*

"Thank you, Mr. Madison. You may be seated." The judge shuffled the papers and photos and pursed his lips as he appeared to study each one again.

Sam rubbed her cold hands. Did she dare hope he would be on her side? She glanced back at Electra who bit vigorously on a thumbnail. Teresa raised her eyebrows and nodded. The courtroom was silent except for the papers and an occasional throat-clearing or foot-shuffling. The wall clock ticked in slow motion.

At last, the judge gathered up the paperwork, tapped it on the desk, and removed his glasses. He stood and walked around to stand in front of the Smythes. "Todd, do you know that endorsing that check and selling property that doesn't belong to you is a crime? Something that could send you to jail for up to five years?"

The boy's face turned pale.

"Mr. Smythe, you are the boy's guardian. Do you want to press charges against your nephew?"

The man's face was equally pale. "No, your honor, I do not."

"All right. I will let you handle that on your own." The judge narrowed his eyes at Smythe. "As for you... in my opinion, this horse looked to be nearly dead when Ms. Moser attempted to rescue him. The photos show a marked improvement by the time you demanded his return, and now..." Pepperman reached back and picked up yesterday's photo, "it appears he is nearly as bad as he was in the initial photos."

"Well, Sebastian is an older horse and—"

The judge waved off Smythe's protest and half-turned toward Sam. "This court and this case is for monetary awards only."

Sam's heart sank. It was too much to hope they'd get Apache back. Electra stifled a small cry behind her.

"I'm ordering you, Mr. Smythe, to repay Ms. Moser the five hundred dollars plus reimbursement for her vet bills."

Her lip quivered. *At least I'll get my money back.* Her body going numb, she bit back her disappointment. Electra would need a lot of comforting in the next few days. Numbness blanketed her and muffled the sounds of the courtroom. She turned and took the girl's hand in hers. Tears streamed down Electra's cheeks.

"However, due to the circumstances and appearance of this horse, I am calling this a case of animal neglect and abuse, and in lieu of allowing the sheriff to file charges, I am recommending you also return the horse to Ms. Moser."

Sam heard the judge's voice, but the words didn't register. Her chest was tight, her heart like a stone. Teresa's "Yes!" startled her. Brad's face broke into a huge grin. Sam frowned. What was happening? She turned back to the front.

"Can I expect compliance from you, Mr. Smythe?"

The man's face darkened. "Yes, your honor. I will write out a check right now, and Ms. Moser may come and pick up the horse whenever she wishes."

Sam blinked. *Pick up the horse?*

Electra's eyes widened, and her mouth fell open. "Sam? Is it… are we…?"

The words finally registered on her brain. *We're getting Apache back.* It was all she could do to keep from jumping up and whooping aloud. The courtroom buzzed with reactions as everyone seemed to speak at once.

Judge Pepperman banged his gavel. The sharp report quieted the audience. "All right. Mr. Smythe, come forward and write out your check and make arrangements with Ms. Moser to retrieve the horse. This court is adjourned."

Teresa leaped from her chair and grabbed Sam in a bear hug. "I knew it! I knew you could do it. Congratulations!"

Electra squealed. "We're getting Apache back! We're getting Apache back!"

As if floating inches off the floor, Sam moved to the judge's desk, where Smythe handed Pepperman a check. The judge looked it over and gave it to Sam. "Okay, young lady." He looked at Smythe. "And the ownership papers?"

"I'll put 'em in the mail." His answer was curt.

The judge shook his head. "You'll need to sign papers right now to transfer ownership to Ms. Moser. You can do that with my clerk at the window."

"All right." He bit the words through thinned lips.

"Thank you, Judge. Thank you, Mr. Smythe." She fought her urge to wave her victory in his reddened face. "This afternoon all right to pick him up?"

"Whenever," Smythe grunted and walked out of the courtroom.

Sam couldn't help grinning. She waved the check at her group. "We did it!"

Brad stepped forward and offered his hand. "Congratulations."

She shook his hand, her anger at him melting. "Thank you, Brad. I think your photos tipped the verdict. Thank you so much."

"Glad to be of service, ma'am." He gave her a little-boy grin. "May I buy you ladies lunch to celebrate?"

"Oh, thanks, but I need to get home, get a trailer, and come back for Apache right away."

Electra squealed again. "We're getting him today? Really? Yes!" She high-fived Sam and skipped from the room.

Sam rolled her eyes and chuckled. "We best be going. Thanks again, Brad. See you later."

As she and Teresa exited the room, Sam caught sight of the Custer County sheriff, his face about an inch from

Warden Madison's crimson one. "I've half a mind to fire you right now."

"B-b-bu—" The warden's lower lip quivered like a scolded child. His face reddened, and veins bulged in his neck.

The sheriff's finger jabbed Madison's chest. "I don't *ever* want to hear anything like this again. Do you understand me?"

The warden's head bobbed up and down in rapid fire motion.

"I'll be personally supervising your calls and reports from now on." The sheriff stepped back. "Now get to work."

Sam and Teresa exchanged a grin. Sheriff O'Connor came up to them. "Congratulations, Sam. Glad this worked out for you."

"Thank you for all your help, Sheriff. I appreciate it."

He put his hat back on, touched the brim with two fingers and walked down the hall.

CHAPTER TWENTY-NINE

On the drive home Sam bounced as much as Electra in her excitement. She whooped and sang at the top of her lungs, Teresa harmonizing and giggling. Electricity sparked from one to the other.

"I can't believe it!" Electra repeated over and over.

"I can't either." Sam shook her head. "Oh, Teresa, I was so nervous. I thought I was going to melt into a big steaming puddle in the middle of the courtroom."

"I knew you were, but you spoke very well, and I could see that your story touched the judge, especially about Electra's transformation." Teresa glanced into the rearview mirror at the grinning girl. "I'm so proud of you. You've done a good thing here."

Sam blinked away a sting in her eyes. "Thanks. And thank you for being here with me. That means so much. You are a good friend."

"You're welcome. But you gotta give Brad some credit too. He's been a big supporter of yours, and those photos..."

Sam looked down at the floorboard. "I know. He didn't *have* to do that, especially since I've been ignoring his calls lately. I dunno, I was just so mad at him for doing that stupid documentary for the Big Open people."

Teresa nodded. "I can understand why you were, but he was merely doing his job, one that he'd been contracted for before you even met him."

Her insides twisted. "Yeah. I guess you're right." She gave her friend a lopsided smile and then turned to Electra. "So, what do you think we should do first thing after we get Apache?"

The teen sobered. "Should we take him to the vet again, make sure he's really okay?"

Sam nodded. "Y'know, that's a good idea. We should get him checked out."

At home, Teresa stayed to help Sam and Electra hook up the borrowed horse trailer. "Good luck. Let me know how things go." She got into her SUV, waved, and drove off.

"Okay, let's go get Apache." Sam jumped into the pickup, and Electra bounded onto the passenger seat.

"Yeah! Let's go! Can you drive faster?"

Sam chuckled. "Not with this trailer and not on these dirt roads. We'll make up some time when we get to the highway, but we don't want to get into an accident before we even get him."

Electra punched on the radio, and they soon wailed to an oldies country station. Sam grinned. Another thing that'd changed. Electra wouldn't have been caught dead listening to country music when she first got there, much less the oldies.

When she turned up the dirt road toward the pasture, her stomach tightened, remembering the goon who'd greeted them last time they'd come to see the horse. She wouldn't be shocked if Smythe changed his mind and wouldn't let her take Apache. A glance at Electra revealed a tight face. Apparently, she remembered that incident too.

The windmill came into sight, blades spinning in the hot wind. Dust swirled from the pasture across the road. Sam held her breath. She didn't see the horse.

"Where's Apache?" Electra leaned forward and peered through the dirty windshield.

Sam drove over a little rise.

"There he is!" Electra cried out, and Sam exhaled.

The horse stood near the water tank, head down, just like the photos Brad had taken. Sam gulped as she pulled up to the gate. Almost before the truck stopped, Electra was out of the door and strode toward the horse. She crawled through the barbed wire fence and made little mewling sounds as she slowed and approached, hand outstretched.

Apache raised his head and blinked huge, liquid brown eyes as if he couldn't believe what he saw. Sam stopped at the fence. Electra held her hand out so he could smell her. The gelding blew softly, bobbed his head, and then whickered. With a big smile, Electra smoothed her palm over his nose and up his face to his ears. "Hello, boy. It's okay. I'm here now." She threw her arms around his neck and buried her face in his dirty, matted mane.

Sam's chest heaved, full to bursting. *They are meant for each other.* Just like Sugar was meant for her. She raised her eyes to the fluffy clouds floating in a sea of blue. "Thank you, God," she whispered.

After a few minutes, she crossed the fence and approached the pair. Electra turned toward her, tears streaking muddy tracks through the dust on her cheeks. "I'm so glad to see him." She sniffled.

Sam handed her a tissue. "Me too." She ran her hands over his neck and down his legs, checking for bumps or sores. "Easy, boy, easy." She spoke in a low, soothing voice. "Well, other than being very thin, I don't think he's in too bad shape." Glancing at the empty feed trough and the few inches of scummy water in the tank, she gritted her teeth. "I forgot the ramp for the trailer, so I'm going to pull into that coulee there, and we can get him loaded."

Electra nodded. "Okay. I'll stay here with him till you're ready."

Sam drove to the wash and backed down into it but shook her head. This wasn't going to work. Where had she loaded him before? She glanced around. A little way down was a flat rock ledge that jutted out from the opposite bank. A perfect ramp. "That's it."

She backed again, got out, drove forward, backed again, trying to get the trailer to line up just right. As she was about to scream with frustration, she saw someone in the side mirror motioning. Brad! Her writhing mass of nerves quieted. She waved, turned the wheel, and backed up.

"Good," he yelled.

She jumped out, almost giddy with satisfaction of a job well-done. "Whew! Thanks. I was about ready to *ride* him home."

Brad chuckled at her joke.

Electra led Apache to the trailer, and the three loaded him without any trouble. He bobbed his head, his eyes brighter, and stepped into the trailer eagerly. Immediately he moved to the front where Sam had placed a small feedbag with oats.

Brad's warm brown eyes shone as his face crinkled into a smile. "Horse rescuer extraordinaire. I'm so proud to know you."

Sam's heart thudded. "Thanks. You had a hand in this too—it wasn't all me."

He scuffed his boot in the dirt. "Naw. I didn't do anything."

"No, really. I couldn't have done it without you and your trusty camera." She wiped sweaty palms on her jeans. *C'mon, Sam. Get a grip. No time for mushiness.* "Well, I gotta get going. We're going to get Apache checked out before we take him home, so…"

"Okay, that's good. Um… I guess I'll see you around then." Brad touched two fingers to his hat brim.

"Yeah." Sam nodded. "See ya." She got into the truck, pulled out of the coulee, and they drove slowly over the dirt road toward town. She glanced in the side mirror to see Brad pull out behind her.

Electra turned to look through the back window at the horse in the trailer. "Oh, Sam, I can't believe it. We got Apache back!" Her face glowed with her huge smile and a tear trickled from the corner of one eye.

Sam smiled. "I can hardly believe it myself. This poor guy needs a good home, good food, and somebody to love him."

"Yeah." The teen settled back in her seat. "Y'know… what Brad said… you are a horse rescuer. And…" she swallowed, "you're my hero."

A lump rose so quickly in Sam's throat she nearly choked. She blinked rapidly to keep the tears from flowing. "Oh… oh, Electra… th-that's the nicest thing anybody has ever said to me." She reached over and squeezed the girl's arm. "I'm so glad you were here to help me. You're a hero too—Apache's hero."

Now they were both sniffling. Electra rummaged in the glove box for a packet of tissue, took one, and gave one to Sam. She giggled then, and Sam felt a happy bubble float from her heart to her throat. She whooped, Electra joined in, and turned up the radio until the music reverberated through the cab with their laughter.

The vet unloaded Apache, ran his hands over the bay's body, checked his teeth, took his temperature, and drew blood. "He is still very underweight and weak, but not quite as bad as he was last time you brought him in." He turned toward the office. "Do you need some more of the vitamin supplements?"

Sam nodded. "I still have some, but probably will need more."

"Okay. Keep dosing him and feeding him as we planned last time. I'll give you a call if the blood tests indicate any problems."

"Thanks, Doc." Sam wrote him a check, relieved she'd received her money back from Smythe, and they loaded the horse. She stopped at the Tasty Freeze for burgers and fries and then headed home.

Sugar greeted them with a rumbling nicker and pranced around the corral as they unloaded Apache. The mare ran up to the gelding. They touched noses, and then she arched her neck and raced around the paddock again. Apache bobbed his head and whinnied after her.

Electra giggled. "They're glad to see each other."

"Yeah, I think they are."

The women gave Apache his feed and vitamins, got him settled into a stall, and fed Sugar. Electra grabbed a brush and currycomb and began to groom the bay. Dust and matted hair floated to the ground and Sam could see his reddish-brown coat once again. "Good job, Electra. Well, I'm going up to the house now."

"Okay. Uh...Sam?"

She turned. "Yes?"

"Can I sleep out here tonight?"

"In the barn?"

Electra nodded, eyes bright.

"Um...well..." Sam shrugged. "I guess so. If you want. It's not going to be very comfortable."

"That's okay. I don't mind. I'll bring my sleeping bag down and make a bed of hay, and we'll be fine."

Pride rose like water in a new-dug well. This girl had changed so much in just a couple of short months. Sam smiled. "All right then. You want to come up for supper?"

"Yeah, ah, okay, but can I just dish up and bring it back here?"

Sam chuckled. "Sure. How about I bring a plate for both of us, and we'll have a picnic here with Apache and Sugar."

Over the next several days, Electra opted to stay home while Sam went to work at Clyde's. She didn't want to take her attention off Apache for even a few hours. The horse lifted his head, whickered, and came to the fence whenever he saw her.

CHAPTER THIRTY

One evening after chores, Sam sat in her rocker reading, occasionally looking up to drink in the lowering, velvet shadows of dusk. Electra had just come in from the barn, finally able to leave Apache for the night, and washed up in the bathroom.

The phone shrilled into the peacefulness. Sam jumped, hurried into the kitchen, and picked up, wondering who would be on the other end. "Yes?"

"How's my favorite horse rescuer today?" Brad's cheery voice sang over the line.

She chuckled. "Oh fine. Just relaxing."

"And how's Apache doing?"

"Electra's taking good care of him, and he's getting stronger every day. His coat is shinier and his eyes are clear. I think he's happy."

"That's great! Wonderful news. Say, I wanted to let you know, KULR has scheduled my documentary tomorrow at 5:00 as their Sunday feature."

"Oh!" Sam paused. "Well…that's good…isn't it?"

"Heck, yeah. Listen, how about I buy you gals dinner at the Jersey Lilly, and we can watch it there?"

"Sure. That would be nice. Thanks."

"See you then."

Sam hung up, and her stomach contracted. Would she look like a stupid fool on television?

"What's the matter?" Electra peered from the doorway.

She told her about the program. "I'm not so sure I really want to see it."

"Why not? You rocked the interview. B'sides, I want to see it—me and Sapphire and the kids from the group home are in it. It'll be fun." Her face glowed with excitement. "You're not really going to skip it, are you? Please? Please?"

Sam rolled her eyes. "No. We'll go. Brad is buying us dinner. And I do want to see the part with Ellie and Trixie and at Clyde's and all." She reached into the cupboard for a bag of chips. "I hope he didn't mess with it like he did with the Big Open documentary."

"He didn't." Electra's voice held a strong, confident note. "Sam...?"

"Yeah?"

"You got your five hundred dollars back from Mr. Smythe, didn't you?"

"Yes."

"And Miss Ellie said she would sell Trixie for five hundred dollars, didn't she?"

Sam nodded. "She did."

"So...are we—you—going to buy Trixie?" The girl's eyebrows and voice rose at the same time.

"Well, I've been thinking about that a little. I sure would like to. And it is the exact amount I need." She paused.

"And...?"

"And now we have another horse to feed and with his medicine and supplements and all, it's going to cost a lot more to do that." She looked down at her boots. That five hundred was all the cushion she had—for any emergency expenses.

Electra's brow knitted, a furrow running between her eyes. "But what will happen to Trixi? Miss Ellie said she can't keep her and she really likes us and she want us to have her and now we have the money and..."

"I know, honey. Let's watch the show tomorrow and see what happens. Maybe somebody out there will want to give her a good home."

"Okay." Electra's lower lip jetted out. She sniffled and shoved her hand into the chip bag. "But I can't see you just giving up like that." She crunched on the chips with a vengeance, her mouth still turned down.

An arrow of guilt shot through Sam. She wasn't giving up. She had to be practical, consider the expenses of running the ranch, taking care of the two horses she already had. And if she ever had enough money to breed Sugar, she still dreamed of her herd of Thoroughbreds.

Horace, Clyde and his wife, and Brad were already at the Jersey Lilly when Sam pulled up. Brad met her at the entrance, opening the door with a flourish. "Evenin', ladies. You're both looking mighty spiffy today."

Electra executed a mock curtsey. "Thank you, Sir Brad."

Sam chuckled and smiled at him. He was dressed in black jeans, a crisp royal-blue shirt with an agate bolo tie. Her heartbeat sped up at the wayward curl that fell onto his forehead as he bowed. "You don't look so bad yourself."

"Your table awaits, m'lady." He took her elbow, escorted her into the dining area, and pulled out her chair, then did the same for Electra.

Wow, he's sure putting on the gallant act. Sam's heart skipped. *But I like it.* It was nice to have a good-looking guy's attention. It had been a while since... Kenny.

"Coke for the young lass?"

Electra nodded.

"And for you, Madame, would you allow me to buy a bottle of Billy's best wine?"

"As long as it's not 'Two-Buck Chuck,' sure." Sam giggled.

Brad looked to the ceiling and shook his head. "You doubt me?" He strode to the bar and came back with a nice Merlot and Electra's soft drink. He poured Sam and himself a glass then held it up toward the Bruckners and Horace. "Here's to our 'Horse Rescuer.'" He brought his gaze back to her with an intense look of what she could only guess at—interest? care? "May you rescue many more."

"Hear, hear!" Horace boomed and raised his beer mug high. Irene Bruckner applauded, and Clyde gave Sam a wink and a nod.

Heat rose from her neck into her cheeks, and she averted her attention to her wine glass. This was too much. She hadn't done anything.

Billy brought out chicken-fried steaks for Sam and Brad and a big, juicy cheeseburger for Electra. They all tucked into their food like starving ranch hands while Billy found the right channel on TV and adjusted the volume.

The program began with a shot of a horse herd—bays, blacks, roans, and palominos—muscles rippling under sleek coats, and their manes and tails flying in the wind as they raced across a green prairie.

"Modern horses have been near and dear to our American hearts since the Spanish Conquistadores reintroduced them to the continent in the sixteenth century." Brad's voice narrated as the camera panned the beautiful, strong animals and the rolling hills against a clear, ultramarine sky.

Sam glanced at him, her eyebrows raised. "Wow," she mouthed. He winked and smiled.

"Horses have been used for transportation, working fields, rounding up cattle, and for entertainment in rodeos." As he spoke, the documentary showed clips of horses in various occupations.

"Many today are beloved pets and part of the family." A smiling family gathered around a sleek black mare, brushing, petting, and hugging her.

Then the scene changed to a still photo of Apache, his head hanging, ribs showing through his dirty coat. Sam and Electra both gasped.

"And yet," the narration continued, "there are those who abuse or neglect these animals who have given us so much.

This is Apache, a horse discovered almost dead recently near Miles City, Montana."

Sam sat up straight when the next scene showed her riding down the hill toward the camera. "This young woman, Samantha Moser, came to the rescue." She felt the flush rise again. *Oh my. I really don't want to be in the limelight.* She shook her head.

Electra grabbed Sam's arm and held on tight while Brad went on to tell the story with its happy ending. Sam blinked back tears and bit down hard on her lip.

"Now, we have another horse who needs to be rescued. Many of us are familiar with the illustrious career of Miss Ellie Hunt and her famous trick-horses. All of her horses have been named Trixi, in honor of another famous trick rider, Trixi McCormick. This is the last one she's trained and exhibited for the past twenty years." Brad continued the story with Ellie's background, photos from her performances, and then showed Trixi as she lay down and let Electra mount.

The audience in the Jersey Lilly applauded, and it was Electra's turn to blush.

Brad continued interviewing the tiny but feisty older woman leaning on her walker.

"Now, I can't live on my own anymore, and I'll be moving into an assisted living facility." Ellie looked directly into the camera with a tear glistening in the corner of one eye. "I can't take my dear Trixi with me, and I want her to go to a good home, with someone special who will love her as much as I do." She turned to Sam on-camera. "Someone like this lovely young woman."

Sam closed her eyes. Guilt crashed over her like an icy tidal wave. She had the five hundred now. Maybe she should take the risk and buy the mare. Things had worked out with Apache.

Brad went on to talk about some of the experiences from the group home kids at Clyde's, including snippets of the interviews with Electra, Robin, Sapphire, and how they'd been impacted by interacting with horses.

Electra bounced in her chair. "Look," she whispered to Sam. "That's me. Cool!"

She smiled at the girl, glad she was enjoying her five minutes of fame. Clyde flashed them a thumbs up, Mrs. Bruckner gave a proud nod, and Horace beamed.

Sam turned her attention back to the TV as Brad the narrator came on screen. "So, you can see what miraculous things can happen when horses—and kids—are rescued. Miss Ellie and Miss Moser need another miracle to save Trixi." The segment focused on a picture of Ellie and Sam talking, with Trixi in the background, reaching her head expectantly over the fence toward them. "Cowgirls Don't Cry" played as the photo faded and the credits rolled.

Sam found herself holding her breath and slowly exhaled as the Jersey Lilly group applauded and whistled. Everyone abandoned their tables and hurried over to congratulate Brad and hug Sam and Electra. "You were wonderful," Irene Bruckner whispered.

"Way to go, little gal!" Horace clapped Sam on the back and then hugged Electra who blushed again.

"Good job." Clyde clasped Sam's hand. "I'm proud of you."

"Thank you." Her cold hands shook with the aftermath of nervous jitters, and she alternately flushed with pride and embarrassment and guilt. "I really didn't do anything. This is all Brad." She turned to him, her heart full of gratitude. She wanted to hug him but held herself back. "That was awesome. You... I..." Her throat closed, and she couldn't speak. Fighting tears, she had to face away.

Irene encircled her with a warm hug. "It's okay," she whispered. "It's okay."

Sam leaned into her motherly embrace for a long moment, then she drew back with a smile. "Thanks," she whispered back. She turned to Brad. "Thank you again for all your help. I just hope... this will help find Trixi a good home."

"B-b-but," Electra sputtered. Her voice rose as she continued. "Miss Ellie said she wants *us* to have her, and, and now you have that five hundred from Mr. Smythe and we could buy her and bring her here and she'd be so good for those kids from the group home and other kids and I want to learn to trick ride and..." Her words faded as she ran out of breath. "Please." Her eyes grew big and moist, her brow furrowed, and her mouth turned down.

Sam's heart lurched, but she nearly laughed. Electra looked like a puppy about to be disciplined. "I know, sweetie. I agree with you, and I'm really torn. There will be lots more expenses on top of the purchase of another horse. I'm not sure what I should do." She addressed the group. "I think I need to go home and think about this, sleep on it. Thanks again, everybody, for all your support. I do appreciate each one of you."

She turned away before they could see the tears and headed out the door.

CHAPTER THIRTY-ONE

After a restless night tossing in bed and turning over ideas and numbers, Sam slept late, awaking hungry. Clyde had told her to take the day off, so for breakfast she made pancakes—"flapjacks" as Grandpa Neil and Great Grandpa Jake called them. Then she and Electra saddled the horses. "We'll just go out a little ways and see how Apache manages," she said. "I don't want to fatigue him or hurt him."

Electra shook her head vehemently. "No way."

They rode the horses at a walk to the nearest pasture to check on the grass and water for Murdock's cows. "He's doing really well." Sam watched Apache who held his head high and flicked his ears back and forth as they talked. "He's come a long way in a short time—thanks to you."

Electra's face shone. "Thanks. I'm so glad to have him back."

Sam took in the fresh air, and her shoulders relaxed in the warmth of the sun. The weight of the world seemed to float away when she was outside, on horseback. She turned to Electra. "I've made a decision."

"Oh yeah?" The girl raised her brows.

"When we get back, I'm going to call Miss Ellie and tell her I'll buy the horse."

"Yes!" Electra squealed and Apache flinched. "Oh sorry, boy." She sat up in a more sedate manner. "What about the money? You won't have anything extra if... like if Apache or Sugar got sick or something."

Sam nodded. "I know. But I didn't have that money before the court stepped in. So, it's kind of like a bonus now. And it's the exact amount I need to buy Trixi. I almost feel like it's a message, a gift..." she looked up into the sky with its wisps of angel hair clouds, "maybe from above."

"Cool." Electra studied the horizon. "Mom always says that if you step out in faith, God will provide."

Sam glanced at the girl. "Really?" She certainly hadn't gotten the impression that Alberta and her daughter were particularly religious. But then, she'd only known the mother for a few days. And Electra, with her Goth-Girl persona, certainly had not given her any impression of faith. "That sounds pretty wise." She raised her eyebrows. "Let's hope it's true."

After checking and counting the white-faced Herefords and their growing calves, the two turned the horses toward home. Even though Electra sat quietly, an aura of nervous energy thrummed around her. Sam grinned. "I'll call Miss Ellie as soon as we get home."

A huge grin split the girl's face. "Oh, goody."

At the barn, they unsaddled and brushed the horses and then headed up to the house. Sam punched in the number and put the phone on speaker. Miss Ellie answered after the first ring. "Oh, Samantha, I'm so glad you called. I was hoping… I don't have your phone number."

"I've been doing a lot of thinking, and I've decided I want to buy Trixi." She explained her feelings about the "gift" and that she thought the horse was meant for her and Electra.

"What I wanted to tell you is my phone has been ringing off the hook this morning after that wonderful show," the older woman gushed. "I've had a number of offers …"

Sam gulped. Oh no. Had someone else come up with more money? She could barely breathe. Beside her, Electra's eyes were wide.

"But, my dear, none of them have come close to the feeling I have about you. I want *you* to have my Trixi."

"Oh!" Sam could hardly believe what she'd heard. "Thank you."

Electra gave a little squeal then clapped her hand over her mouth.

"I'm so happy. I knew the moment I met you that you were the right person." She paused. "You won't regret it."

Sam allowed herself a slow smile. "I think you're right."

Ellie chuckled. "So, Trixi is yours. With the caveat that I get to come visit her now and then."

Electra ran around the kitchen, whooping now.

Sam and Ellie both laughed. "I think your girl is excited," Ellie said. "I am too."

"Me three!" Sam slapped her thigh. "And yes, you can come visit as often as you want. We'll even come to Billings to pick you up sometimes, if you'd like."

"That sounds just wonderful, my dear." The woman's voice hitched a little. "I can make my move now with a great deal of peace."

"I have to work the next couple days, but we'll come in Saturday to pick her up." Sam said her goodbyes and disconnected. For a long moment, she looked at Electra who quivered in the doorway with a look of triumphant joy. Then Sam gave a whoop too and rushed to wrap the teen in a giant bear hug. Together they jumped up and down like two ten-year-old schoolgirls.

"I can't believe it! I can't believe it!" Electra kept repeating. "I gotta call Mom. Is that okay?"

"Of course. You do that, and I'll make us some lunch."

Sam looked up from the sink when she heard a vehicle outside. A white sedan pulled up the incline to the house. She frowned, not knowing anyone with a car like that. Her hands poised above the soapy water as a man got out of the driver's side and walked around to the trunk.

Kenny!

Her mouth dropped open. For a moment the world stood still, and she was paralyzed. Then she grabbed the towel and wiped her hands as she headed to the door. Heart thudding, she stepped onto the porch and then froze again.

Kenny unfolded a wheelchair and brought it around to the passenger door. He lifted someone out and onto the chair.

Sam's mind floated above the scene, as if looking down on herself standing inside a glacier. Wind roared through her ears and scrambled her brain. Pieces of pictures blew by—the crumpled blue car, Kenny's defeated look, the plane taking him away, her dead horse. She reached out to catch them, but they were lost. Lost. Lost.

"…ghost…" A voice penetrated the hurricane.

Sam gulped in short pants of air. Frozen hands uncurled. Her heartbeat slowed. As if moving through Jell-O, she took a step forward.

"You look like you've seen a ghost," the woman repeated.

"Jace." Sam's voice shook. "Kenny. What are you doing here?"

Kenny grinned, his white teeth flashing through his tan. "You wouldn't return our calls, so we thought we'd come up for a visit and surprise you."

"Oh." Sam still could barely move. "Well… um… it's a… surprise all right."

"Can we come in?" Jace brushed back shoulder-length black hair.

"Um, yeah. Sorry. Yes, do come in."

Kenny turned the wheelchair backwards and pulled it up the steps.

"Can we just sit out here on the porch?" Jace smiled up at Sam. "It's such a beautiful afternoon, and Kenny told me all about how you guys restored this porch and the house."

Still in a daze, Sam nodded. "Of course."

Electra opened the screen door and stood beside Sam, looking at her quizzically. "Hi."

"Hi," Sam replied. The fog continued to swirl in her brain. She couldn't even think.

"I'm Electra." The girl held out her hand to Jace and then Kenny. "Would you like some iced tea?"

"Oh. Yes. I'm sorry." Sam shook her head to try to clear the clouds. "This is my friend Electra who is helping me out this summer. Iced tea sounds great, honey. Could you bring us all some?"

The teen went back into the house, returning in a few minutes with a tray of glasses and a plate of chocolate chip cookies.

Jace helped herself and bit into one. "Mmm. Home-made. Did you bake these?"

Electra nodded. "Sam and I did." She sat on the porch swing next to Sam, looking from Jace to Kenny and back again. "Do you guys like horses? We have two now. Sam already had Sugar, and we just rescued Apache, he was almost dead from starving and we had to go to court but now we have him and next we're going to Billings to buy Trixi, an awesome trick horse, she was going to maybe go to auction if we couldn't rescue her because her owner is going to a nursing home and…"

"Whoa." Jace held up her hand with a chuckle while Kenny guffawed from his perch on the porch railing. "Sounds like you two are quite the horse women. I always knew you loved horses, Sam. Take after your great-grandma, huh?"

Sam nodded. "I guess so. Yes. I can't stand to see any animal suffering."

Jace smiled. "Remember the time when we were kids, we went to this riding class and you saw a baby bird on the ground? We just had to stop the whole group while you located its nest up in a tree, picked up the little creature with your gloves on so it wouldn't have your scent, and climbed up there to put it back."

A flush heated Sam's neck. "I do remember that. The instructor was so 'by the book' and insisted we had to get back before a certain time, and I was holding up the lesson."

Electra turned to her. "Wow. That's so cool, Sam. You really are a rescuer."

Sam shook her head. "Well... I don't know about that. I do what I think needs to be done."

Jace gazed around the yard at the cottonwood trees rustling in the breeze, the corrals, and the red and white barn. "This is such a nice place. It's so peaceful." She leaned back in her wheelchair. I can understand why you don't want to leave."

Kenny snorted. "Well, you ain't seen the winters. Snow up to your neck and cold enough to freeze the brass ba—" he threw a quick glance at Electra, "er, doorknobs off a monkey." I darn near died out here... in the middle of nowhere." He gave Sam a knowing look.

She opened her mouth to shoot him a biting response when a white pickup drove up the incline.

Brad.

Sam gulped. *No, no, no! Not now!* She rose and walked to the edge of the porch as he got out of the vehicle and bounded up the steps toward her. *What is he doing here?* Her heart pounded like a bass drum, and her mind raced, but she couldn't take another step or utter a sound.

"Hi, Sam." He gave her a quick peck on the cheek, then glanced at the group staring at him.

"Hi, Brad!" Electra called out. When Sam made no introductions, she continued, "These are Sam's friends from Phoenix, Jace and—"

"Kenny." He stuck his hand out. "Sam's fiancé."

Brad's mouth dropped.

"No. I…" Her chest locked up and the winds roared in her ears again. Inside her head she shouted *No, No, No,* but no sound came out.

His face went blank. "Oh. Well, I'm sorry to interrupt. Just had some news about the documentary. I'll talk to you later." Brad turned abruptly on his boot heel, strode to his pickup. and drove away, gears grinding and dust spraying behind the tires.

Sam tried to move, to run after him, to explain, to tell him the truth. But he was gone.

Her hands clenched, cold and sweaty. She opened her mouth and closed it again like a fish gasping out of water. Then she turned to face Kenny.

"That…was uncalled for. An out and out lie. You are NOT my fiancé." Her voice was icy, though her insides boiled. "You. You are the one who left me. You are the one who can't understand my connection with this ranch. You are the one who couldn't hack it here. You!" Her body shook as though from an earthquake tremor.

He held out his hands, palms up. "I tried to compromise with you. Made all kinds of suggestions—come back to Phoenix and save up more money, spend winters there and summers here—"

Sam stepped closer and jabbed her finger into his chest. "You never intended to come back here. And I don't want you here now." Her voice rose. "Get out! Get the HELL out of here. I don't *ever* want to see you again."

Kenny took a step back. "Now, now, let's just talk a little"

"No! I'm done talking. I've started my life here, by myself, thank you very much. Now get out of here. Go!" Sam screamed, her face flaming.

He started toward the car and then looked at Jace.

She waved him off. "You go. I'll be okay."

Still shaking his head and muttering, he stomped to the car and roared off.

CHAPTER THIRTY-TWO

Tears sizzled down Sam's cheeks. She stood rooted to the spot, every nerve and muscle trembling, her thoughts jumbled and confused.

"Sam? Sam?" Jace's voice penetrated her deep, dark fog.

"Are you okay?" Electra touched her arm.

She swiveled her eyes to the side and tried to focus on her young friend. *What just happened?* "Uh… I… don't know." Had she gone crazy? She allowed Electra to lead her to the porch swing and took the offered glass of iced tea. Her still-shaking fingers registered the cold and wetness of the glass. She took a drink and swallowed with difficulty. A dirt clod seemed to have lodged itself in her throat. Her breaths came rapidly, punctuated with tiny sobs.

Electra sat in the swing beside her and put an arm around her shoulders. Jace rolled her chair nearer and took her icy hands. She sank into her friends' embrace until her breathing slowed and her body stopped jittering.

She inhaled and let out a long sigh. Looking up from her lap, she saw two concerned faces and tried to smile. "I…guess I lost it."

The teen grinned. "Yeah, you kinda did. You were awesome."

Jace squeezed her hands. "I think that needed doing."

Sam shook her head. "Maybe…I guess. But that's not me. I don't lose my cool—usually." Then another reality sank in. She gasped. "Brad. He's gone. I let him go. I didn't stop him. I froze." Another tear followed the tracks on her cheek. "Oh my gosh, what have I done?" She buried her face in her hands and sobbed again. The other women patted her and murmured soothing sounds.

Finally spent, she leaned back in the swing. "I think I'm okay now. I'm… I'm sorry, you guys."

"No need to be sorry," Jace said.

Sam took a long swig of tea. "What was Kenny thinking anyway? I never realized he was so manipulative. What a jerk! He's the one who left me, but he won't let go. He wanted things to go his way, not *ours*."

Jace nodded. "It does seem that way." The young woman paused. "But he did get me here."

Sam looked at her childhood friend. She seemed thinner, older than her years. "Yeah. What *are* you doing here? We haven't spoken in years."

Jace lowered her gaze, her dark hair falling forward. "I know. It's my fault. I'm sure you blamed yourself... for our fight, and what happened..." She gestured at her legs. "And for a while I did too. Anything to not have to own up to my own stupidity."

"I should've tried harder. Wrestled the keys away from you. Knocked you down. Something!" Sam shook her head vehemently. "But I didn't. I just let you go."

Electra peered at Jace, hunched in her wheelchair. "You were in a bad car accident?"

Jace nodded.

"My brother was killed in an accident. My dad blamed himself, and he went away." The teen bit her trembling lip.

"I'm so sorry." Jace sighed. Her navy blue eyes clouded. "For years, I've been bitter, blaming everything and everybody. I pushed everyone away, just wallowed in self-pity. And I continued to drink... to numb the pain, the loss."

She gave a mirthless laugh. "But of course, that made everything worse. I lost everybody who tried to help. My own family gave up on me."

Sam chewed her bottom lip. *And I left her too.*

"About a year ago, I really hit bottom. I was living—well, existing—in an abandoned house, a foreclosure owned by the bank. Nobody ever came by so a bunch of us just flopped there. Most everybody was on drugs. I did a little, but mostly booze—all I could afford."

"Oh my gosh, Jace. I had no idea." Anguish crushed Sam's heart.

"Nobody did." Her friend lifted one side of her mouth in a wry smile. "I got so sick. Malnourished, no heat, got pneumonia. I was fortunate that one of my roommates was finally sober enough one day to get me to the hospital."

Electra sat still, her eyes and mouth in matching "O's". Sam's heart pounded.

"For the second time in my life I saw the white light and felt something so peaceful beckoning me. I almost followed." Jace shrugged. "But something called me back, and when I woke up, I realized I'd been given two second chances, and I'd better not blow this one."

Sam took her friend's hand and gave it a squeeze.

"The chaplain came by every day. At first, I resisted the idea that I had a problem. One day he brought a 'friend' to visit. I was ticked when I found out she was in AA. But they both kept coming, and I had a lot of time to think about my situation. I've been going to meetings ever since." She smiled, her face lighting up. "And I just got my one-year sobriety chip a week ago."

"That's wonderful!" Sam gave her a hug. "I'm so happy for you." She huffed a little laugh. "And I was just about to offer to get us something stronger than tea, after all this."

Jace laughed. "Nope. Thanks, but that did not solve my problems. I can look back and see that I never wanted to take responsibility for my own actions. Taking another drink was my way of escaping."

Sam inhaled sharply. Is that what she'd been doing? Her eyes flicked toward the kitchen and the high shelf that contained her vodka bottle.

"Trouble had a way of always finding me, no matter how hard I tried to get away." Jace took a sip of her iced tea. "Anyway, you've heard of the twelve-step program, right?"

Sam nodded.

"One of the steps is to make amends to the people you've harmed with your addiction."

Sam blinked and cocked an eyebrow. Amends? What was she talking about?

"You were my best friend. I pushed you away. You were hurt by my actions and my accident. I haven't been able to find a way to get here before now, but I wanted to apologize in person to make things right." She brushed a strand of dark hair out of her eyes. "I hope you'll forgive me."

Sam stifled a gasp. Silence hung over the two women as she struggled to process what her friend had said. Her tongue thickened. "I..." Her voice squeaked. "Forgive *you*? I don't think *you* need forgiveness. I—"

"Yes, I do." Jace's eyes glistened. "I can't move on and heal—mentally or spiritually—until I own what I did and receive atonement."

Sam leaned forward and took Jace's hands. "Of course. I forgive you. But... I am to blame for our relationship dying too." Hot tears stung her eyes. "Will you forgive me?"

Her friend nodded. "Yes. I forgive you."

They embraced for a long moment until Electra cleared her throat. Tears ran down her cheeks, but she smiled. "That is so cool. I'm so glad." She took an audible breath. "I wonder if Mom knows how to contact Dad. Maybe if he... Do you think I...?" Her eyes shone with hope. "I'm going to go call Mom. If that's okay."

Sam squeezed the girl's arm. "Yes. Call your mom."

The women sat on the porch the rest of the afternoon, sipping iced tea Electra kept refilled and catching up on their lives. As the sun dipped toward the far butte and turned it to molten gold, Electra broke in. "I'm getting hungry. What if I fix some hotdogs?"

Sam leaned back in the swing and laughed. "I've completely lost track of time. Let's go inside and have some supper. Yes, please get the hotdogs started, and I'll make a potato salad from the leftover spuds." She opened the screen door for Jace to wheel through.

She turned to Electra. "Say, did you talk to your mom?"

The girl's face fell. "Yeah. But she said she didn't know how to get ahold of Dad." She gave Jace a tiny smile. "But maybe if he gets to a certain point, like you did, he'll call us."

"Yes." Jace smiled back. "I think he will."

After supper and visiting until late, Sam changed the sheets on her bed downstairs for Jace and spread out a cushion and sleeping bag in the second bedroom upstairs for herself. Electra frowned. "You take my bed. I can sleep better than you on the floor."

Sam gave her a hug. "You're so sweet. I'll be okay. You don't need to do that."

"No. I want to. It'll be like camping." Electra stripped the sheets off her bed for Sam. "I like camping."

***

Despite having a bed and not the floor, Sam lay staring at the ceiling. The day's events kept looping through her brain like the replay of the movie *Groundhog Day*. Kenny showing up, telling Brad he was still her fiancé. She clenched her fists as anger rose again with bile in her throat. Then fear drenched her in a cold sweat. Brad had looked so shocked. She'd probably lost him—or the potential of him.

She pictured calling him to apologize and explain, rehearsing one conversation and then another. No matter how hard she tried to anticipate his reaction, she could only hear the disappointment in his voice and the negative response: "It's over." Before it even started. They hadn't even shared a real kiss.

Groaning, she sat up and threw her pillow on the floor. That vodka bottle was still half-full. Just sitting there in the cupboard. Calling for her. Waiting to numb the pain. She stood and reached for her robe.

But Jace. She had gone through hell with alcohol. Her stories about the horrific life she'd led flashed through Sam's mind again. *But I haven't sunk that low. I wouldn't put the booze first in my life.* She belted the robe and took a step toward the door. One or two drinks now and then didn't hurt anything. She crept down each stair, stepping to the side to keep it from creaking.

In the kitchen, she reached into the high cupboard and took out the bottle, resting its cool promise against her cheek.

Jace's voice came from the back of her thoughts. "Taking another drink was my way of escaping."

Is that what I'm doing—trying to escape? She sat in a kitchen chair, still holding the bottle to her chest. She thought back to Kenny leaving her, to Murdock wanting to renege on the lease, to losing Apache, to her money worries. Every time something bad happened, she'd turned to the vodka.

Jace's words came again. "But trouble had a way of always finding me, no matter how hard I tried to get away."

That's what they'd fought about—Jace's drinking and self-destructive behavior. She couldn't be repeating the thing she hated in her friend. Could she?

She gazed out the window at the crescent moon hanging in the ebony sky. "Hey, God. It's me again." She swallowed. "I guess I need some help figuring this all out. I think you helped me sleep several times, and you helped me get Apache back. So, if you could... would you please help me get through my troubles... without turning to this." She stood as slow as old Horace, walked to the cupboard and put the bottle back. *One step at a time, right?*

The next morning, her heart pounding like a tom-tom, she punched in Brad's number, counting the rings that echoed in the silence. One...two...three... It went to voicemail. She took a ragged breath. "Brad, it's Sam. I need to talk to you. Things are not what they seem." She paused. "I'm sorry. Please. Call me."

CHAPTER THIRTY-THREE

With reassurances from Jace that she'd be all right by herself, Sam and Electra headed off to work at Clyde's. Two couples from Portland, Oregon arrived in time for lunch, eager to experience horseback riding in the "wild west."

Sam tried her best to visit with the women over venison burgers, but her mind wandered back to yesterday's events. Hands clammy and shaky, she sneaked her cell phone from her pocket several times, checking for messages.

After lunch, she and Electra introduced the women to the horses, showed them how to brush and comb and bridle and saddle them. They practiced several times, and then just before supper Electra took them on a tour of the ranch yards, corrals, and barn where the growing kittens frolicked in the sun's rays.

Arriving home again, Sam immediately glanced at the answering machine. No blinking light. She hugged Jace. "Did anyone call today?"

"Nope. Not even a telemarketer." Her friend raised one eyebrow. "No word from Brad?"

Sam shook her head and tried to will away the choking sensation in her chest. She busied herself fixing tomato soup and grilled cheese sandwiches.

The rest of the week followed suit. No phone call from Brad. But the dudes were attentive and cooperative, for a nice change of pace. "We just love this country," one woman gushed.

The other agreed. "This is the most fun vacation we've ever taken."

"We'll be back next year," her husband added.

Clyde beamed and pumped the men's hands. After they drove off, he grinned at Sam. "That was a great bunch. Wish they were all like that."

She nodded. "Yeah, that's for sure." She turned to Electra. "Well, we'd better head for home. Gotta stop by Horace's and pick up the horse trailer."

The girl danced on the balls of her feet. "Yeah! We get to go get Trixi tomorrow. Yay!"

Clyde chuckled. "You gals have fun. Drive safe now, ya hear?"

The next morning, Sam loaded Jace's wheelchair in the back of the pickup and helped her into the passenger side. Electra slid into the middle, and they took off for Billings. Jace and the teen chattered about horses and life on the ranch versus the anthill hustle in the city.

Sam retreated into her thoughts. *Well, I seem to have screwed up royally with Brad. I'll probably never hear from him again.* Her heart felt squeezed by giant, cold hands. She vacillated between letting him go or calling him again to give him the full explanation. But if he was going to be scared off by a stupid thing like that, then maybe he was not worth getting involved with.

"...huh, Sam?" Electra's voice broke her trance.

"What? Sorry, didn't hear you."

"Will Miss Ellie teach us the commands for Trixi, so I can learn trick riding?"

She glanced at the girl's eager face and smiled. "Yes, I'm sure she will."

Electra squirmed in the seat. "I can't wait! Can't you drive faster?"

"Not towing that trailer." Jace looked out the side window. "I don't want to be in another wreck."

"Oh, sorry." The teen's face fell.

Jace chuckled and cuffed Electra's shoulder. "It's okay. Just joking. Sam's a good driver." She turned up the radio, and they sang along as they covered the last miles to town.

A plump, motherly woman met them at the door. "Hi, I'm Doris, Ellie's caregiver. Come on in. She's so excited to see you."

Electra ran into the living room and gave the old woman a hug and a kiss on the cheek.

"Hello, dear." She smiled at Sam. "This is a happy day indeed. I'm going to move to the Manor on Monday, and now I know Trixi will have a good home." She scooted forward in her chair and grabbed her walker. "Let's go out to the patio, and you can say hello to her."

Doris helped her up, and Sam pushed Jace's wheelchair outside. Electra immediately hurried to the fence and whistled. Out in the pasture, Trixi's head lifted from grazing, her blonde mane shifting in the breeze. She trotted to the girl's outstretched hand and lipped a carrot from her palm. Sam joined them and caressed the mare's face and scratched behind her ears. Trixi blew softly and leaned into her.

Electra's eyes shone as they exchanged a glance. "I can't believe we're getting her."

"I know. Me too." Sam swallowed. *I just hope spending that five hundred isn't a mistake.* She shook off her doubts. "Let's help Miss Ellie get a little closer, and she can show us some of her signals."

The caretaker brought a patio chair out into the yard, and Miss Ellie shuffled out to it. Jace's chair bumped over the grass to join her.

"Okay, the first thing. If you want her to lie down so you can get on, you do this." She made a motion and the horse got down. She motioned again, and Trixi stood. "Now you try it."

Electra looked at Sam. "Can I?"

"Of course."

The girl mimicked Miss Ellie's hand motion, and Trixi lay down again. Electra climbed on, they rose and walked around the pasture.

"Good job." Ellie beamed her approval.

Jace's eyes were wide. "Wow. That is awesome."

Sam nodded. "Isn't it though? I'm so impressed, Miss Ellie. I wish I could've seen some of your exhibitions."

The woman's white curls bobbed. "Oh, it was a thing of beauty. And most of all, we had such fun together. She's really my favorite of all my trick horses. She understood me almost immediately, like we were one."

Ellie continued with her lessons, first Electra, and then Sam giving the signals. Jace applauded with each successful execution.

At last, Sam returned to the old woman's side. "Well, I suppose we should get her loaded and get on the road before it gets too late. Let me grab my purse, and I'll write you a check."

"Oh, my dear, I almost forgot." Ellie gave a cackle of delight. "You know that program that delightful young man did—Brad, was it?—has resulted in several very nice donations. But when I contacted the people to try to return the money, they wouldn't accept it."

Sam furrowed her brow. *What did this mean? Is Miss Ellie going to keep the horse now?* Her heart turned to a lead weight. They'd made the trip in good faith, and now...

Ellie looked into her face. "Goodness gracious, you look like you've been hit with a horseshoe. I'm not reneging on the deal. You still have a horse, a wonderful horse. But..." she smiled, "...I'm not taking your money. I'm set up pretty well now with this money and with the sale of my house, I'll be comfortable in my 'golden years.'"

Sam shook her head, her face still scrunched in disbelief. "What did you say?"

Ellie laughed. "I'm giving you my horse, dear. You don't owe me a dime. Just take good care of my baby."

Relief flooded Sam like a warm summer shower. "Oh." A weight flew off her shoulders. "Oh my goodness. Are you sure? I mean..."

"Of course, silly girl. But I'm going to be coming out to visit...often!" Ellie stood. "Before you take off, please come in and have some coffee and cookies. Doris baked them in your honor."

Sam almost giggled. "We'd love some. C'mon, girls."

***

Electra kept swiveling her head and craning her neck to look back at the horse trailer. "I just can't believe this. Can you believe it, Sam? Can you, Jace? We got Trixi, and Miss Ellie *gave* her to us. I can't believe it!"

Sam exchanged a grin with Jace. "I know. Isn't that the best thing ever?" No, she couldn't quite believe it. One part of her mind still clouded with doubts—was this real? Was she taking on too much? Would Miss Ellie change her mind? Then reality zinged through the clouds. *Yes, this is real! You now have three rescue horses. You've accomplished something good.*

Electra kept up her patter. "I can't wait to get home. I want to try all those things I learned. I want to be a trick rider like Miss Ellie. Do you think I can?" She turned to Jace.

Jace nodded. "Yes, I do. You are an incredibly determined young woman, and I know you can do whatever you set your heart on."

Sam blinked. Good advice. Nice to hear her friend sound so confident after everything she'd been through. *Probably good advice for me too.*

When they got home, Sam unloaded the wheelchair and helped Jace into it so she could watch the unloading procedure. She backed the trailer up to the chute, getting it aligned after a couple of false starts. Electra had already climbed over the fence and was trying to open the doors by the time Sam came around.

"Take it slow now. We don't want to scare her." She unlatched the fasteners and talked softly to the mare as she stepped close to her head to untie the halter rope. Trixi blew, and as if on cue, backed out of the trailer. "Good girl. Easy as pie. You're so well-trained." Sam led her into the corral. "Such a good horse." She patted her neck.

"Can I ride her now?" Electra reverberated beside her.

"Let's let her roam the corral for a while and get used to her new surroundings, meet the other horses over the fence. Later I'll take her into the barn and feed her. She's really a good horse, but we need to let her be for a bit." She turned to push Jace up the incline. "Let's go in and fix supper. It's been a long day."

As Sam walked into the kitchen, her eyes automatically shifted to the answering machine. The light was blinking. Her breath caught. It was the first time all afternoon she'd thought about... She hit the play button.

"Hey, Sam, it's Brad."

Her heart thudded.

"Sorry, I didn't get your message until today. I've been working out of state, out of cell range. Uh... anyway, I'd like to talk. I left a message on your cell too. Give me a call."

She fished her phone out of her pocket. Funny, she hadn't received a call. The cell was dead. "Oh, I forgot to charge it last night." She looked at Jace. "With no cell service here at the ranch, it's hard to remember sometimes."

Electra's dark eyebrows arched. "Are you going to call him?"

Sam's head jittered in small movements up and down. "I think so." Her focus wavered and the room shifted slightly.

She sat. "Oh my. I don't know. Maybe we should…" she looked at her friends, "…should eat first."

"No!" Electra nearly shouted, but then her face softened into a pleading smile.

Jace laughed. "Call him now. We'll go in the living room and give you some privacy." She wheeled her chair around and beckoned Electra with her head.

With cold, shaking fingers, Sam punched in Brad's number. He answered on the third ring.

"Hi, Brad. Got your message. Th-thanks for calling me back." The words stuttered out like ice cubes from an ice maker.

"Yeah… Um… So, I'm back home in Billings for a few days. Can I come out tomorrow to see you?"

Sam hardly dared breathe for fear of sobbing. *He wants to see me.*

"Yes." The word finally choked out. *Maybe it's not too late after all.*

CHAPTER THIRTY-FOUR

The next morning, Electra barely took two bites of oatmeal before she fixed on Sam with intense dark eyes. "Can we go out and work with Trixi now?"

Sam swallowed her own bite to keep from laughing. "Well, I don't see why not." After all, Brad wouldn't be there until later in the afternoon. Might as well keep busy. "But..." she quickly added as Electra picked up her still-full bowl and pushed back her chair, "you need to finish breakfast first."

"Aww..." The teen slumped back into her chair, but then straightened her shoulders. "Okay. We need nourishment to work, right?"

Jace hid a smile behind her napkin. "You're absolutely right. I think I'll have another piece of toast. Watching you guys is going to take a lot of fuel."

Sam chuckled and passed her the plate of buttered toast and the strawberry jam.

Soon the three were on their way to the corral, Electra leading the way with a half-skip. The sun hung warm and bright in the clear blue sky. Sam inhaled deeply the familiar perfume of the dried grass, musty corrals and horses.

Trixi hung her head over the fence where Apache and Sugar stood on the other side, looking like gossipy old ladies. Electra climbed into the corral and approached Trixi with a cake pellet. She scratched the mare's neck, then leaned through the fence to give Apache, then Sugar, a treat. She turned to Sam who wheeled Jace through the gate. "I probably should brush Apache first. I don't want him to be jealous."

Sam nodded. "Good idea. Let's give our babies some attention before we start working with Trixi." She let the two horses into an adjoining pen.

Electra hugged Apache and gazed lovingly into his eyes. "You're my boy. I'm not abandoning you. We'll go for a ride a little later, okay?" The gelding nuzzled her neck.

After Sam and Electra spent a half hour grooming the two horses, Trixi whinnied from the other side. Electra laughed. "Okay, girl, it's your turn now."

Sam offered Jace a brush. "Want to help?"

The young woman's face lit up. "Sure." She wheeled closer. While Sam and Electra worked on Trixi's withers and back, Jace brushed the horse's shoulder and caressed her legs. Trixi stood patiently, with a look of contentment on her face. "Such a pretty girl," Jace murmured, "such a good girl. I wish I could ride you."

Sam and Electra stopped mid-brush and exchanged a glance. "Why couldn't she?" the teen asked.

A momentary chill ran through Sam's body. "Oh. Well. I don't know." Visions of her friend falling from the great height flashed into her mind. "Maybe it's not..."

The teen was already kneeling beside Jace's chair. "Why not? Trixi is trained to lie down. We can help you get on, and we'll be right here beside you. Do you want to?"

Her friend's eyes widened. She looked at Electra. "I would." Then at Sam. "Can I? Please?"

At Sam's continued hesitation, Electra pleaded, "Sam. Trixi is meant for this. Don't you see? We were meant to get her because of Jace. C'mon. Let's do it."

She let out a pent-up breath. "Well, okay. Go get your saddle and bridle." As Electra raced to the barn, she reached out and touched Jace's shoulder. "You sure you want to?"

"Absolutely!" Jace grinned. "Nothing ventured, nothing gained, right?"

When Electra had the horse saddled, she gave Trixi the signal. With a nod, the mare bent one knee, then the other, and came to a rest on the ground with all fours under her. Jace wheeled up closer to her side, scooted her body to the edge of her chair, and with her arms, lifted her right leg onto the saddle. Sam stepped forward to help her, but she shook her head. "Let me try. If I start to fall, catch me." She grinned, grabbed the horn with one hand and the cantle with the other. With a grunt, she heaved herself up and inched her way to a sitting position on the saddle.

"Woohoo!" Electra high-fived her. "You did it."

Sam grinned, pride expanding her heart. "Good job. That's great."

Electra gave the signal and Trixi stood. Sam and Electra put Jace's feet into the stirrups, which were the perfect length. Jace gave the reins a bit of slack and clucked, and she rode around the corral, first at a walk, then a trot, reining like a pro.

"Oh my gosh, oh my gosh!" Electra vibrated beside Sam. "She's riding! Do you see that? She's riding!"

Sam tried to hold back the gushing emotions that churned just beneath the surface. Then she broke into a grin and whooped. "Yes! She's riding! Jace, you're riding!"

Jace cantered up to them and reined the horse in. Her face glowed. "This...this is amazing. Thank you." Tears glistened in her eyes. "Thank you so much."

They took a break for lunch and after a short nap for Jace, she wheeled back out to the porch where Sam paced, and Electra sat. "Could we go for a real ride, the three of us?" she asked.

Electra jumped up from the swing. "Yeah! Let's!"

Sam glanced at her watch.

Jace grinned. "It'll keep your mind off Brad..."

Sam shook her head and laughed. "You're right. Okay. We have time for a short ride."

Once again, Trixi got down into a sitting position and Jace pulled herself onto the saddle. She wiped the sweat from her forehead. "Hard work!" She gave the signal, and Trixi stood.

Electra led Apache and Sugar into the corral, already saddled, and Sam and she mounted. The horses ambled calmly through the pasture toward the small, nearly dry reservoir nearby. A gentle breeze cooled the hot August sun, insects whirred and clicked as hooves disturbed their resting places, and meadowlarks trilled to each other from their perches on fence posts.

Electra led the procession, and Sam rode beside her old friend, keeping a close eye on her balance. She sat strong in the saddle, with no problems.

"What a beautiful day. I love this place." Jace beamed. "I feel whole. For the first time in years, I'm not handicapped. I feel normal."

Tears stung Sam's eyes. She tried to speak but the words stuck in her throat. A sensation like a warm light flowed through her body. Another miracle with a girl and a horse. She reached out, took Jace's hand, and gave it a squeeze. Looking skyward, she whispered, "Thank you."

As they rode up a small rise back toward the corral, Sam's heartbeat tripped when she saw the white pickup parked by the barn.

"Brad's here!" Electra shouted and urged Apache into a trot.

She swallowed. *Here it comes. The moment of truth. Do we have a chance at a relationship, or did I screw things up royally?* Her stomach flip-flopped. She forced herself to ride sedately into the corral next to Jace and nodded at Brad who smiled and touched a finger to his hat.

Electra was already unsaddling Apache and talking at him a mile a minute. "Do you see this? Jace is riding and Trixi is perfect for her. She gets down and lets her get on. Oh, it's so cool. Just watch!" She pointed at the pair as Trixi lowered herself to the ground, and Jace maneuvered herself back into her chair, with Sam's help.

Brad gave an appreciative whistle and flashed a thumbs-up as Sam and her friend approached him. "Awesome, ladies." He switched his penetrating gaze to her. "Hello, Sam." His voice was even, friendly.

Her neck and face heated under his scrutiny. "H-hi, Brad." Her fingers were ice-cold despite the heat. "How ya doing?" Acutely aware of Electra and Jace watching her every movement, she turned to the teen and handed her Sugar's reins. "Would you go ahead and unsaddle all the horses, and maybe you and Jace could brush them? Thanks."

Brad stepped forward. "Let's take a walk." He touched her arm to guide her. Electricity prickled her skin, and she pulled back without thinking. They headed out into the pasture, dried grass crunching under their boots.

"Brad."

"Sam." They both spoke at the same time, then laughed.

He gave a half-bow. "Ladies first." His white teeth flashed against his tan.

All the tennis-playing butterflies in the world rose up to compete in her chest. "Brad, I'm really sorry about what happened last time you were here." She took a breath to steady her voice. "We haven't actually known each other long enough to get into past history, so..." She swallowed. "Anyway, Kenny *was* my fiancé. We moved here from Arizona, and he helped me rebuild the barn and house and fix up this place. We had big plans for the future. I thought."

She scuffed her boot in the dust. "But the first winter blizzard hit, and...he couldn't handle it. He left. My dreams and his were apparently not the same." She raised her head.

Brad's dark eyes caught and held her gaze. "Do you still love him?"

"No. It's over." She bit the inside of her cheek. "But he keeps calling every once in a while, trying to get me to move back to Phoenix. Then he just showed up out of the blue with Jace." She explained about her best friend and the accident, tears threatening to spill.

"I'm sorry. I'm kind of blathering on, and I know there was no excuse for me not to say anything that day." She shook her head. "But it shocked me so much, I just froze. And then you were gone. And then you didn't return my calls. I was afraid..." The corners of her mouth trembled.

Brad took her hand. "I understand. You've had a tough time. Meeting him was a bit of a shock for me when he introduced himself." He grinned. "I guess I froze too. Had to get out of here before I busted his chops."

Sam smiled. "I almost wish you had."

"That would've been interesting." He chuckled. "No. Glad I didn't. But I needed a little time to cool off and think."

"You said you've been out of state working, out of cell range?"

He nodded. "Yeah. Down in Wyoming. Strangely enough, for Roberts and his crew." He held up a hand as Sam drew back. "Now before you get upset, hear me out. The good news is, they've given up their quest to create a 'Big Open' in Montana. They're working with a group that's evaluating Wyoming for a project to bring in kangaroos."

Sam felt her mouth drop open. "Kangaroos?"

Brad grinned. "Yup. They're serious, and they claim the Wyoming Wild Game Department is going along with it."

She rolled her eyes. "Unbelievable."

"And, they've hired me to document the process. It's good money, and as a freelancer, I can't pass up the opportunity."

Sam sighed. "I understand. You have to make money when and where you can. Wow. This just seems so far-fetched. But... I'm really glad they're gone from here."

"Yeah, I think they got the message loud and clear from the guys at the Jersey Lilly that night." Brad laughed. "Plus, nobody was selling."

"That's very good news."

"Oh, yeah. And I have more. In fact, this is the reason I stopped by that day. I wanted to tell you that as a result of my program about Miss Ellie and you…" he paused and put his hands on her shoulders, heating them like a branding iron, "I set up a bank account with donations that have been pouring in for you and your rescue horses. As soon as you can come to town, we'll get it transferred to your name."

Sam jerked her head back. "What?"

His smile broadened and he reached into his shirt pocket, taking out a deposit slip, and showed her the amount.

Sam's knees buckled and the world spun.

Brad caught her before she went down, his warm arms holding her close. She rested her face on his shoulder and inhaled his clean, spicy scent. For a long moment she was content right there. Then the outside world nudged her thoughts. *Wait. What just happened?*

Sam pushed herself away and peered into his face. "Tell me again. Money? For me?"

He grinned, his eyes twinkling. "Yup. All for you." He picked up the paper that had fallen and handed it to her.

She stared it the document. More money than she'd ever seen associated with her. "This is for real?"

"Yes. For real."

"Oh my gosh, Brad. Do you know what this means?" She shook her head. *I must look like an idiot with my mouth hanging open.*

"Well, I know that now you can take care of the three horses you own without worrying about whether you can feed yourself too."

Sam nodded. "We've got to go back and tell Electra and Jace." She turned and strode back toward the barn.

Brad trotted to catch up and grabbed her hand. "So, are *we* good then?"

She studied him with a frown. "Good? Yeah. Sure." *What is he talking about? I just got the news of a lifetime. Of course, I'm good.*

"I mean, you and me. You're not upset with me?"

Sam stopped and faced him. "Of course not. You are the bearer of great news, why would I be upset?"

"So, you don't mind if I call you and come around to see you on a more regular basis?"

"Oh!" The realization suddenly penetrated her fog. "You mean…"

He nodded, and the dark lock of hair fell onto his forehead. "I'd like to get to know you better."

"Yes." She smiled. "Yes, I would like that." For a moment, her gaze held his, and she leaned closer to push the curl back.

Horses! Money! Excitement broke the spell. She grabbed his hand and pulled him forward into a run. "C'mon. We've got news to share."

He laughed as they sprinted toward the barn.

Jace and Electra waited expectantly by the corral gate. "Well?" Electra peered into Brad's face and then hers.

"Brad just gave me the most wonderful news."

"Yeah? What?" The women waited expectantly.

She held up the bank statement and shared with her friends what had happened.

Electra whooped and leaped in the air, her fist shooting toward the clouds. Brad stood off to the side, grinning broadly.

Jace applauded and wheeled closer to him. "You're our hero."

"Naw. I'm just the messenger." He looked down at the ground, a flush rising to his cheeks.

Sam touched his arm. "Yes, you are a hero. Without your pictures, I probably wouldn't have gotten Apache back, and without your feature story, I wouldn't have this." She waved the paper. "I have steaks in the freezer. Let's go up to the house and celebrate. I'll call Teresa and have her come over too."

She set up a table on the front porch, and Brad barbecued the steaks. Teresa arrived with a bottle of wine and corn on the cob. Soon they were laughing and eating, toasting Brad who blushed and kept denying his hero status.

"So, what are you going to do with the money?" Teresa pushed her plate back and leaned toward her. "Invest it, buy the ranch, more horses?"

Sam shook her head. "I don't know. I haven't had much time to think about it." She chuckled. "I could afford the breeding fee for Sugar now, and maybe I could start my Thoroughbred herd."

Brad cocked his head to the side. "Thoroughbreds, huh?"

"Yeah, it's been a dream of mine for a long time." She gazed out over the maize-colored prairie. "But I have to be practical too. It wouldn't take long to burn through the money if I just go following dreams. I have a lot of thinking to do."

The group sat visiting by lantern light as the moon rose and stars dotted the darkened sky. Finally, Brad stood. "I'd better let you ladies get your beauty rest."

"Yeah, we have to work tomorrow. Another group of dudes coming in this week." She nudged Electra. "And your mom will be here Friday."

The teen nodded, uncharacteristically quiet. Her eyes glistened in the lamplight. Sam put an arm around her shoulder and squeezed.

"I don't want to go." Electra sniffed. "I mean, I'm really happy to be seeing Mom, but..." Her voice broke, and she buried her face in Sam's shoulder. "I'll miss you" came the muffled words.

Her heart lurched. She bit her lip and blinked back tears as she hugged her young friend.

Brad gently touched Sam's shoulder. "I'll call you."

Torn between Electra's need and her own, she nodded and mouthed, "Thank you."

CHAPTER THIRTY-FIVE

The following Thursday, Sam sat at the kitchen table with Clyde and Irene Bruckner at the end of a busy dude-wrangling day. It was the first opportunity she had to talk at length with them about her new financial status, other than quickly relaying the news on Monday. Tomorrow Electra's mom would arrive, and the Bruckners would be hosting the end-of-the-week barbecue for their clients.

"So *nouveau riche*, huh?" Clyde quipped.

She rolled her eyes. "Well, not exactly rich..."

Mrs. Bruckner cuffed her husband's shoulder. "Stop teasing her and showing off, dear." She gave Sam a warm smile. "This is such fantastic news. What are you planning to do now?"

"That's part of what I want to talk to you about. I'm not sure if I should squirrel the money away in savings or some kind of investment. I could get Sugar bred now, but I don't know if that would be the best use of the money. I thought maybe you guys could give me some advice."

"Good questions. I can see you been thinkin' on it a bit." Clyde leaned back in his chair and rolled a toothpick from one corner of his mouth to the other. "Off the top of my head, I'll tell ya, you won't be earning any interest if you put it in savings, and it would be tempting to dip into the account whenever you wanted, so investing would be the better of those two options. I could put you in touch with my accountant."

Irene poured more coffee for them. "I know you've had this dream of starting a Thoroughbred herd. Have you done any research on that?"

Sam nodded. "Yes, and I was shocked at the breeding fees. That plan may still be way out of my league." She shifted in her chair. "And after being here for a couple of years now, I'm questioning whether this would really be a good area to raise Thoroughbreds."

Clyde took a sip of his coffee and silently traced lines with a finger on the plastic tablecloth. "Well," he looked into her eyes, "here's another thought. I've seen what you've done with Electra and the kids from the group home—nothin' short of miracles. You already have three rescue horses. Why don't you consider maybe starting a non-profit to continue that work with kids and horses?"

Sam jerked her head back. "Really? Me? Wow." She rubbed the back of her neck. "What would I have to do?"

"I think you oughta talk to my accountant. He can give you the particulars on that." He grinned. "And what if we kinda become partners? I have the facilities—at least until you figure out the logistics and whether you'd want to set up at your place."

She felt her mouth drop open. *No way. It's too much. I can't do that!* "Oh my gosh, Clyde. I…I don't know what to say. This is incredibly generous of you." Her hands trembled.

He waved off her words. "Pshaw. I'll give you Milton's phone number if you want to talk to him. You think on it a while. No need to rush."

She got up, went around to his side and gave him a hug. "Thank you, Clyde. I will do that."

***

Friday lunch was a hubbub of conversation and laughter as the three visiting families rehashed their week. "Such fun!" "Never thought I'd enjoy being out in the middle of nowhere, but I want to come back." "When does hunting season start?" "Can we go for one last ride this afternoon?"

Sam and Electra were finishing the last bites of their sandwiches when a white car drove into the parking area. A dark-haired woman got out and stretched.

240

"Mom!" Electra shrieked and ran toward her. The two reunited with a long hug and tears. Electra pulled her mother by the hand toward the picnic area. "...come and meet our clients and there's Sam and oh, Mom, you gotta come to our place and meet Apache and Trixi and just wait till you see..."

Sam chuckled as the teen tried to fill Alberta in on the whole summer all at once. She stood and went to greet the woman with a hug. "Welcome back."

"Oh, it's so good to be here. I've been looking forward to this ever since I left." She gave her a huge smile, hugging Electra close with one arm. "This one has grown a couple inches, I think."

"Mom, Sam and I are going to take the kids out for a short ride now. Do you want to come along?"

"I sure do. Let me go get my boots out of the car."

"Your mom would probably like some lunch before we go." Sam turned to Alberta. "Have you eaten?"

"No. A sandwich would be great."

After Alberta had eaten and Sam rounded up the kids, they took off for their ride over the sun-kissed prairie, trotting though low coulees and over rolling hills.

"I can't believe the change in Electra. It is absolutely night and day." Alberta shook her head. "I really felt bad leaving her with you last spring, with her attitude the way it was. She's a different person."

Sam grinned. "It was Apache, our rescue. Those two bonded immediately. She helped save his life."

Alberta's eyes glistened. "And he saved hers."

She nodded. "Yes, he did."

When the group returned to the corrals, Sam saw a white truck parked nearby and a familiar dark-haired figure leaning against the poles. Her heartbeat quickened. "Hey, Brad." She waved as she trotted by him and stopped by the barn to unsaddle and supervise the kids as they untacked. She worked with quick efficiency to make sure the riders properly stowed the gear in the barn and brushed down their horses. Acutely aware of his gaze on her back, she tried to ignore the prickly but pleasant feeling.

Finally, they were all ready to troop off to the house for lemonade. "Hiya, Brad." Electra bounded over to him, her mother in tow. "This is my mom. Mom, this is Brad." She raised her eyebrows and emphasized his name.

"Alberta." She put out a hand to shake.

Sam walked up beside them. "Thanks for introducing your mom, Electra. Would you like to go see what Clyde needs us to do to get everyone ready for the hayride and barbecue?"

"Sure. See ya later, Brad. You're coming too, aren't you?"

He nodded. "Wouldn't miss it." As Electra and her mother moved off, he grinned at her. "Good week?"

"Pretty good. This bunch hasn't been as…challenging as some." She sighed. "But I'm still glad the week is over."

He touched her arm. "I missed you."

Heat raised the hairs on her skin where he touched, and nerves skittered in her stomach. "Yeah. Me too." She glanced toward the group at the house and swallowed. "Um… I'd better go up and help."

"Sure. I'll tag along, if you don't mind." He fell into step beside her.

Dang. C'mon, Sam, you're an adult now, not a silly teenager. Images flashed of her as a tongue-tied schoolgirl not knowing how to talk to a boy she had a crush on. *C'mon, ask him something, comment on the weather, something.* Yet, for the life of her, she couldn't come up with anything. "See ya." She split off from him and hurried over to the Bruckners.

For the next hour, she bustled around, helping Irene load food into the old-fashioned, canvas-domed chuck wagon as Clyde and Brad hefted hay bales onto the other flatbed wagon and hitched up the team.

"Okay, everybody," Clyde announced. "Time to load up."

The kids ran to the hay wagon, jostling each other to be the first and get the best seat in front. The adults followed somewhat more sedately but climbed aboard with enthusiastic shouts and laughter.

Sam jumped onto the chuck wagon seat beside Irene and the procession took off toward the rocky outcrops in the pasture, where Clyde had prepared a fire ring. The early evening sun hung low on the horizon and painted a golden promise of a spectacular sunset. The breeze cooled the day's heat and crickets chirped a symphony in the sage.

At the site, everyone piled out. Irene opened the back of the chuck wagon and Sam helped her open the steaming pot of barbecued beans, bowls of potato salad, baskets of home-made rolls, and all the fixin's. Clyde dug into the fire pit and brought out foil-wrapped packages of beef. The aroma made her mouth water and her stomach rumble.

The families and their kids fell in line to dish up, exclaiming over every platter and bowl. Carrying heaping plates, they settled on logs around the campfire, and dug in with enthusiasm.

Brad came up next to her. "Your turn to eat now?"

She smiled. "Yeah. I'm starved." They filled their plates, and he steered her to a log a little to the side of the rest of the group.

Between bites and "mmm's" of ecstasy over the melt-in-the-mouth beef, she stole glances at Brad, catching him doing the same.

"So, what did—?"

"How was—?" They both spoke at once and then laughed.

"We gotta quit doing this." Brad shook his head. "I want to hear about you. Have you thought any more about what to do with your money?"

"Oh. Yeah." *I do have things to talk to him about.* "Had an interesting conversation with Clyde." She related her boss's proposal and idea to meet with his accountant. "I hadn't really thought of that angle, but it is something that intrigues me."

"But of course." He set his plate on the ground. "You're a natural. And you have a great start already."

She shrugged. "I don't know if I could pull it off, as a business. This is such an out-of-the way area. Where would I find clients? What about wintertime?"

"You can do it. I have confidence in you. With Clyde's help—he already has his dude ranch clientele—and I'll help in any way I can, you can do it." His chocolate eyes searched hers.

She gazed, mesmerized, into their dark pools. As the last rays of sunlight faded in a fiery production over the purple west butte, someone strummed a guitar and a soft baritone sang.

Brad took her plate and dropped it on the ground. He scooted closer and gently cupped her cheeks between his warm palms. "I want to be here for you."

Her face heated beneath his hands. She could barely breathe as he leaned slowly closer, his sweet barbecue-scented breath washing over her face. Her heart thudded. She held his gaze as he tilted his head, then closed her eyes when his lips touched hers. Soft at first, then more intense, he wrapped his arms tighter around her. Warmth and tingling spread through her body, and she melted into his embrace. This was so right. This is where she belonged.

CHAPTER THIRTY-SIX

Sam wasn't sure how she got home. Maybe she'd ridden on a magic carpet. Finally, the kiss. It was everything she'd dreamed of, and more—of promise. For the first time in a long time, she held onto hope and optimism and... maybe love.

Alberta and Electra were already at the house, chatting with Jace around the kitchen table. As she walked in, they all gave her a smiling, eyebrow-raised look.

"Well...?" Jace cocked her head.

She merely grinned, walked to the high cupboard and took out the vodka bottle. She turned to see Jace and Electra with open mouths.

"Uh... Sam..." Jace stammered.

She pivoted to the sink and upended the bottle, spilling the remainder of the liquor down the drain. Then she lifted the empty bottle toward the women.

"Here's to a bright future. For all of us. We have so much to be thankful for, to look forward to. To my friends." She raised the bottle high, then dropped it in the garbage.

**Enjoy this book?
You can make a big difference.**

Reviews of my books help bring them to the attention of other readers.

If you've enjoyed this book, I would be very grateful if you could spend just five minutes of your time leaving a review (it can be as short as you like) on the book's Amazon page.

Thank you very much!
Heidi

Next Book in the Rescue Series
The sequel: *Rescuing Hope*. Samantha continues her quest to buy the ranch her great-grandparents once owned. More rescue horses come her way, as well as a group of veterans working to overcome PTSD, and her mentorship of a troubled teen continues with more twists and turns. A serious vehicle accident threatens her relationship. Can Sam overcome her own inner demons and come out victorious?

ABOUT THE AUTHOR

Heidi M. Thomas grew up on a working ranch in eastern Montana, riding and gathering cattle for branding and shipping. Her parents taught her a love of books, and her grandmother rode bucking stock in rodeos. She followed her dream of writing, with a journalism degree from the University of Montana. Heidi is the author of the award-winning "Cowgirl Dreams" novel series and *Cowgirl Up: A History of Rodeo Women.*

Seeking the American Dream and *Finding True Home* are based on her mother who emigrated from Germany after WWII. She makes her home in North-Central Arizona.

Rescuing Samantha, Heidi's eighth book, is the first in a new series, continuing the fictional Moser family story.

Made in the USA
Middletown, DE
12 October 2021

49713710R00151